THE TRAVELERS : BOOK ONE

DARK
INVASION

NATHAN HYSTAD

D1738426

Cover art: J Caleb Design
Edited by: Christen Hystad
Edited by: Scarlett R Algee
Proofed and Formatted by: BZ Hercules

ISBN-13: 9798378039630

Part One
The Island

1

Sunlight penetrated the store's front glass, temporarily blinding me. I squinted and returned my focus to the customer at the sales counter. She'd been here for a few minutes, trying to offer a phone number that worked.

"If you don't have your card, it's no big deal." I knew exactly who she was. Bell Island was a small community, and she'd been coming here for years. Since this was my second shift after returning from college, she'd probably forgotten my face.

Mrs. Walker glanced at my nametag. "Elliot, can you rent me the movie? It's my anniversary, and since my husband didn't book a dinner reservation..."

"Sure thing. I went to school with Lance," I told her.

"Elliot Hoffman?" Her expression softened. "I'm so sorry to hear about your mother."

"She's going to be fine." I accessed her account and entered the information. "There it is, Mrs. Walker. That'll be $2.99."

"$2.99! That's outrageous!"

I closed my eyes and took a deep breath. I had a feeling I'd be doing that repeatedly over the course of the summer. "Do you want it or not?"

She paid and I gave her change, which she promptly pocketed, rather than adding to the Take-a-Penny-Leave-a-Penny tray. Mrs. Walker snatched her romantic comedy and stormed out, almost knocking a new patron aside in the process.

"What's her problem?" Bones asked.

"Marriage issues," I answered.

Bones. My best friend in the world. We'd known each other since we could walk, and I still found myself adjusting to the dramatic alteration in his appearance since I'd left for college. He'd gone from preppy to punk in the course of one semester. His red-tipped mohawk freely defied gravity tonight.

"You're early," I told him, checking the clock. I had another thirty minutes before my shift ended and we closed up for the night. Nothing on Bell Island stayed open past eight o'clock except the diner, and that was my destination after work.

Bones stopped next to a life-size cardboard cut-out of Sylvester Stallone with boxing gloves. "You really think he's this tall?"

"I don't know, Bones. Why don't you peruse the horror section, and I'll be with you when I'm done?" I peered at Mark's office to find him watching me through the window. He adjusted his glasses and sat at the desk, pretending to be busy.

The phone rang. "Island Video. If we don't have it, the next one's on us," I answered. The policy was full of asterisks and fine print, and rarely ever paid out. Given the exorbitant cost to purchase a VHS, we generally carried two of any new release, but Mark refused to change the tagline his ex-wife had chosen before leaving him a year ago.

"Elliot. It's me. Mark," my manager said.

He stared at the wall with the bright red phone in his grip. He rarely left that office.

"Mark, what's up?"

The door chimes jingled and in walked a family of five, eager to choose a Friday night movie before we closed. The boys broke off, running to the kids' section while the parents stalked to the new releases, a bewildered look on their faces. I'd seen it a million times after a long week. All they wanted was a flick and some popcorn before sleeping in tomorrow while their children watched cartoons.

"When you've finished replenishing the shelves, I'd like a word with you," Mark said.

"Am I in trouble?" I kind of needed this job, although I wouldn't admit that out loud.

"No, I just have something important to discuss." The phone clicked, and I hung up.

"Do you have anything with aliens in it?" one of the boys asked. He was maybe ten, his blond hair spiked.

"Sure, what kind of aliens are you after? Big robots? Little green men?" I furrowed my brow.

His younger brother arrived, and the older stuck a hand into his own shirt, pretending he was breeding a monster inside his stomach. "I want aliens that bust out of your body!" He wiggled his fingers from beneath his collar.

"Mom! Tell Brad to stop scaring me!"

They ran off, Brad punching his sibling in the arm.

"Precious, aren't they?" Bones asked. "I used to babysit them ages ago. They were even worse then, if you can imagine." He leaned on the counter, the chain clipping his wallet to his belt banging against it.

I rented them five movies, none of which contained violence or aliens, and when they left, it was almost closing time. Bones helped me restock the popcorn shelf, and he thumbed through the previously viewed VHS tapes, clutching a slasher flick. "Should I buy it?"

"You know we can rent any of these for free, right?" I reminded him.

"Sure. I guess I forgot," he whispered. "It's not like you've been around much."

And there it was. Bones scratched the bald side of his head and skimmed the end of his mohawk.

"It only took you a few days to start the digs," I said.

"What? You've been gone for three years at that fancy college of yours, and all I get is a lousy call when you're in town for a holiday. Which hasn't been very often, I'll note." Bones crossed his arms, and his tough exterior vanished. He resembled the thirteen-year-old I'd gotten into trouble with.

"Sorry, dude. It's been rough." He didn't know all the details about my family issues, but enough that he nodded and pretended to let it go. Which was his default, because Bones took much longer to process stuff than the average human.

"We still going to hang later?"

I was meeting with my girlfriend in…I glanced at my digital watch…ten minutes. "Come to the diner."

"I don't want to be a third wheel."

"Maybe Bethany can bring someone. Should I call and ask?"

"Elliot, have you forgotten that we know every single girl on this damned island?" Bones huffed a breath and faced the exit. "Looks like you have another customer."

I'd already closed the till.

The front door opened slowly, the bells jingling with his arrival.

"Who's that?" I asked.

"Oh yeah, you haven't met Sarge before," Bones said quietly.

"Sarge?"

"No one knows his real name. Always wearing that military stuff." Bones averted his gaze when Sarge approached the center aisle.

He stopped ten feet away, his hands on his hips. "You have any recording devices?"

"We rent movies, sir," I said, my voice catching. Rough stubble covered his cheeks and chin, more gray than black, but it was his eyes that stood out. One was blue, the other brown, and they'd likely seen countless horrors.

"What about video cameras?" he grumbled.

"Uhm…" I peered to Mark's office. "I was told it came in last month."

I went to the storage room to retrieve the metal case and set it on the counter. I opened the latches and swung it wide.

Bones whistled. "Talk about the AV club's dream."

There were numerous attachments and cords, along with a thick manual. "The Movitron 2000," I said.

Sarge picked it up, stuck it to his eye and grunted. "Lemme have it."

I did the paperwork, and asked him for ID.

"I'd rather not," he said.

"I need it for your address."

He gave a phone number and dropped three one-hundred-dollar bills down before closing the case. "Consider it a long-term rental."

The veteran exited without another word, and I followed him, locking the latch. "That was weird."

"What do you think he's going to film? I bet he's hunting deer, skinning them," Bones said.

"Where do you get that idea?" I asked, genuinely

curious. It wasn't often that Bell Island had a newcomer, especially one so colorful.

"He's in the old Reeve farm. I've seen that barn light up at all hours," Bones told me.

"And why are you snooping around his farm in the middle of the night?"

"Dude, you have no idea how boring the Island has been without you." Bones shoved his hands into his pockets. He pulled out a pack of smokes and lit one in his mouth.

"Smoking?"

"Whatever. You can ride your high horse to the parking lot when you're done." He strolled outside.

I walked to Mark's office and knocked.

"Come in."

Mark's elbows were on the desk, and he nodded to the chair across from him. "Have a seat."

I was decidedly uncomfortable. "Sir, if I did anything wrong…"

"Nothing like that. Elliot, you've worked here for five summers now. Do you enjoy it?"

No. I'd rather poke needles in my eyes than spend another day renting movies to… "I love it."

"Good." He steepled his fingers and leaned back with a smile. "I want to name you assistant manager. It comes with a lot of responsibility. More hours, and some tough decisions."

I cleared my throat. "You're promoting me?"

"I've met someone." He glanced at the wall, and I saw the gilded frame showcasing the late great ex-wife, Carol. Her hair was huge, her smile fake. He must have noticed, because he got up and tugged it off. The paint looked fresh behind it. He rammed the photo into the desk drawer. "We're going to Europe for a couple of weeks, and I need someone reliable to watch over things. This store is my legacy, Elliot. Maybe one day, it can be yours."

I tried not to cough and put a fist over my lips. "I'm still in college."

"Finance, right?" he asked.

"Yes." Though I wasn't certain if I would ever return. Not after the recent news.

"Think about it. I trust that you and I can go far together, buddy." Mark thrust his hand out. I shook it and walked away.

"I appreciate the offer. Can I let you know tomorrow?"

"Not tomorrow." He grinned. "It's your day off. Thursday is fine. Have a good Fourth of July."

"You too." I shut the door and gawked at the store with the lights off. Movie posters everywhere, the smell of musty carpet and bonbons. The pinball machine beeped and buzzed in the corner. Could I spend my life here?

My watch alarm sounded, reminding me that Bethany was waiting. She'd been in town for a few weeks. My own homecoming had been delayed, since I'd had to stick around for a condensed course after I flunked my third-year accounting, and that meant I had missed my mother's breakdown.

"He fire you?" Bones asked when I emerged. The sun was almost setting, casting long shadows from the park across the street. There were already benches and streamers set up for tomorrow's festivities.

"The opposite. He wants me to be his assistant manager."

"You told him to shove it, right?"

"Nah. I'll think about it." We strolled down the sidewalk, traveling past the bakery, the library, and Cliff's Records. The Open sign was flipped to Closed, but I poked my head in, finding Cliff at the till.

"Hey, man. Good to see you. I got the new Van Halen restocked."

"Cool. I'll swing by next week."

"What about you, Hank? Still want the Ramones special edition I ordered?" Cliff asked.

"Bones. My name's Bones." He pointed to the skull tattoo on his forearm.

"Whatever. It's here when you're ready." Cliff's phone rang, and he answered it.

"We're going to be late." I waved at him and rounded the corner to the side lot. Staff weren't allowed to park here, not when space was so limited downtown. That being said, I didn't think I'd ever seen it at capacity.

"It looks even more mint, if that's possible," Bones muttered.

"Thanks. Waxed it when I got home." I loved my Camaro. Black with white hood stripes. 1967. It had been my uncle's favorite possession and became mine three summers ago when he drowned. She was the only thing I had to remember him by, and I was determined to take care of her.

Bones slammed his door shut, and I glared at him. "Sorry. I don't know my own strength." He started to light another cigarette, and I slapped it away.

"Don't even think about it."

He lifted his hands up. "Fine."

The diner was a few blocks ahead, and I noted how quiet the area was. "Where is everyone?"

"Oh, some big Fourth of July festival in the city. A bunch of people left on the ferry to start a day early, I guess."

There was only one way to Bell Island, and that was the ferry. I didn't mind the nearly one-hour ride when I came home. It was nice to watch the waves and consider my future. Now I wasn't sure what that would entail. It wouldn't be what I wanted, not with my family's current situation. My foot pressed harder on the pedal, and we flew the last block.

"Easy, Speed Racer." Bones climbed out when I parked.

"Can you give us a few minutes?" I saw Bethany sitting at a booth inside, primping her hair. She was beautiful as usual.

"Sure. I'll be at the counter." Bones meandered left when we entered, and I wandered to my girlfriend.

The moment I sat beside her, I knew something was wrong. "What's going on?"

She didn't look up, but her hand touched mine. "Elliot…"

I shifted farther away. "What is it?"

I knew this tone. It was the same one she'd used the first time we broke up, before college. "Not again," I managed.

Bethany finally made eye contact. "Elliot, I know your mom is gone, and your dad lost his job…"

"And you chose this special moment of my life to break up with me," I finished, moving to the far side of the booth. "You're unbelievable."

"It's not like you've been attentive."

"I've had other things on my mind!" I shouted, and the few people inside quieted. I paused until they returned to their own meals.

"That's the problem, Elliot. Your head is always in the clouds. You live in some dream world. Well, I'm graduating next year, and I want to move to the city. Maybe out of state. I'm done with this place. And from what I can tell, you won't even finish your degree."

"That's not true," I mumbled.

She stood up. "I'm sorry about your mom, but you have to get your shit together." She stared at me like I was a lost cause. "Goodbye, Elliot."

Bethany walked away, and I didn't let myself watch her go until she was in the parking lot. I heard the engine before I saw Cooper's Mustang, and cringed when she went into his car. "You've got to be kidding me."

It all became clear. How long had she been pretending we were still together? A month? A semester? A year? We'd only seen one another on the rarest of occasions, and the letters and phone calls had drastically reduced since I hadn't shown up for Easter dinner. I pictured Bethany drinking in the bar, deep into a glass of wine while Cooper perched on a stool beside her.

"That's so heinous," Bones said, plopping into her seat. He eyed her untouched soda and started to slurp it through the straw. "What a spaz."

Cooper ripped out, tires spinning on the pavement. Bethany glanced behind her, lifting her hand for a last wave. I didn't return the gesture but contemplated giving her a different one. "My life is falling apart."

"Chin up, old chap," Bones said. "It's only uphill now."

"Who ordered the grilled cheese?" a woman's voice asked.

"She bailed," I mumbled.

"Right here." Bones tapped the table. "And how about a burger and fries for my heartbroken friend?"

"Heartbroken?" the waitress asked, and I glanced up. She had curly blonde hair, and the most genuine smile I'd ever seen. "Don't tell me it was that chick you were talking with."

"Yeah, Bethany."

"She's been around a lot. Usually with some other guy.

He still wears his letterman jacket from high school," she said with a laugh. "Unless you guys are total nerds and think that's cool."

"Quite the opposite," Bones said with a mouth full of fries.

"He's a loser," the waitress added.

I liked her. "That's Cooper." I sat up straighter. "He's always wanted to date Bethany, ever since we were juniors."

"Guess he got his wish." The waitress made notes on a small pad. "How about I toss in a milkshake with that burger? My treat."

I grinned, suddenly feeling better. I looked at her nametag. "Leia?"

"It's actually Kimberly. Kim is better. I don't want to be the same person every day. Plus, who doesn't dig a good science fiction heroine?" She winked and headed for the kitchen.

Bones finished the soda. "You're extraordinary, Elliot."

"Why?"

"Because you just got dumped, and this betty is into you. It's not fair."

"She wasn't flirting with me," I said.

"She definitely wasn't flirting with *me*..." Bones took a bite of his sandwich and made a satisfied smack of his lips. "How can bread and cheese be so tasty?"

Something flashed outside, drawing my gaze. The sun had set in the west, leaving Bell Island in a state of darkness. It was normal growing up here, but after being in the city for months, seeing just how bleak it became was unsettling.

Another crack of light was followed by a booming thunderclap.

"Storm's coming," Bones said, as if he were a sooth-sayer.

"Very good, Nostradamus. However did you extrapolate that bit of information?"

"Extrapolate. You have been paying attention in class." Bones shoved his plate at me, and I picked a couple fries off. "Can I ask you something?"

"Sure."

His demeanor changed to serious. "Is what your mom has hereditary?"

I swallowed and clenched my other fist beneath the table. "I don't know."

"I can change the subject if you want."

"It's fine."

"What happened? I was with you at Christmas, and she seemed okay."

I recalled the late phone call to my dorm from my father a month ago. "*Your mother had an incident. They're taking her to Pacific Northwest Hospital.*"

"*Is she hurt?*" was the first thing I'd asked.

"*She… she's seeing things, Elliot. Like before.*"

"One burger and a shake." The plate rattling on the table broke me from the memory.

"Thanks, Kim."

The diner was mostly empty, and Kim scooted in beside me. "What do you guys do for fun?"

I glanced at Bones, silently willing him not to answer. "Dungeons and Dragons, video games… I listen to music. The Cure is my favorite." He pointed at his t-shirt.

"How anti-establishment of you," Kim said, and Bones perked up, like she'd thrown him the world's best compliment.

"What about for the Fourth? Any good spots to watch the fireworks?"

I didn't mention that Bethany and I usually parked at Cove Peak every summer.

"Cove Peak," Bones said, smirking at me. "Right, Elliot?"

"You guys gonna be there tomorrow?" she asked.

"I don't…"

"Of course we are. Wanna meet us?" Bones suggested.

I braved the question. "How about I pick you up? You working?"

"'Til seven. Closing early for the holiday."

"Seven it is," I told her.

The diner's owner stood with his arms crossed near the cash register, and Kim hurried from the booth. "My irreplaceable skills are required elsewhere. See you then." She locked gazes with me as the lightning flashed outside, and I felt something in my chest, different than anything I'd experienced with Bethany.

"Can I have a bite?" Bones asked, and I cut it in half, dripping grease on the table as I set it on his plate.

"You were asking about my mom."

"You don't have to tell me."

"She's always had what the doctors called delusions. She met aliens once, when she was a kid. So did her brother."

"Uncle Taylor?"

I nodded. "They were on Bell Island, at their acreage out by Dawson Road."

"Where the drive-in is now," Bones said.

I took a single bite and let it go. My appetite was suddenly gone. "Want to bounce?"

"We can watch a movie at my place, if you want?" Bones lived in his grandmother's guest house, which was really just a converted garage. But it was his.

"Nah, I better go home. Check on my dad."

Kimberly was at the register with an older couple, and I waited until they were done to hand a twenty over. "Keep the change."

"How boss of you," Kim said. She grabbed her notepad and scribbled on it, tearing the page free. "That's my number. I'm staying at the motel."

She didn't have to say which chain, since there was only one.

"You really are new to town."

"Not many rental options on Bell Island."

"What are you doing here?" I asked, and the cook rang a bell from the kitchen.

"That's a surprise." She walked off, and I did my best not to stare.

This was either the best or worst day of my life.

Time would tell.

2

"You sure you don't want to hang? You just came to town. It's been so boring without you," Bones said.

He'd attended one semester at the community college on the edge of the city, and had quickly returned home without an explanation, but it was definitely related to his parents' departure. It wasn't my fault he'd never tried again or had any sort of meaningful employment. He currently worked at the local mechanic shop, rotating tires and changing oil for Lawrence Banner, the Island's biggest entrepreneur. He owned half the businesses out here.

"Tomorrow. I promise."

Bones hopped from my car, carefully closing the door. His grandmother's lights were off in the living room, and I could see the TV was on. Wind blew heavily, shaking the giant white oak in her front yard. A small branch fell on my hood, and I moved to avoid any more debris. I waved at Bones and sped from his home.

I'd told Bones I wanted to talk with my dad, but the truth was, we didn't have much to say to one another. Never had. He'd worked hard his whole life, and I thought my parents had an okay relationship, but now I understood there was a big difference between okay and great.

It was only ten PM, but the streets were empty, the storm growing more violent with each passing minute. I needed to go home. Instead of taking the direct route, I went the long way, circling the town to the edge of Bell

Island. The road forked, and I had two options: go toward the beach or head up to Cove Peak. I chose the latter, and my engine grumbled and roared as I hit the gas, speedily ascending the high-grade incline.

There were no couples making out here tonight, and I parked in the open, not wanting to risk damaging my car with a fallen tree. You could see the city from here, twenty miles in the distance, the lights a welcoming beacon. Here on the Island, it was the opposite, a darkness spread out like a blanket on the ten-mile-wide piece of land.

I stared at the beach, finding the parking lot for the ferry, the boat docked in the city for the night. The man who operated it didn't live on Bell Island, but he'd be here at eight AM like clockwork, ready to usher the handful of people working on the mainland to their places of business.

The lighthouse was on, the bright beam slowly spreading over the channel. As a kid, I'd always loved the lighthouse. I thought Mr. McIlroy was a hero, keeping boats safe from our coastlines.

The marina was mostly empty, a few boats clanging to their moors in the heavy waves.

I couldn't stay here. Bell Island was dying, and I was only twenty-two years old.

My thoughts drifted to Kim, and I realized how relieved I felt since Bethany dumped me. She was something else from my past I'd been clinging to, but in reality, she dragged me down like an anchor.

Thunder shook my car windows, and a flash of lightning struck a pine twenty feet away. I jumped in my seat, and decided it was time to go. My tires spun in the water, and I drove slower down the decline, not wanting to hydroplane into the forest. The estates were to the left, and I exited for the area of the Island designated to the rich and wealthy. Most were from the city, looking for a mansion to remove themselves from the ever-growing pressures of the work week. I drove past the first few, with their big, gated driveways, and poorly lit yards.

I hit the brakes as I neared Cooper's house and parked across the street. His living room was bright, and one of their four garage stalls had the door open, displaying his Mustang. He must have been in such a hurry to get Bethany inside, he'd forgotten to shut it.

What was I doing here? I pressed the gas and used the cul de sac to head the other way. Bell Island had me in a rut, but that wasn't necessarily the island's fault. I'd been in one for longer than I could remember.

It was time to go home and face the music.

The trip took ten minutes, and the storm had begun to ease. The skies occasionally flickered with forks of lightning, but the thunder took longer to relay, meaning it was heading east.

I turned onto my street, feeling a moment of jealousy after being in Cooper's neighborhood. Here the homes were older, built in the boom of Bell Island, when people thought it would become a prosperous fishing community, maybe a tourist attraction from the city and even farther into the United States. But that had never happened. There was always a setback, starting with World War II, and the island didn't recover. Those were the stories I'd grown up hearing about at the dinner table. My father told them like he was a skipping record.

My dad would rather complain about his situation than take ownership of it and change something. I had a feeling I wasn't the only son to recognize this. But he provided food and shelter, and that was about as much as my sister and I could expect from him.

My mom's van was parked out front, leaves sticking to the windshield. It was strange being home without her around. I pulled into the driveway, behind my dad's yellow and white truck, and sat in the driver's seat of my Camaro, feeling the vibrations of the powerful engine for a moment before turning the key. I didn't have much, but this car was mine.

The house was a four-level split, with bedrooms on the right and a living space on the left. It didn't look like anyone was home.

I tested the handle, and it was unlocked. That wasn't a shocker, because my dad didn't believe there was any reason to secure yourself in Bell Island. If he'd ever spoken to the police about break and enters, he'd know that wasn't true, but he preferred to stick his head in the sand on most things.

I stepped one foot in, only partially committing. "Dad?"

"In here." His voice was gruff, and I glanced at my car. Then I shut the door, firming my resolve. If I was going to make this work, we needed to have a discussion.

I kicked off my wet shoes and went into the kitchen. Dad was at the table, head in his hands. A glass of whiskey sat in front of him, and a mostly full bottle, but neither looked touched.

"Grab a seat," he said.

I obliged, taking the one opposite him. I could see where my mom used to dance through the kitchen, wearing the floral apron Cindy and I bought her for Christmas in '78. She would smile as she made a roast or baked a loaf of bread. I missed her, and felt a wave of guilt, because I hadn't even visited the hospital yet.

"How was work?" Dad asked.

I suddenly realized how old he was. Maybe not in years, but in life. The lines surrounding his eyes were deep, his skin sallow, his hair gray and receding. I'd only been gone a semester and a half, but it seemed like a decade.

"Work was good. Mark offered me a promotion," I said.

He lifted an eyebrow. "Really? That's my boy. Already moving up in the world."

"I'm not sure if I'll take it."

He lost his grin. "Son, with the way things are going, we need you to pitch in a bit."

I knew this was coming. "I still have another year. I can't stay."

"It's not like I wanted your mother to have a psychotic break. We've been struggling, Elliot. For years. The health plan from her school package isn't that good. She's been on these no-name drugs for some time, and there's not much work for boat repair. Not since Reagan stopped spending on our infrastructure."

We'd reached the blame game portion of the conversation. "What happened, Dad?"

"To your mother? She was good until Taylor died, then it all fell apart."

Three years ago, and I'd been so focused on school that I hadn't even known. Uncle Taylor had drowned right here off the shore of Bell Island, and I'd returned for the funeral, inheriting the car posthumously. I hadn't asked a lot of questions. "Why?"

"They were close. You know that, in the way only twins can be. They experienced something profound when they were kids, but until recently, she never really expanded on it, and I wasn't one to pry."

I wanted to shout at him that he might have been able to help her, but didn't have the energy. My father was the type of man you couldn't argue with, because he'd fail to see the other perspective in the conversation. "And before she left?"

"Aliens, Elliot." He mopped his face with his hands. "They came to their farm. Landed out back. For some reason, she was triggered by Taylor's drowning, and no matter what she tried since then, the nightmares continued. I haven't told you this, but…"

I dug my fingernails into my palms. "What?"

"She was in the ocean. I found her van by the marina. She was trying to…" He cleared his throat and drank from the glass, shooting the whiskey.

"She wouldn't do that to us," I managed.

"I'm glad you're home, Elliot."

I looked around. "Where's Cindy?" Outside, the storm had returned with a vigor. The trees swayed in the yard, the sky continually flashing brightly.

He seemed to break from his daze. "She's at Yolanda's. Said she'd walk home."

"In this?" I rushed to the phone on the wall and pulled it free. My finger hovered near the dial, but the line was silent. I tapped the receiver a few times, with the same result. "Phones are dead."

"They always are during a storm."

"I'll go look for her," I said.

"I can help."

"No. Stay here in case she comes home." I grabbed a jacket, my old yellow raincoat, and an umbrella, hearing my mother's cautioning voice in my mind. *Be prepared for anything. Bell Island is full of surprises.*

The gusts of wind almost sent me flying from the front step, and I crouched as I ran to the car. I dumped the umbrella into the seat behind me and backed up, struggling to see.

Yolanda lived nearly two miles from us, and I knew that path well. I used to hang out with her older brother when we were kids, and later, when I could drive, my parents made me pick up my sister a couple of times a week.

I rolled at twenty as I scanned the neighborhood, trying to spot her in the darkness. The streetlights were few and far between, their light casting a dull orange glow that seemed even more bleak tonight.

When I reached the edge of our area, I turned right, heading past a playground. Lightning bolts darted over the park, and I thought I saw something standing near the slide. I slammed on the brake, wondering if that was Cindy trying to take a shortcut, but this was far too big to be my sister. When the lightning returned, the figure was gone.

I kept driving.

Water gushed across the road, the storm drains not able to handle the sudden onslaught of precipitation. My tires splashed as I crawled past the pool. With any luck, Cindy had decided to wait out the downpour.

The housing gave way to forest. I'd always warned Cindy about this stretch, because there was a blind corner and people didn't pay much attention to speed limit signs. I crested the turn carefully, but Cindy wasn't anywhere to be found.

Finally, I made it to Yolanda's place and parked in the front. I pulled the slicker tight to my neck and ran up the sidewalk centering their yard. I banged on the door impatiently, and someone opened it almost immediately. It was Bruce, her brother.

"Elliot? What are you doing here?" he asked.

"Is Cindy inside?"

"Sure. I offered to drive her home, but my parents said to stick it out." He turned and cupped his hands to his mouth. "Cindy! Elliot's here!" He shrugged. "Sorry to hear about your mom."

"Thanks." I didn't know what else to say. Apparently,

word had spread quickly. I'd forever be known as the guy with the insane mother. "What have you been up to?"

"Not much. Painting this summer. Mostly fences and stuff. But it's good money and I'm outside. Hey, me and the guys will be at the fireworks tomorrow. You interested? They'd love to see you."

"Sure. Maybe," I lied. They were the same bunch that had picked on Bones until he nearly quit school. I'd confronted them, led by the one and only Cooper, and found myself ostracized by the entire clique. Which I was totally okay with. That was ages ago, but I'd never forget.

Cindy appeared, clutching her ET backpack. Her cheeks were red, her eyes wide. "What were you up to?"

"Don't tell Dad, but we were watching *Halloween*." She made a show of shivering her entire body. "That Myers is scary."

I waved at Yolanda, and Cindy and I left.

"I'm glad you stayed put," I said.

Cindy huffed and jogged to catch me. "You thought I'd leave in this? I'm fifteen, not stupid."

My Camaro fired up, and I sat there for a second. "Cindy, did you notice Mom's behavior change?"

She stared out the window at the raging rain. "I guess so. I didn't think much about it. She kind of just locked herself in her room. Said she wasn't feeling well."

"Let's go before this becomes worse."

I neared the sharp corner, and saw the shape before I had time to react. My muted headlights reflected off the deer's eyes, and I hit him, his giant body smashing into my hood and cracking the windshield. I slammed the brakes, my car skidding sideways, and I slid into the ditch. The deer fell clear, and I could do nothing to prevent Cindy's door from hitting an oak tree. Cindy's screams were short-lived, and the moment we stopped moving, I turned to her, grabbing her shoulders. "You okay?"

Her eyes were filled with tears, and she unbuckled her waist, patting herself on the legs. "I'm fine. That deer came out of nowhere." Her voice wavered.

It struck me. My car was ruined. In a flash, I recalled the first time I'd seen Uncle Taylor bring it over to our house, taking the ferry from shore with the shiny muscle car. I remembered the feeling of the keys in my hand the day he let me borrow her to take Bethany to prom, and the opposite sensation when the lawyer passed them in an envelope after the wake. And then I was back inside the car, thunder booming, rain threatening to wash us farther into the ditch.

Cindy tried to open her door, but it was crumpled inward. Mine worked fine, and I stepped into the soggy ditch, the water instantly dampening my shoes and shins. Just when I thought things couldn't become any worse, they had.

The deer was ten yards away, and I walked to it, seeing its front legs twitch. It made eye contact for a moment, and a wave of sadness and guilt washed over me. And it stopped, the black eye glazing. It was dead.

Cindy stared at it beside me and slung her pack on. "Let's get home."

I returned to the car, shut the lights off, grabbed my keys, and took the umbrella. I handed it to Cindy, and we began the long trudge home in the middle of the night.

It was the worst day of my life after all.

"Where's Bethany?" Cindy asked.

"Keep walking."

3

I woke to birds chirping, the sunlight gleaming through my window, past my blinds, and directly into my eyes. Nature wanted me to get up, and who was I to deny her?

I'd dreamt of hitting the deer, but when I went to the body, Cooper was on the road instead of the animal.

"My car…" I swung my legs from the blankets and slid into my fuzzy Garfield slippers.

I had the holiday off, and now I had to waste it attempting to have my Camaro towed to Bones' shop. The first thing I did was test the phone. Dial tone. I took the small victory as an omen for a better upcoming day.

I dialed Bones, and he answered on the second ring. "Hey, buddy, I've been thinking… we should definitely ask Kim to bring a friend. Maybe she's from the city and can find someone on short notice."

"Bones, I have a problem."

"Sure, don't we all?"

"I had an accident last night."

"You wet the bed? I thought you stopped that in middle school."

"Funny. Seriously, though, I went to pick up Cindy and rammed into a deer."

"Bummer. Where's the car?"

I told him, and he repeated it as he wrote it down. "Is that necessary? You know where it is, Hank."

"Don't call me that," he said.

"Okay, sorry… Bones."

"Meet me there in an hour. I'm watching cartoons." The call ended.

"Good old Bones. Never change."

I had to share a bathroom with Cindy, and her damp towels were on the floor. I kicked them aside, seeing piles of her hair in the sink and on a pink brush. I really needed to get the hell out of here. I showered, dressing in a pair of shorts and a white t-shirt, and headed to the kitchen. Dad was at the table again; this time, his whiskey was replaced with a cup of coffee. The paper was spread out wide, and he didn't react as I grabbed a piece of buttered toast from the countertop.

"You talk to Hank?" he asked, still reading.

"Bones, Dad."

"I don't understand what happened to that kid."

I wasn't willing to discuss the deep inner workings of Bones right now. "He'll be there soon. Can I take the van?"

Cindy was in the living room, giggling at the loud TV.

Now my dad glanced up. "Your mother's van?"

"Just until mine is fixed," I said.

"Do you have any idea how much that'll cost? You should see if Lawrence Banner will buy it off you as is. It's probably worth a couple grand even busted up," he told me.

Not on my life. "We'll see." There was no world where I sold that car.

"Keys are in the junk pile." He returned to his paper, and I opened the overstuffed drawer near the stove. It was filled with old take-out menus and pens that had dried out years ago. I saw a therapist's business card near the top and found the keys beside it.

"See you later." I tied my shoes while eating the toast and stopped at the doorway. "Would you mind doing a load of laundry, Cindy? And for the love of God, can you clean the bathroom?"

"Mom always does that," Cindy said, still in her pajamas.

"Well, she's not here, and we have to take over."

"What about you?"

"I'll cut the grass later!" I shouted as the front screen door slammed closed.

It was beautiful outside, and I took a moment to let the morning air settle on my skin. The lawn was getting long.

Mrs. Lutz from across the street sat on her front steps, clutching a coffee mug. She had rollers in her hair, and a potent menthol cigarette in her lips. "Morning, Elliot."

"Hey, Mrs. Lutz."

She gave me a sad smile. "Back for the summer?"

"Think so," I muttered. She seemed confused by my response, so I elaborated. "It's nice to be home. Less pressure than college."

"I hope those blasted fireworks don't scare Mitsy." Her dog scratched at the front window and let out a yip. The dog looked older than Mrs. Lutz, if that was possible.

"Have a good day." I got into mom's van and sat there for a moment. It was fairly clean, as she preferred. The little tree hung from her rearview mirror and still smelled of pine. I turned the key, and the engine started, the radio playing from the speakers.

"We had quite the storm last night. I haven't seen a light show like that since the Rolling Stones concert. How about you, Terri?"

"I agree with you, Phil. We're celebrating this nation's independence today in the city, and you don't have to wait until it's dark to enjoy the festivities. Come downtown this afternoon and join us for the wiener roast. I'll personally be there, grilling dogs, and you can win prizes from the radio station. How about a new boom box, courtesy of Vance Electronics?"

"That sounds great to me, Terri. Now, something new and fun, a track from Lionel Richie...."

I shut it off and drove to the site of my crash. The deer was gone, and I had no idea who would have removed it on such short notice. I couldn't call the county last night, considering the phone lines had been down.

Bones was using a winch to drag my Camaro out of the ditch. The tow truck was marked as such, and painted in yellow and black, a buzzing bee indicating you couldn't *Beet* their prices. My friend grimaced when I came over. "Sorry about the car," he said. "When you said you hit a deer, I pictured a busted windshield, not mass destruction."

"Not your fault... but thanks. Think they can fix her?" It looked even worse in the comfort of the morning light. The bashed fender, the hood caved in, the windshield covered in spiderwebbing fractures. Bits of blood clung to it, dried and ominous. I fought the tremors coursing through me. My last connection to my uncle was lying here, a fraction of its previous self. He'd trusted me with her, and I'd failed him.

Bones didn't reply instantly. "For sure, but it's going to take a lot of overtime and favors to get it done for cheap."

The fact that he was open to helping meant the world to me. I patted his shoulder. "You're a good friend."

"The best." He flashed me a smile. Bones' uniform was comprised of a t-shirt with a black vest, jeans, thick black boots, and a wallet chain dangling down his leg.

"Don't you ever get hot?" I asked, trying to forget that my only worldly possession resembled a crushed soda can.

"Nah. I run cool. You know that."

"The coolest," I joked.

He had the car on the tow truck. "Let's bring her to the shop. Want to follow me?"

"You bet." We went slowly, and I could tell Bones was

being extra careful, since it was my car attached to the truck. The shop was closed, the *Open* sign dimmed, but he unlocked the bay door, and we placed the car in without any issue. I was already sweating, and it was ten in the morning. Today was excruciatingly humid.

Bones flicked the lights on and cranked the radio. "Love this song."

The singer was barely coherent, but I had to admit the British punk movement was still killing it. I circled my Camaro, examining the damages one more time. The trunk was popped, and I tried to close it. It wouldn't clasp.

Bones poked his head in, showing me the faulty latch. "What's this?" He reached deeper, grunting as he stretched the entire way. He emerged with a piece of paper. He flipped it around, handing it to me. "It was under the mat. Must have slipped loose."

I held the notepad paper, unsure of its meaning.

D.R. x R.S. 100 NE 100 NW 50 W

"That's weird," I whispered.

"Probably nothing."

I agreed and put it in my pocket. "When can we get an estimate?" I asked.

"Since there's no one around, it has to be Thursday. But given the holiday, probably Friday," Bones said.

I could live with that. It wasn't as if I couldn't drive a van for a couple weeks. My mom wasn't here to use it.

We exited the shop, and Bones closed up the bay, securing it with a thick padlock. "What do you want to do?"

I had a rare free day, and we weren't meeting the new girl in town until later. I had promised to cut the grass, but wasn't in the mood, given my current situation. My mom deserved better than I'd given her.

"Bones, I know I've been a bummer since I came home, but I have to do something else today."

Bones looked at the ground, kicking a rock. "No probs. I'm used to being alone."

I hated to see him like this. We made quite the duo. "Come with me to the city."

He grinned. "Seriously?"

"I need to visit my mom, but then we can check out that big record shop. The one you like," I told him, hoping to appease my best friend.

"And the Thai place?" Bones crossed his fingers, holding them up.

"Totally."

Bones patted the door on the van and hopped into the passenger seat. "I've always wanted to see a psych hospital."

"Why?"

He shrugged and changed the radio station the moment the van was running. He always did that. "Guess it's kind of messed up. They were normal people who had something inside them. That could be me."

"It won't."

"How can you be sure? It happened to your mom," he said.

"She experienced trauma. That's what they called it. From when she was a kid."

"And I didn't?" Bones rolled his window down. Bell Island's industrial area consisted of a fish processing plant, a lumber yard that doubled as a storage field for Lawrence Banner's construction equipment, and a bottle depot, all of which were closed at the moment.

"You're fine."

"Now. You remember my dad," Bones said.

I certainly did. He was a piece of crap, and the last time he hit Bones, my friend had had enough. He called the cops, who didn't believe him. Turns out his dad played poker with the old sheriff. We were both glad Sheriff Parker had since taken over. When his parents ran out on him, Bones' grandma took him in, and that was where he remained. Another reason I regretted abandoning him for college.

"We're going to have fun today, I promise." I lifted my fist, and we tapped knuckles three times, making a thumbs-up gesture to finish off our private handshake.

"We better. I love the Fourth." Bones pointed at the church when we drove by it. People stood in front with banners and billboards, talking about Satan's influence on the youth of Bell Island. From what I could tell, the Island was doing better than the city. Sometimes being isolated was refreshing. "Can you believe these guys? Like rolling dice and fending off cave trolls is going to make us kill someone."

There were only a few of them, and the pastor made eye contact with me as we drove by. He'd counseled my mom for years, and probably wondered who was driving her van. "Let's go to the ferry."

When we reached the bay, only a couple of cars were parked in the lot. I waited first in line at the long blue gate, and Mr. Webb waved at me before opening it.

"Morning, Elliot." He peeked past me, finding Bones. "I haven't seen you in a while, Hank."

"Bones."

"Right," Mr. Webb said. "Tell you what, you can pay half price for the return trip. It'll be leaving at three."

I did the math, and that would give us a few hours in the city. "Deal." I handed the five bucks over, and guessed he was generous because of my situation. Everyone knew that my father didn't have work, and my mom had been hospitalized. Welcome to Bell Island, the birthplace of gossip.

The wheel locks popped up under the van, securing it, and I exited. The ferry wasn't big like the intercity ones north of us. Only a trickle of residents made the commute each day, and it had the capacity for twenty vehicles at any given time. Now there were three, since two more loaded after us. We walked to the top deck, staring at the water. You couldn't see the city in the daylight, but it was there, under twenty miles away.

Bones lit a cigarette, puffing on it with little effort. "This is nice."

I had a gnawing feeling in my gut after the last twenty-four hours, but tried to stay positive. "It is, isn't it."

We clutched the railing, the blue paint chipped and worn, and Mr. Webb brought us out, moving from the shore. The lighthouse was to the side, atop a small cliff, and I peered behind us to Cove Peak.

"Do you believe in aliens?" I asked Bones, and he coughed as if the question caught him off-guard.

"Aliens?"

"That's what Mom said. She and Taylor saw them when they were kids. Dad said she suppressed it for years but couldn't let it go. And ever since he..." I looked at the waters around us, knowing my uncle had died not far from this very spot. "She's gotten worse."

"I sure as hell hope they're real," he said, flicking the butt into the channel.

"Really? Why?"

"Because this can't be all there is."

What could I say to that? I nodded along.

We chatted about the mundane for the duration of the trip. The weather. Our favorite music, movies, and TV shows. When we docked, Mr. Webb reminded everyone he'd be returning to Bell Island at 3 PM sharp, and if they were stuck across, it wasn't his fault.

I drove the van off, waved at the operator, and headed into town, nervous to see my mother for the first time since her breakdown.

It wasn't far, since the hospital was on the edge of the city. No one wanted a psychiatric facility in their backyard. From what I could tell, they took good care of the place. The driveway was clean, the landscaping lush and filled with colorful flowers. My mother loved to garden, and this probably soothed her mind.

I parked near the entrance, which was easy, given how few cars were here. The staff lot beyond was packed.

"You want to stay put?" I asked, and Bones glanced at the entrance, then nodded.

"Take your time. But not too much. We have a record store and Thai to crush," he reminded me.

I entered at the front doors; a friendly woman smiled at me from the desk. "Hello. Do you have an appointment?"

"Did I need one?" I asked with a smile, trying to be affable.

"The doctors prefer it. Who are you here to visit?" she asked, flipping open a giant book.

"Lorraine Hoffman." I noticed a slight tic in her cheek at the mention of my mother.

"One moment." She lifted a finger, picking up the phone, and spun the opposite direction so I couldn't see her face. She whispered into it and hung up. "She just had her afternoon medication. Maybe another time…"

"I'm her son, Elliot. I've been at college and would really love to visit her. Let her know I came." I stepped closer, and she leaned in, her expression softening.

"Sure thing, honey. We'll make an exception. Please write your name down. Quiet time is coming up, so you won't have long." She waved at a man in a white coat approaching from the hall. "Xavier will take you."

"Thank you," I said.

"This way, sir." Xavier didn't make small talk as he escorted me through the facility. People lingered in a common space, some playing games, others reading books. Classical music echoed from old speakers, the sound even more antiquated by the ancient sound system.

And there she was.

I didn't know what I expected. Somehow I pictured her as a frail white-haired version of herself, but she looked great. She'd lost a couple pounds, which she'd always wanted to rid herself of. Mom called them "pastry pounds," and would laugh like it was a private joke between her and the world. Her cheeks had color, her hair was neatly styled. She seemed healthier than ever.

"Mom?" I crossed the room, and Xavier glanced in, as if to ensure I had the right person.

She had been staring out the window, and she rose, astonishment painting her expression. "Elliot. You came."

"Sorry about that." She met me halfway. The space was tight. There was a single bed, a nightstand, and a tiny television, with a chair perched near the window. From there, she had a view of the gardens.

We hugged, and she pulled me tight, her face pressed into my neck. I felt tears.

"I'm doing better," she said before I could ask. "They think I can go home soon."

"And the…" I didn't want to say *delusions*.

"I realize it was only my imagination. I was mistaken, and so was Taylor. When he… died, it broke my heart. I had to buy into the concept that he'd done it for an otherworldly reason, because why else would my sweet brother end his own life? But I was wrong. It's all so clear now, and I can come home to take care of my family."

"That's great," I said, hugging her again.

"You and your sister mean everything to me. How was school?" She sat on the bed, and I joined her.

"Great," I embellished.

"Did you pass?"

"Yeah, second chances sometimes pay off," I told her.

"And Bethany? Any wedding bells in the future?" she asked, her smile too wide to deny.

"Not quite yet, Mom."

"And the car?"

I cringed but kept a straight face. "Running like never before." That wasn't technically a lie.

Her eyes were watery, and I reached into my pocket, grabbing a tissue. The piece of paper fell out. Mom's gaze landed on it, and she picked it up from the carpet. "What do you have there?" she asked.

"I found it in the Camaro."

"I've seen this before," she whispered.

"You have?"

"It's Uncle Taylor's handwriting. D.R. is Dawson Road. Where we used to live."

"Making the R.S. stand for Royal Street?"

She nodded, and the next part made sense. It was directions. From the intersection at Dawson and Royal. Shivers darted down my spine. I folded the note and shoved it back. "Don't mind that. It's nothing."

Mom didn't seem sold, but she peered into the hall, where Xavier was waiting, pretending not to eavesdrop.

"When can I bring you home? Can you leave now?"

She patted my hand. "Not quite. Another week. Maybe two."

"That's great!" I was ecstatic with the news.

"Time's up, kid," Xavier said from the entrance.

"Tell your father I love him. And give Cindy a kiss for

me."

"How about a punch in the arm instead?" I asked.

"One day you'll realize how important your sister is to you, and you'll regret not being closer when you were young," she said somberly. Her eyes began to droop, and I guessed her afternoon meds were kicking in.

"I love you," I told her.

"Happy Fourth of July, son," she said. "Be careful. Bell Island has a colorful history on this day."

"What do you mean?"

"The storm. Thirty-five years ago, to be exact. We were almost washed out… that's when the… never mind. It was only inclement weather. Have a good night."

"You too."

I left her there, hating seeing my mother in a place like this. But she seemed well-adjusted and, by her own admission, almost ready to leave.

Dawson Road and Royal Street. What did it mean?

"Everything good?" Bones asked. He was leaning on the van, one foot on the door, a smoke in his mouth.

"She looked happy."

"Stick enough lithium in a person, they'll fly to the moon," he muttered, but I didn't let his skepticism affect me. I felt a million times better having visited her.

"Hungry?" I laughed when Bones rubbed his stomach.

"I could eat."

4

*M*r. Webb was closing the gate when we arrived, my palms sweating from fear of missing the final ferry to Bell Island.

"Cutting it close, boys."

"Sorry, Mr. Webb."

He swung it wide, letting us through. It was busier now, and I spotted Cooper's Mustang across the lower deck. "Great," I murmured.

"One more minute and you'd have been camping out for the night," he said, and I drove by, parking as far from Cooper as I could.

The sun was high in the sky, the cloudless day a complete reversal from yesterday's storm. Bones and I stayed in the van while the ferry undocked, comparing our record score. I'd bought three used vinyls and admired a mint Journey album I'd been wanting.

"Journey," Bones complained. "You may as well listen to Tony Bennett."

"Give me a break. At least you can understand what Steve Perry is singing."

We argued about the merits of our own favorite genres for a while until we exhausted all avenues, and I found the bag of leftovers. I unwrapped a spring roll and bit into it. "What are we even going to do tonight?"

"Buy some beers. Watch the fireworks." He slapped a palm to his forehead. "You forgot to ask her about a friend, didn't you?"

"It's not like I have…" I'd forgotten that she'd given me her number. "She's probably at work already."

"Then let's make a visit," Bones said.

I chewed the spring roll. "We just ate."

Bones rubbed his stomach. "I could use a burger."

"Where does it all go?" I asked, and he shrugged. His eyes narrowed, and I followed his gaze.

"Cooper," he muttered. The ex-high school football quarterback wandered to his car, a girl on his arm.

"That's not Bethany," I said, getting out of the car.

Bones trailed after me. "What are you going to do? Yell at him for cheating on the girl that cheated on you?"

I tried to follow his logic, but it escaped me as I marched across the deck. Cooper wasn't wearing his stupid jacket, but I saw his prestigious college name on his t-shirt. It was another reminder we came from different worlds. The girl looked younger than us, and she was probably attracted to his wealth.

"What the hell do you think you're doing?" I asked him.

Cooper acted surprised by my sudden appearance. "Elliot."

"Who's this?" The girl chewed a big piece of pink gum and blew a bubble.

"Nobody," Cooper said. "Now go back to the hole you crawled out of." Cooper turned away from me, wrapping his arm around his date.

I wasn't done. "What about Bethany?" I grabbed his shoulder, and he shoved me the moment we faced off.

"What about her, Elliot?"

"I thought you were an item," I said.

"An item? What decade are you living in, man? This is the eighties." He poked a finger toward me, and I swatted it away.

"Who's Bethany?" The girl seemed more interested now.

"Don't worry about her, Katie." Cooper put himself between her and me, and I noticed a few Bell Island locals watching us.

"She doesn't deserve this," I mumbled.

"And you deserve an ass-kicking." Cooper's fist was clenched, and I guessed he was looking to punch me. But he didn't.

I wasn't about to fight him for Bethany's honor, no matter our history. She'd walked away from us, and they were free to date and do whatever they wanted.

"Maybe I do, Cooper, but I already decided to have a better day. So how about you leave us alone, and we call it a truce." I smirked at him and caught Katie's eye. She smiled at me, twisting her hair with a manicured finger.

"Would you cut that out," Cooper muttered. "We're almost there. Get in the car."

Katie followed, but not before giving me a wave behind Cooper's back.

I waited cross-armed, while Bones laughed. "You should have decked him."

"Whatever. Not worth it," I said. The small crowd dispersed when the threat of violence had subsided, and there stood Sarge, wearing black and green camo pants and a black tee.

"You were too lazy," he told me.

"Lazy?"

"That man was ready to strike, and your left foot was too far in your stance. You'd have lost your balance if you needed to counter him," Sarge said.

Bones rolled his eyes. "Okay, GI Joe."

"Thanks. I'll remember that."

"See that you do. And out here, don't worry about rules of engagement." He grabbed a pack from between his feet. It looked heavy, judging by the vein bulging in his forehead at the effort.

"What rules?"

"Look them up, kid. And do the opposite. Because the real world isn't equipped for regulations. I've seen that firsthand more times than I can count." He left us, heading to an old truck.

"Let's go to the van. We're about to dock." Bones and I watched as the ex-soldier tossed the duffel bag into the box, and it landed with a loud clang.

"What do you think he's got in there?" Bones whispered.

"I don't want to know. Come on."

A few minutes later, we were driving onto Bell Island, and the adrenaline from my confrontation dissolved. I even forgot the smug look on Cooper's stupid face.

"Check the diner?" Bones asked.

"One stop first," I told him, determined to visit my mother's childhood home. It was a stark contrast from the stories she'd shared when we were younger. Now there were mini malls, a tennis court, an outdoor swimming pool, and a drive-in-movie theater, all of which were favorites of ours growing up.

"We don't have time for this," Bones protested.

The pool was packed, a hundred screaming and joyful children jumping off diving boards, lying on plastic tanning chairs, and cannonballing into the deep end. I spotted a small boy, a green alien floatation device wrapped around his waist. He jumped in, shrieking in delight.

I proceeded until we reached the sign.

"Royal Street." I signaled and saw the arcade between us and Dawson Road.

"Hey, pull up," Bones said, and I parked at an angle, shutting the engine off. He jumped out, patted his hair as if to ensure it had kept its height, and walked up to a girl.

I had to assume it was the elusive Reaper Bones was always talking about. He looked annoyed when I came over, but recovered quickly.

"Elliot, this is Reaper," he said.

"How's it going?"

"Fine." Reaper was skinny, with pink hair cut short at the back and sides. She had a hooped nose ring and torn jeans. "Didn't expect to see you here."

"Why not?"

"Because you said you were spending the holiday with your old friend. Assuming that's you?" Reaper asked.

"Yeah, Elliot Hoffman."

"Cool." She glanced into the arcade, which was mostly filled with teenage boys, each vying for the record on whatever game was trending at the moment.

"Anything cool going on tonight?" Bones asked her.

"We're hanging at the reservoir. One of the new guys built a half pipe there, and it's pretty rad. You guys should show," Reaper said. I saw the tattoo on her arm, a long scythe clutched by a shadowy cloak. These guys literally inked their monikers on their bodies, but I couldn't blame them. It was an artistic expression, something I'd never been good at.

Bones looked at me for guidance. "Sure, we could stop by," I said, taking the lead. "Nice to meet you, Reaper."

"Likewise. Stay chill."

Bones was smiling when he was in the van. He was still grinning when I reached the intersection. "You haven't asked her out?"

"Nah." Bones cracked his neck, turning his head side to side. "She's an enigma. Doubt she'd see anything in me."

"You won't know unless you try," I told him.

"Gnarly. Now you sound like my grandma."

"Dawson and Royal." I grabbed the notepad and held it on the steering wheel. "What was Uncle Taylor intending with this?"

Bones peered at it. "Let's hit the diner. There still might be time to find me a date."

"I'm not even on a date," I reminded him. "We're just showing Kim how lame a Fourth party is on Bell Island. That should be enough to send her home… wherever that is."

Bones grated his teeth, and I could tell I'd done something to upset him. "Why do you always do that?"

"Do what?"

"Put down Bell Island. Elliot, you grew up here. Didn't we have fun?"

"I guess." Our recollections were slightly different.

"I mean it, man. We did whatever we wanted. Those epic bike rides, or paddleboarding in the channel. Remember that time we tried to make windsurfers, and almost got lost at sea?" He laughed, and I couldn't help but join him.

"You're right, we had some good times."

"Then don't make it seem like returning to the Island is this horrible penance you have to overcome. Some of us choose to stay." Bones stared at the street signs. "And not everyone had the chance at education."

His parents were basically out of the picture, not even bothering to send him a card for his birthday, and I knew Granny didn't have much other than her dead husband's retirement income to keep her afloat. "I hadn't really thought about it."

"Of course you didn't." Bones stuck his arm out the window.

"How about that burger?" I said, and he didn't

respond.

I wasn't hungry when we drove up to the diner. It was remarkably busy for four in the afternoon. The glass was painted with fireworks, the daily deals included beneath them.

"A burger for a buck. Count me in." Bones was practically out of the van before I parked it, and I leaned over, rolling his window up with the crank. He always left things open.

"Half the town must be there." I pointed across the street, where festivities were set up for kids. People walked around with red, white, and blue face paint, matching their tank tops and socks. American flags fluttered on plastic handheld poles, and the Boss echoed from a big speaker near a bandstand.

The party was in full effect. Eventually, parents would drag their exhausted kids home to barbecue with the neighbors and friends while drinking too many beers. The next day, they'd nurse their hangovers and sunburns, but all would recall the night with great fondness. At least, that was how I envisioned it. I'd yet to have a fantastic Fourth, contrary to what Bones suggested.

Last year, I'd worked a shift at the video store, then found out Bethany was sick with the flu. I spent all night with her, holding her clammy hand while she apologized for her poorly timed illness. Every other year was a variation of that, but I was determined to make this one better the moment I spotted Kimberly serving someone's meal in the restaurant. She made the pale blue smock appealing.

She chewed on the end of her pen, then scribbled down a family's order. The kids threw straws at one another while their parents ignored their shenanigans. Kim looked flustered as someone shouted at her for a refill.

Bones went to our usual booth, which was somehow

vacant, considering how busy the joint was. He gazed out the window, frowning toward the festivities. "They all seem so happy. It disgusts me."

I saw my sister walking with a group of friends. A boy was particularly close, and he kept staring at her. "Who's that?" I asked Bones.

"The kid ogling Cindy? That's Ben or Benji… I don't know. It's getting harder to care," he said. Bones flipped the giant laminated menu, running a finger over the options. He did this almost every time, but always ordered the same thing.

"I'll be right back." I ran for the exit, jogging to catch up as they crossed the street. "Cindy!"

She turned around, her expression full of embarrassment at the sight of her older brother. "Elliot, what's up?"

"Hi, River. Hey, Becky." I waved at her best friends, and they smiled back. "Did you finish cleaning the bathroom?"

"Jeez, Elliot. Yes, I did." She grabbed my arm, dragging me away. "Can you stop humiliating me?"

"Don't want to look bad in front of… Benji?" I glanced past her at the guy, who had to be a grade or two ahead of them.

"It's Ben, and he's got a cool car."

That was the best reason to date someone when you were fifteen and bored to death on Bell Island. "Just be careful, okay?"

"You don't have to do this," she whispered, her anger subsiding.

"Do what?"

"I already have a father." She went to her friends, linking arms with each girl as they wandered to the event.

I sighed and noticed something near the trees. The light reflected off the camera's lens, illuminating Sarge hiding in the shadows, filming the crowd. "What the hell is that guy up to?"

I heard a knock on the window and saw Bones impatiently waiting for me inside the diner. "Sorry about that." I plopped into the booth.

"Kim is swamped," Bones said.

She finally arrived at our table a few minutes later, her fun and playful demeanor from yesterday replaced with exhaustion. "Hey, you two. I apologize for the holdup. Looks like everyone decided to take the day off and forgot to tell me. What'll you have?"

We gave her our order, and she lingered for a second. She looked directly at me. "You still showing me around tonight?"

"Yeah, if you're not too tired."

"A couple shots of Dale's black coffee and I'll be good for hours," she said.

"You don't… have any friends you could bring along, do you?" Bones asked, finding his voice.

"Sorry, hon. I've only been here a few weeks, and everyone I work with is sixty plus, unless you want Liz to teach you to salsa dance." She jabbed a thumb toward the owner's wife, sitting on a stool behind the counter. She filled sugar containers so slowly and methodically, I thought she might be sleeping.

"No worries." Bones slid his menu to the edge of the table, and I added mine to the pile. Kim reached for them, and our fingers touched. I let my hand linger, and she smiled, taking the menus with her.

I needed to know more about this woman. Why was she on Bell Island when there were so many other places in the world? No one moved *to* the island, just away from it.

Bones talked about what we could do, and that we

needed to hit the beer store, but I only half listened as I watched Kim from the corner of my eye, tirelessly drifting between tables, filling coffee cups, retrieving dirty plates. It was like an art.

"What do you think?"

I snapped my attention back to the conversation. "About?"

"Dude, did you really not hear me?"

"Sorry, I'm distracted today."

"Today? Bethany was right, man. Your head is always in the clouds."

That stung, but they weren't wrong. I focused on my friend and lifted my fist. "I'm here, buddy."

He bumped it three times, breaking away with a thumbs-up like we'd done for the last decade. "Okay. I appreciate it. I also have a surprise."

"What's that?"

"We need to swing by my place to grab it." The mischievous smirk made me laugh.

"Whatever you say. We should have enough time between food and picking Kim up," I told him.

The doors opened, and Sheriff Parker entered. He stood with his hands on his hips as his gaze surveyed the crowded diner. Our eyes locked, and he sauntered closer. We hadn't interacted much in the past, but he'd gone to school with my father back in the day.

Parker was a hard man, with a handlebar mustache and a permanent scowl. "Hoffman. Larson."

Bones leaned on the table with his elbows. "Sheriff. To what do we owe the pleasure?"

He remained at the end of the booth, and most of the diner watched not so subtly. "You were in an accident last night?"

"Yes, sir. I went to pick up my sister and hit a deer."

"We found the blood. Someone called it in," he said. "Why didn't you?"

"Didn't I what?"

"Call it in?"

"The lines were down. I had it towed."

"Where is the deer?" he asked, his tone accusing.

"I couldn't say. It was gone when we got there this morning," I told him.

He rubbed his chin and took off his hat. I could smell the sweat-soaked fabric from my seat. "Are you certain it was a deer?"

I glanced at Bones, who shrugged. "Yeah, I know what a deer looks like, sir."

He patted his thighs and nodded a couple times, his frown lessening. "Okay, son."

"What's this about?" Bones asked.

Sheriff Parker lowered his chin and voice. "We've had some... missing cattle at the Mackenzie Ranch. And a couple dogs."

"The Mackenzie Ranch is next to the Reeve place, right?" I asked, thinking about Sarge, and Bones' comments about the man being up at all hours of the night in his barn.

"That's the one." His gaze narrowed. "You know something, son?"

"Sorry, I don't."

"All right, then. Stay safe, gentlemen." The sheriff went to the counter, and Kimberly dropped what she was doing to give him a cup of coffee in a Styrofoam cup. He glanced around one more time and exited the diner.

"That was strange," Bones said.

"No kidding. Was he implying someone took the deer?"

"They must have. Unless it wasn't dead," Bones

suggested.

"It was gone." I'd witnessed the moment it lost consciousness, the life draining from the deer's eyes, its chest no longer heaving with panicked breaths.

Kim came with our two plates, and I didn't have an appetite. "You two aren't the town criminals, are you?"

"Don't think so," I said.

"Drug dealers? Pimps?" she asked with a grin.

"Not even a little bit," Bones said.

"Then what did he want?" She took more time at our booth now that another waitress had arrived. The older woman flashed an apologetic nod at Kim and started serving coffee refills. Her name was Nadine, and she'd been here since the dawn of time, or so it felt to me. I guessed she was probably only around forty.

"He said some animals had gone missing. He was asking about my accident last night," I said, and quickly realized Kimberly didn't know about my crash.

"Accident?"

"I ran into a deer during the storm. Crushed my Camaro. The deer died, but it disappeared this morning," I mumbled.

"What a bummer. Sorry, Elliot." When Kim said it, I sensed her empathy. "I better check on Nadine. She doesn't look so hot." Kim hurried off, and Bones didn't waste any time mowing down his burger.

I ate half of my food and picked at the fries, thinking about Sarge. What was he doing filming the Fourth of July festivities, and why were cattle and dogs going missing on the farm beside him? Were the two things related? I mentioned it to Bones, and he nodded emphatically.

"I'm telling you, the man can't be trusted," he said. "He's got a few screws loose, like lots of those guys."

"What guys?"

"Vietnam. Man, they had it rough."

We'd all heard about the conflict in school. I'd been a little boy when they were overseas, fighting a war no one could ever win.

"Let's just forget about the deer and my car, and most definitely this Sarge character, and have a fun night," I told him.

"Deal. You going to finish that?" Bones stared at my plate.

Kim was huddled with Nadine in the corner of the restaurant, and I wondered why the woman was crying.

5

*I*t was after five when we rolled down Main Street, waiting at every corner while residents crossed to the celebration. I waved at a few people and went to the convenience store, parking in the gravel lot.

"Damn it," Bones muttered.

"What?" Then I saw Cooper's convertible. Katie and Bethany had been replaced with his old high school buddies, and they lingered near the store's entrance.

"If it isn't the freak parade," Paul said. He was a big guy, more muscles than brains.

"Get out of my way." Bones tried to walk past him, but the brute stood in his path.

"Let us through. This isn't high school," I said.

"That's right. It's the real world now, Elliot." Paul glared at me.

I suddenly missed college, where the students just focused on finishing their assignments and partying on weekends. These childish games had vanished the moment I set foot on the mainland, leaving the island behind.

Cooper and Bruce exited the store, each with a case of beer in their possession. Bruce perked up, grinning at me. "Hey, Elliot. You gonna hang with us tonight?"

Cooper shot daggers at him, but Bruce didn't seem to notice. "Nah, looks like Paul has other ideas."

Bruce set the beer down and pushed Paul toward the parking lot. "What's wrong with you, doofus? Elliot was our friend." He looked at me. "Sorry, bud."

Paul didn't answer, and their group filed into the convertible. Cooper started the engine, his glam rock blaring from the speakers as he sped off, tires spinning.

"You good?" I asked Bones.

"Always."

We entered the air-conditioned building and stocked up on supplies. Bones grabbed a bottle of butterscotch liqueur, and we found a dozen cheap beers, along with a case of wine cooler for the 'ladies,' as Bones put it. Bones put on a show of searching for his wallet, and I paid, knowing he was probably more broke than me. If this kept up, I really would need to spend my life in servitude to the video store. I'd been trying not to think about my future today, but worry kept creeping through.

Maybe my mother was right, and she could come home soon. Then she'd be able to return to work this fall at the middle school, and Dad would find a job. I could leave to finish my degree, and never come back to Bell Island.

Thinking about it with Bones beside me made me sad for him. It just meant I had to ensure nights like tonight were entertaining, and we could remember them forever.

I dumped a bag of ice into a cooler in the back of the van and placed the drinks inside.

We loaded the snacks and booze before returning Bones to his grandmother's house. She was on the front step, eyes closed, with the sun on her face.

"Nana, you okay?" Bones asked.

She smiled and opened them. "Just peachy. Elliot, how's your mother?"

"Fine, ma'am."

"That's swell. Would you boys like some lemonade?"

"Sure, ma'am." I was hot, and she always made the best: never too tart or overly sweet.

Going into her house was like traveling to the 1950s. The walls were painted green, the furniture covered in plastic. The wooden coffee table had been waxed so many times, I was certain I could dig a fingernail a half inch into it if I tired. Despite the ancient feel, it smelled comforting, with the tinge of liniment oil and baking. It was Bones' childhood in a bottle.

His grandma had lost her husband when we were young, maybe ten, and she'd persevered ever since. "Here you go." She carried a tray with a wobbly grip, and I took it from her, setting it on the table.

"Thank you," I said, filling the three glasses to hand out. I tested mine and smacked my lips. "Still the best, Nana."

"You're a good boy. Bones is lucky to have you," she said, almost falling into her favorite chair. It had an indent in the cushions and was only suitable for her at this point. "How's school?"

"Great. I'll have my degree in a year."

"Then what?" She sipped her beverage.

"Uhm, I'll get a job."

She nodded. "As one does."

"Yeah. I guess so."

"Bones has applied for the fall," she said.

I almost spat my lemonade out. "Is that true?"

Bones looked uncomfortable and took a drink before answering. "It's not college, Nana. It's a trade school."

"Mechanic?"

"Nah, I don't want to deal with that all my life," he said. "It's a tattoo program in Nevada."

"Nevada?" No wonder he'd been clinging to the past so much. He was the one about to leave.

"It's just a year. Then I'll need to work under someone for a while. What do they call that?"

"An apprenticeship?" I asked.

"Right. But it's not a big deal," he said dismissively.

Nana reached over and set a hand on his. "You're a good boy, Hank. I know you're going to do very well."

This time, Bones didn't correct her. Nana had permission to call him by his given name, even if it rankled Bones. "Thanks, Nana. I hope so. They still have to accept me."

"Have you checked the mail?" she asked.

"Not yet." Bones finished his lemonade and peered at the door. "We should…"

I lifted a finger and cut him off. "Nana, you've lived here your entire life, right?"

"Not quite. Moved here before the rush in the thirties. My father was one of the first landowners. He sold most of our property to the developers in the late forties, when people were desperate after the war. If he'd have held on another year or two, we would have been rich. But that was my Pappy, always looking for a quick buck. Why do you ask?"

"My mom mentioned something from her childhood. Think it happened around this time. Maybe a storm thirty-five years ago."

"Oh yes." She sat up straight, her smile vanished. "It was worse than last night. Thunder and lightning like we'd never seen. Half the island was flash flooded, separating the two halves of the bell. Animals went missing. Some were found dead in the aftermath. My husband lost a truck to the ocean. Drifted off the property. Insurance don't wanna cover that kind of thing. Said it was God's doing, but I don't think God wanted to break so many people."

"Anything else?" I whispered.

She adjusted her red-framed glasses. "It might be the distorted memories of a tottering old lady, but I remember fragments. I asked about it later, and they said maybe it was ball lightning. I guess it could have been."

This triggered a reaction in me, like the story was familiar somehow. "Where was it?"

"Out by the Dawson land. Think it's a drive-in now."

Bones and I shared a look. "What did it do?"

"I went searching for Hank's father. He always ran around with that girl. Long before your mother, dear," she added. "The road was torn in half! Water pouring into the earth, and this light rose. I don't know what else to say. Well, enough about that. You two have a fun night and stay out of trouble. You both have bright futures ahead of you. Take it from someone who's seen it all."

"Thanks, Nana," I told her.

The TV turned on before we were out the door, and I recognized the gentle rocking of her chair. "Did you hear that?"

"Yeah, it's a soap opera," he said. "She calls them her *stories*."

"No, about the ball lightning. That's where my mom and Uncle Taylor saw something," I blurted.

"That's heavy." Bones rushed across the yard, heading to his garage suite. He unlocked the door with a quick turn of his key, and I was transported to another world. Movie posters lined an entire wall, ranging from the original German version of *Nosferatu* to the more recent slasher flicks. Band t-shirts were hung on a stand-alone clothing rack, with a mixture of more black vests, and a couple pairs of tall leather boots sat near the exit.

His bed butted up to the garage door, and his room was surprisingly organized and well kept. There were no dirty dishes and no dishevelled laundry piles, and it actually smelled fresh. It had been a long time since I'd stepped foot into his lair.

"Expecting company?" I asked, pointing at a vanilla

candle on his coffee table.

"Shut up," he barked. "Okay, so Nana confirmed there was something strange going down during the storm. But what about that piece of paper?" He made a 'give it over' gesture, and I grabbed the note, unfolding it.

"What do the numbers mean? 100 NE?"

"Directions. Northeast," Bones said.

"100… steps!"

"Could be," he added. "If that's the case…" Bones faced the north, holding the page. "A hundred paces northeast from the intersection at Dawson and Royal. Then another hundred northwest. Followed by fifty straight west."

I nodded along, trying to picture the area. "We have to check it out."

"We're running out of time, my friend." Bones went to an old trunk by his bed and knelt in front of it. He lifted a massive iron lock and used a key from a chain around his neck. He'd worn it since we were kids. He craned the lid open and grabbed an object wrapped in brown packing paper. With a flip of the corner, I saw what he was so excited about.

"Fireworks? You're more likely to blow yourself up. Do you remember the last time we tried this? You almost fell down Cove Peak," I said, laughing at the memory.

"You're exaggerating." He looked at his forearm, where a scar sat beneath his skull tattoo.

"If you say so. What do you plan on doing with those?"

He waggled his eyebrows. "Light up the night sky."

"You could have told me about going to Nevada instead of giving me such a hard time about leaving," I muttered.

"I know. I just wanted a fun summer with you before we go our separate ways again. I doubt I'm coming back when I'm done. There's barely any tattoo parlors around here, so I'll probably stay in Vegas or Reno to train. Maybe afterwards I'll come home and open a shop," he said.

"On Bell Island?" I pictured the church protestors picketing his doorstep, attempting to shut him down for satanic rituals.

"Maybe. Or not. It's tough… with Nana."

"She seems to get by on her own," I said.

"Tough old cat, that one." Bones slid the fireworks into a backpack and shoved it at me. He went to his nightstand to retrieve a new pack of smokes. "Now we can go."

"Five thirty. Gives us time to check this out." I held the paper up.

"Fine." Bones went to a cabinet and grabbed a spade shovel. "It's good to be prepared." He continued rifling through the shelving, throwing some duct tape and twine into the bag.

"Are you planning on kidnapping someone?"

"You never know when you need a shovel and rope, okay," Bones joked.

Bones locked his door when we emerged, and I noticed his grass was overgrown. "I forgot."

"What?"

"I said I'd cut the grass today."

"Seriously? Why?"

"I offered to help out around the house, and since my dad seems incapable of stepping up, I want to be a good influence on Cindy."

Bones cursed under his breath. "Let's make it quick. I don't know why I let you rope me into these things."

With over an hour before I needed to pick up Kim from the diner, I could return home. The neighbors' house had a bunch of cars parked out front, many of them lined all the way up the street. One was half-blocking my driveway, and I managed to sneak by the big boat.

When I ran inside, Dad wasn't there, and I peeked through the kitchen window, seeing him in the Bradshaws' yard, sipping a cold beer. His wife was in a hospital, and he was relaxing with the neighbors. I'd never been close with the man, and this was yet another reason why.

"Come on. Let's do this."

"Let's?" Bones lifted his eyebrows.

"It'll go faster if you help." I went to the back, stalking angrily to the shed. Bones accepted the trimmer like it was something he'd never seen before. "Give me that." I primed it and started the tool for him. "Just do around the fences and the flower beds."

Despite my mother's absence, her gardening work in previous years had paid off. Bright white and pink flowers covered the area, and I thought how nice it would be when she returned home. I wouldn't let this place go to hell in the interim.

The lawnmower was loud, and I hoped my dad could hear me doing the work while he was enjoying himself. When we finished, I was sweating, and Bones had somehow cut part of his bootlace off. He struggled to even them out.

By the time I freshened up, it was six thirty. I thought about the note from the Camaro, and realized we'd have to investigate that later. With Bones about to leave for school, and me eager to complete my degree, life would change forever.

This night on Bell Island might well be our last chance at freedom. I hadn't committed to working at the video store as an assistant manager yet, but that was inevitable. It was the best way to save some cash to move out. I bet Cooper didn't have to worry about this kind of issue. His parents had probably already bought him a condo with a view.

I couldn't let the dread of my mother's hospitalization, my busted-up Camaro, or my breakup with Bethany drag me into a spiraling depression. Not tonight. If anything, I'd do it for Bones, the only true friend I'd ever had.

The moment I started the van, I noticed the fuel gauge nearing empty. "Out of gas," I said.

"You were never in the Boy Scouts, were you?"

"You know I wasn't."

"I'll lend you the guidebook." He rolled the window down as I drove for the gas station.

It was halfway to the diner, and I stopped, rolling to an empty spot. A pimply kid popped out of the store and lazily walked to the van.

"What'll it be?"

"Fill her up," I said, and he moved even slower.

"Kids these days," Bones muttered. "No ambition."

I smirked while watching him from my side mirror. "You realize he was us five years ago, right?"

"I was never like him. Okay, I'm a bit listless, but that's all about to change," he said.

"What did you think about Nana's talk? The ball lightning?" I asked.

"She's old. Maybe she's misremembering it," he replied.

"It's possible, but..." I glanced to the west, seeing the hint of a dark cloud far in the horizon. "Is there supposed to be a storm?"

"Didn't hear anything on that." Bones changed the station, which had been playing rock music on the lowest volume. He cranked it up so we could hear.

"It's the Fourth of July, but there might be more than fireworks tonight in the city. We're going to be caught with our flags up. We're getting word that another storm, possibly worse than last night's, is

drifting in. Batten down the hatches, folks; she's coming."

"Thanks, Dan. In other news, the fires in British Columbia continue to ravage…"

Bones flicked it off. "This blows."

"Totally."

The kid finished and lingered at the window with his palm raised. "Nineteen bucks."

I opened my wallet, noticing how quickly my cash reserve was being depleted. "Keep the change."

"Thanks. Aren't you Elliot Hoffman?" he asked.

"Maybe."

"You have the record for runs made," the kid said.

"Still?"

He nodded and patted the door. "Stay cool."

"It was ten years ago, Elliot. Don't be too proud of it," Bones said.

"Just because you were the team's worst outfielder ever, doesn't mean you should…"

"Whoa now, I caught a few of them," Bones countered.

With a glance at the clock, I decided there were more important things than discussing our old little league days. "We're going to be late."

"Because of these stops," Bones complained. "We're hitting the reservoir later, aren't we?"

"You want to see Reaper?"

"I guess."

I pulled onto Main Street, which was more packed than earlier. I let the sounds of the festivities course through the van's open windows, and it made me smile. It smelled like hot dogs and fire pits, and even Bones seemed content. "No, we're not stopping for wieners."

"You're always stifling me, Elliot."

I parked two blocks from the diner and hopped to the

street, sensing a change outside. I suspected if I had a barometer, I'd find a shift in the atmospheric pressure. The air was electric.

The roads were choked off with red barricades, a handful of deputies trying to manage the crowds. Even though a percentage of our residents went to the city for the bigger events, having most of the Island's population in one area made it feel crowded.

I scanned the area for my sister but couldn't see her or her friends. The church folk were there, carrying signs at the edge of the park, and beyond them, I noticed Sarge again. "Bones, give me a minute."

"Where you…"

His comment was lost among the multitude of voices as I wound my way through the crowd and into the park. I went by the fountain, where kids ran around the water, some jumping in for reprieve from the heat. Parents everywhere were attempting to humor their young ones, and I walked by a giant line for an ice cream truck.

When I reached the picketers, Sarge was gone.

"Where did you go?" And better yet, what was he doing filming the people of Bell Island with the camera I'd rented him? The forest he'd been occupying was rife with thick oak trees, their leaves hearty and green this time of year. I entered the meadow, and the noises subsided. It was almost like traveling to another place. The tinny speakers still blared music, but in the cover of the massive tree limbs, it was muted.

I slowly turned around, and when I faced the park again, Sarge was inches from me, the camera in his grip.

"What the hell do you want?" he growled.

"Nothing. I was …"

He stepped closer, and I backed up, tripping on a stump. "You were spying on me. I don't like to be watched."

"What are you doing with that?" I asked, nodding at the Movitron 2000. "If you break the camera, it's my hide."

The veteran smirked, his hard gaze softening. "You're just worried about the camera." He patted it roughly and extended a hand to help me up. I dusted a few damp leaves off my shorts. "It may sound weird, but I'm searching for something."

"Like what?" I peered through the trees at the crowd.

"You wouldn't get it, kid."

"I'm twenty-two."

He lost his smile. "I knew men at eighteen who lost their limbs, or worse, their lives. Twenty-two is different now… *kid*."

I chose not to argue with him about that. I couldn't imagine wearing a uniform and flying overseas to infiltrate another country's jungles, nor did I want to.

"Sorry about that. I'm not used to talking with people," he mumbled.

"My name's Elliot."

"Buzz," he said. "I've heard what the locals are calling me, and it's not a bad nickname, if I'm being honest."

He was referring to the name Sarge. "Is Buzz your real name?"

"Nope."

"Why Buzz?" I asked.

"First day at recruitment, the barber got distracted. I made quite the sight. Pale skin, freckled nose, and ears sticking out like wings. My CO called me Buzz, and it stuck."

"Thanks for doing your country proud," I said, repeating the phrase I'd heard others use when speaking to a veteran.

"Don't. It was hell. Every day wondering if today was

the one I'd be killed."

"You made it back," I said.

"Barely, but that's another story. Anything else?" He tapped his foot impatiently.

"No, sir."

"Don't call me sir either. Buzz will do."

"Okay, Buzz."

The interaction was different than I'd expected. I thought he was going to murder me and bury me in the forest, while the church protested D&D fifty yards away.

I left without any further comment and kept going until I was at the diner where Bones waited. He was smoking again, and I noticed him talking with someone.

"Hey, Reaper," I said.

She didn't react to my arrival.

"We're going to chill for a bit, if that's cool."

I didn't know what to say. He'd been adamant about our plans, and already he was bailing. Reaper watched him with a slight smirk, and I knew he needed this. He'd been pining over the girl for a while.

"No sweat. Where and when?"

"Reservoir at eight?" Bones lifted his chin, almost silently apologizing for the break in our adventure.

"Done. I'll bring the goods," I promised.

"Sweet. Catch ya." We bumped fists, then finished our handshake, and they strolled from the diner.

"They together?" Kim asked from the entrance. I hadn't heard her exit.

"Bones and Reaper? Nah. Not yet."

"What is it with Bell Island and the names?" she asked with a grin.

"We breed interesting characters," I answered.

She'd changed out of her uniform and looked beyond bodacious. Her shorts were red, cut high on the leg, and her white sleeveless blouse had two dangling gold chains. Her hair was curled and blonde, with large red plastic hoops poking out from her ears.

"You look…"

She did a slow spin. "Not bad for a waitress, hey?"

She wasn't kidding. Her confidence was unexpected, and I wasn't sure how to respond. Fortunately, she took the lead. "Can you follow me home? I gotta drop my car off."

"Sure." We took the sidewalk, away from the throngs of people. "Today must have been nuts."

She fanned out a stack of bills and flipped through them like they were a deck of cards. "It has its perks, but my feet are barking."

I'd never even seen that many bills in our cash register at work.

We walked by the video store, and Mark happened to be locking up at that very moment. He reversed the CLOSED sign and smiled as we approached. "If it isn't my best employee." Trudi walked by him, her headphones around her neck.

"Thanks, Mark," she huffed.

I shot my co-worker a knowing glance.

"Elliot doesn't forget to stock the shelves and empty the return bin, Trudi…"

"Whatever." Trudi went in the opposite direction while Mark put his keys away.

"Have you given any thought to what we spoke about yesterday?" Mark asked.

"I have," I said.

"And…"

"And I'll give you an answer on Thursday, if that's cool."

"Certainly." Mark clapped his hands together. "Who's

your friend?"

"Kim, this is Mark, my boss."

"I prefer to think we're friends, Elliot."

I cleared my throat and nodded once. "Yeah. This is my *friend* Kimberly."

"From the diner, right?" Mark narrowed his gaze on her, like he was scrutinizing Kim.

"That's me." They shook hands. "Nice to formally meet you. You're the lentil soup and tuna on rye?"

Mark's eyes widened. "Very good. Keep her close, Elliot."

"Have a good night," I said, and Mark walked to his station wagon, whistling a tune from an old cowboy TV show.

We watched as he drove off.

"Nice guy," Kim whispered. "He never leaves a tip."

"Sounds about right."

"You work here?" She eyed the windows, where a poster of ET faced us. "Ever get tired of it?"

I cocked my head to the side. "Don't you dare…"

She lifted a finger. "Ellllllliooooottttttt."

I rolled my eyes, and she took my hand, pulling us closer. Our noses almost touched, and I could smell her watermelon gum. "It had to be done." She let go, continuing our stroll.

I knew at that moment I was done for.

"So you live here, like permanently?" She stopped at an old car, with rust spots near the wheel wells. There were books inside, and I tried to see what she was reading.

"I'm heading into my senior year. Finance."

"A money man. How exciting," she said. "What's the strategy with that? Work at Bell Island National? Or move to Manhattan, buy a suit and chase the money?"

"I haven't got that far."

"Not a planner? I can appreciate that. Came here on a whim." She opened her car door and rolled her window down with the crank to let the heat out. A coffee cup fell onto the street, and she picked it up.

"Can't wait to hear about it," I said.

"You know the motel?"

"Hard not to when you grew up on the island," I told her.

She got in and started away, driving to the north.

My van was nearby, and I jogged to it, feeling like I might be able to compensate for yesterday's catastrophes. The island was small, and it only took five minutes before we arrived at the motel, her right in front of unit number 111. "I prefer the ground level. For a quick escape."

"What are you escaping?" I laughed, but she didn't join in.

"You never know what might be lurking in the night." Kim unlocked it, and I stayed outside. "Can you give me a minute? I wasn't expecting company."

I waited by the door, facing the parking lot while she shuffled around inside. I heard some thuds and doors slamming.

A couple of people hung out by the pool, drinking beer from a bag and talking loudly about their plans for later. Thankfully, it didn't involve the reservoir or Cove Peak. I didn't want to meet these guys in the wild, judging by their demeanor. Bell Island was a fairly safe place to live, but we weren't impervious to the growing drug problem of the Pacific Northwest. Things like marijuana were always around, but crack and heroin were growing in prevalence. At college, I'd met a few people using the hard stuff, but most were grass smokers.

One of them turned toward me, but I ducked and headed to Kim's room right as she opened the door.

"Make yourself at home," she said.

It was neat after her quick clean-up. The motel rooms had a tiny kitchenette with a two-burner hotplate and a mini fridge. The bed was made, the blankets perfectly tucked, and I doubted anyone working here would have done that for her.

"It's great."

"You're just being nice. It's a dump. But I don't expect to be around long," she said.

"In the motel, or on Bell Island?" I nudged.

Kim shrugged in response. "I'm not a planner either, so time will tell. Sometimes you need a reason to stay."

I could be that reason. I didn't dare say my thoughts, and wondered how she got to me so easily. "Don't I know it."

"Give me a second?" Kim went to the bathroom, where I guessed she was freshening up her makeup.

I saw more paperbacks stacked on the table. "You like to read?"

"Mostly true crime. Some mysteries," she said from the other room.

I picked one up and flicked through the musty pages. A journal sat beside them with her name embossed on the front of the book. This had clearly been a gift from someone that loved her. It looked well made, and not cheap.

She came out, her eyes darker, her cheeks slightly redder.

"Are you ready for a real Bell Island Fourth of July celebration?" I asked her.

"As long as that involves drinking beer around a fire and watching the stars, then sure thing."

"We might have a storm," I said, and her entire demeanor changed.

"Where did you hear that?" she whispered.

"The radio."

"I'd better bring a jacket." She went to the bed and tossed a few items into an oversized bag, including the journal from the table. The last was an umbrella. "I'm ready for some fun."

I suddenly realized that whatever we managed to do tonight would pale in comparison to what Kim anticipated. "Just to warn you, we're not that exciting."

"I have a feeling tonight will be," she uttered, and closed the door, locking it from outside.

6

"Sorry your car was trashed," Kim said as we traversed the back roads. Everyone left on the island was parked along the main drag, and even now, dozens of people took to the ditches, heading downtown. Music carried through my window from five or six blocks away.

"Yeah, it sucks."

"Where did you get it?" Kim asked.

"The car?"

She nodded.

"My Uncle Taylor."

Her eyes widened. "That's one nice uncle. The only thing my family ever gave me was a headache."

"He was the best," I said.

"Was? I didn't know…"

"Why would you? He drowned a couple years ago and left me the car."

"That's terrible. I'm sorry. Not about the car, but the other part." She reached for her chest, as if she could feel the cold water rushing into her lungs.

"He wasn't well." I tapped my head. At least that was the story around town. Add in my mother, and everyone had started treating me as if I'd be next.

It wasn't quite time to meet at the reservoir, so I had to stall. "Want to see the falls?"

"Wait, you have waterfalls on Bell Island?"

"Nothing to write home about, but they're kind of

cool," I said, hoping to temper her expectations.

It was the heart of summer, and the air was heavy with the threat of an incoming storm, despite the current clear sky. Bell Island was split into three sections, with small mountains piercing through the southern side. There were only a few residences overlooking the ocean. They were reserved for the elite city dwellers. One of them was an old politician who'd retired and sold his book rights for a stack of cash. My dad had bought a copy, but I doubt he'd ever read it. Too liberal for a conservative, he'd said. Whatever that meant.

The road narrowed, merging to a single-lane gravel stretch leading to the falls entrance. I parked in a turnabout, facing my van away from the path. "This is it."

"I don't see any falls," she told me.

"We have to walk a mile," I said with a grin.

"A mile?" She glanced at her feet. "Good thing I have sneakers." They were white with a few scuffs on them.

"I should have warned you. There are bugs the size of your thumb out here, but we should be fine."

Kim set her hand on the door handle and watched me. "You're not plotting to kill me or anything, are you?"

I laughed and got out. "You've read too many of those true crimes. But please ignore the shovel in the back."

"You're joking, right?"

"It was Bones' idea. I think he's worried about getting stuck in a mudslide or something," I said. I took a deep breath and grinned. "It's nice."

She joined me, inhaling the fresh air. "A girl could get used to this." She slapped a mosquito, leaving a red streak on her arm. "I spoke too soon."

"You're not from a small town, are you?"

"Nope."

We began the walk, taking the rocky path. Endless

trees with long branches swayed above in the breeze. Bird songs echoed through the area, and insects accompanied them in nature's harmony.

Mount Alexander was named for the creator of the telephone, by some early resident who thought he was being coy. Alexander Graham Bell, since our Island shared a name with him. Unfortunately, it just physically resembled a bell, and had nothing to do with the Scottish inventor.

I could see the peak from the ground, only a hundred yards up. I squinted, noticing a glint of light from the top. I grabbed Kim's hand and pointed. "Do you see that?"

Kim stared with me but shook her head. "What? It's a mountain. A hill, really."

Whatever I'd seen reflecting was gone. We kept going. "So where are you from? You seem to be avoiding my questions."

"Okay. You want to know?"

"I do."

"I lived in Chicago for most of my life. Went to San Diego for my education, and just graduated a few months ago."

So she was slightly older than me. "What did you take?"

"Journalism."

I let that sink in. Kimberly had a degree in journalism and had moved to Bell Island to be a waitress and live in a scuzzy motel. "What the hell are you doing here?" I must have asked it too loudly, because she visibly recoiled. She swatted at a swarm of miniature flies and stopped.

"I needed a change," she said.

It hit me. She'd been in a relationship, and it had probably ended sourly. "That's understandable."

She smiled, and the uncomfortable moment passed. "You look like you need one too."

"A change?"

"Yep. Maybe tonight can start you on a new journey." Kim walked on, and I jogged to catch up.

We rounded a bend, and the tree cover grew denser. It didn't seem like the county maintenance had spent much effort trimming the area this summer. When we entered a clearing, the rush of the falls carried the half mile to our ears. Our pace quickened with the promise of the sight, and I hurried to keep stride with Kimberly.

"What's after Bell Island?" I asked her.

"We'll see, Elliot. One day at a time."

It was as circumspect of an answer as one could give, but I shrugged it off. She didn't know what she wanted and was letting an unseen force guide her. I could respect that.

We neared the water, and Kim laughed when we arrived. "This is beautiful."

I'd seen it a million times. Bones and I used to come here once a week as kids, riding our bikes through Viking territory, avoiding the Sasquatch forest, and evading pirates at the base of the falls. The memories surfaced in my mind as we stared at the gushing stream.

The rocks were slick with dampness, moss covering most of them, and Kimberly stepped closer. The falls fell over a ledge of rock with a pitch-black cave behind the rushing water.

"Have you ever been in there?" she asked.

"Of course." I'd done it once, and only after relentless goading by Bones, when we were eleven. It was scary inside, and the Island was home to a few bobcats that had somehow made residence years before. It was rumored they'd made a nest in there, but I'd found no evidence. The sheriff had started that tale to keep kids from playing around and cracking their skulls open on the slippery stone surface.

Kim kicked off her shoes and wiggled her toes, grinning at me. "Show me."

"Now?" My heart raced, the beats thrumming in my eardrums. I froze in place.

"Is there a problem?" She was knee-deep in the pool. It wasn't very high, and it might only soak the hem of her shorts if she continued.

"Not at all." I turned around, removing my own shoes, and slid my socks off. *You can do this, Elliot.* I smirked to convey a confidence I didn't have and stepped into the water. It was cold, giving amnesty from the early evening heat.

We explored the pond together and slowed down near the falls. Kimberly avoided the splash but stood close enough to feel the mist. I gestured to the right. "Our best bet is to take that side."

Kim went without comment, and climbed from the water, her shins dripping onto the boulders. "It's slick." She lifted her arms to balance on the wet moss.

"Be careful." I got out too, and stared into the void beyond the falls, picturing a massive cat within, waiting to pounce.

"This is already more fun than I've had in months," Kim proclaimed, and ventured into the opening.

I knew there was nothing to fear, but something bothered me. The hair on my arms stood on end, and I reached for her, preventing her from going any farther. She gasped, and I stared past her at a pile of bones.

Kim let out a gurgling sound, and her nails dug into my hand as she clutched it. "What is that?"

Most of the cavern was dark, with the light of day only sneaking through the falls near the front of the space. I trudged closer to the white skeletal remains, wondering if I'd find a human skull atop them, but it wasn't a person. "It's a cow." The skull still had fleshy bits stuck to it. It was clearly bovine.

I could smell it, the scent of death and decay rushing into my nose. Before, I'd thought it was the musk of the water, but now I understood the source. I wasn't sure if it was my nerves, or if something really shifted at the far end of the cave, but I stepped in front of Kim with fists raised.

"Let's go," Kim whispered.

She started to back up and must have tripped on a rock, because she fell, screaming as she splashed into the pond. I didn't want to break my stare with the shadows, but finally spun and dove in after her.

Kim was already on her feet, the falls dousing her head with water. She spat out a mouthful of liquid and lowered into the pool, swimming toward the path. I eagerly caught up, both of us submerged to our necks as we watched the cavern beyond the waterfall.

"What was that?" she asked.

"Bobcat."

"No, Elliot. A bobcat doesn't bring a cow to a cavern. It's not big enough."

We climbed out, and I cracked a smile. Kimberly was soaked. So was I, but her clothing stuck to her body like it was painted on. I averted my eyes, and she started to laugh. "Turn around, Elliot."

I obeyed, and heard her removing her clothing before wringing it out and dressing again.

We slid into our shoes, and Kim's pace on the way back to the van was even faster. Her wet hair was plastered to her face. "Now what?"

"Let's get you cleaned up," I said.

Twenty minutes later, I pulled into my driveway. Dad's truck was gone, as were half the cars from the neighbor's party. They must have left for the fireworks. That was all we needed. A bunch of drunk islanders ripping around the roads.

"This is your house?" Kim asked as she shut the van door.

"Yep. It's nothing fancy," I said.

"I like it. It's quaint."

I was pretty sure that word was used in the same way *cozy* meant *small*. "Thanks."

We went inside, and I grimaced when I saw Cindy hadn't cleaned up the bathroom. "Give me a minute?"

She nodded, and I made do with what I had. When I thought it might be passable for someone like Kimberly, I offered the shower to her, and gave her a couple of fresh towels.

"You sure?" she asked.

"Yeah, if you give me the clothes, I can throw them in the dryer with mine."

She grinned again, and left the door open a crack. The water started, and after a minute, she handed me everything she'd been wearing and closed the bathroom.

I undressed and tossed it all into the dryer in the basement. While I waited, I noticed all my mother's stuff. She had a mannequin with a half-formed dress on it. Her sewing machine was beside it, and I ran a finger over the top, finding a layer of dust. She used to love this space. Mom had once sold her designs at a shop downtown, and occasionally in the city, but she'd stopped a few years ago, probably around the time her brother succumbed to his demons. I put on an old pink bathrobe hanging near her things.

"Come home, Mom," I whispered, and didn't hear Kim's footsteps until she was right behind me. She wore a towel, her hair wrapped in a second one.

Seeing her reminded me of how distant Bethany and I had been. When was the last time she'd set my heart racing like Kim could? Years, probably.

Kim pointed at my robe. "Nice threads."

"Thanks, it's my mom's."

"Does she sew?" she asked.

"Yeah."

"Is she downtown for the fireworks?" Kim touched the fabric on the dress.

"She's in the city."

"For what?"

I didn't want to delve into it, but also felt like I could tell this stranger anything and it wouldn't matter. I'd spent most of my life ashamed, but there was an air about Kim that set me free. "She's at the Pacific Northwest Hospital."

Kim stared blankly, like she had no idea where that was. "Is she sick?"

"It's a psychiatric hospital."

Kim's mouth sealed tight, and she backed up a step, probably not even realizing it. "Why is she there?"

"It's a long story. It has to do with her and my uncle, and…"

"They witnessed something, didn't they?"

"Why do you say that?" I asked, suddenly questioning just who this woman was.

"I've heard the rumors," Kim said, "but didn't know what to make of them. Small towns are full of gossip, but usually, there's a shred of truth to the words on the wind."

The door upstairs opened, and Cindy's voice carried to my ears. Her friends were there, and I glanced at Kim, wondering what my dad would think when he heard about a half-naked girl in our house with me.

"Where's the booze?" It was River, her voice high and whiny.

"Cindy's dad only drinks gross stuff," Becky complained.

I marched up the stairs, ready to tear a new one into my sister.

Cindy jumped when she saw me, and her gaze drifted behind me. "Who's this?" She started to smile, looking Kim up and down. "And what are you wearing?" Cindy poked my arm.

"Oh my, God, it's that new chick from the diner," River said. "She's like totally cute."

"Thanks," Kim whispered. "I'd better…" She paused, heading to the bathroom.

"Cindy, you can't steal Dad's whiskey. You're fifteen," I told her.

"You think I didn't notice you and Hank sneaking into the backyard with his beers when you were thirteen? I was a kid, not blind."

"That's different," I said.

"Why, because you're boys?" Cindy tapped her foot and crossed her arms.

"Just stay out of it. And don't tell Dad about…" I glanced at the hall.

"I won't, but… what is Bethany going to think?"

"We're done," I said.

"You didn't hear?" Becky asked, chewing her gum loudly. Her hair was in a side ponytail, her light jeans jacket covering her pink tank top. "She totally dumped him at the diner. I guess Elliot didn't wait too long to pounce on another chick."

The girls laughed, and Cindy gawked at me. "Beth left you?"

They were close, almost like sisters. Bethany had been around for all the major holidays and weekend dinners when we were both in town. "Yeah."

Cindy barreled into me, hugging me tightly. "I'm sorry, Elliot. I know you think I'm a pill, but this must sting."

"Not as much as you might think," I muttered. The dryer buzzed from the basement. "Get out of here, Cindy, and don't make any trouble."

"Come on, girls, maybe there's something at River's house," Cindy said.

"Totally. My parents are gone and they love wine spritzers." River led the trio from the living room, and Cindy stopped at the exit, holding the knob.

"See you later."

I gave her a smile, and when she was gone, I grabbed the clothing from the dryer. I knocked on the bathroom door and handed it in to Kim. She had it on in no time and entered the hallway looking refreshed. I could tell she'd used some of Cindy's eyeliner, because it was light blue.

"Your turn?" Kim asked.

I checked the time, and we had twenty minutes before Bones was expecting us. "Sure, I'll be quick."

I washed the murky water from my hair, shampooing twice to ensure the smell was gone. I dressed and put on jeans instead of shorts, given the threat of a storm. Like Kim, I grabbed a jacket from the front closet.

I searched for her. "Kim?"

"In here."

She was in my room, holding one of my baseball trophies. She placed it beside a horror novel and lifted an eyebrow. "Sports and academia. Quite the well-rounded man, aren't you?"

I was slightly embarrassed by my room, with a *Star Wars* poster on the wall from when I was Cindy's age, and my collection of GI Joes standing in line above my desk. "We don't want to be late."

"I think it's sweet," Kim said. She strolled up and kissed my cheek before walking past me.

Dad had recently gotten one of these fancy new

answering machines, hoping he could catch wind of any jobs on the Island, or even in the city, but I didn't know how to use it. The red light was blinking, but I left it, not wanting to break anything. He said it cost more than we could afford, but that it might pay off in the end. I remember hearing about the argument between my parents from Cindy, as Mom didn't approve of wasteful spending.

I locked up, and then we were on the road for the millionth time that day. I really wished I was driving my own car, rather than my mother's van, especially because I was escorting Kim around.

She investigated the back. "What's in the cooler?"

"Beer. Some lighter stuff," I said.

"Cool."

"Bones has fireworks too."

"That sounds fun," Kim told me.

The reservoir was across the island, past the turnoff to the docks and Cove Peak, and the farther from downtown I was, the less traffic we encountered. When I parked at our destination, I spotted the first cloud heading to the north edge of Bell Island. A tingle raced down my arms, but I ignored the sensation.

7

The reservoir was along the dammed river that snaked from Mount Alexander, and it wasn't much more than a glorified slough. One side was natural, the other a stone wall, rising five feet over the surface. Someone was walking across the wall, like they were on a tightrope, when we arrived. I clutched the cooler, and Kim had a backpack from the van.

I set it down, my arms protesting after only a short hike. The thing weighed a ton.

"Elliot!" Bones called from a picnic table. He was with Reaper, and a bunch of other people I barely knew. Most of them were a couple years younger, and a few far older. There were ten in total, none of whom seemed pleased by us newcomers.

"Hey, Bones." I set the cooler on the table and opened the lid. There was already a keg near a firepit, and two of the guys were dousing the wood with gasoline.

"Hi. I'm Kimberly." She waved at them, and Reaper gave her a grin in return.

I realized how the pair of us didn't belong among this crowd. They all had dyed black hair, leather, and tattoos. I'd never felt out of place with Bones and his mohawk, but suddenly understood why people looked at him a certain way.

"Nice to meet you, Kim." Reaper cracked a beer, sending a bit of foam down the can. She offered it to Kim, who accepted with a gracious smile.

The fire lit with a whoosh, and one of the men had to pat his shirt when it caught. They laughed about it, and the pit roared with the initial spark, the fuel quickly burning off. It lowered, and the wood crackled.

A girl rolled her skateboard on a homemade half-pipe and did an axle stall, before spinning to the other side.

Kim and I took a seat across from Bones and Reaper, and I grabbed a beer. "How are we getting home?" I asked Bones.

"I hadn't thought that far ahead," he admitted.

"Jeff can drive us." Reaper pointed at a man with gray in his beard. "He owns the arcade. Doesn't drink."

I watched as he puffed on a smoke, and realized it was weed, not tobacco. "We can find our own way," I muttered.

"What did you two do?" Bones sipped his drink.

I told them about our experience at the falls, and Jeff stood up, walking over to the table. "A cow?"

"Yeah. It was the damnedest thing," I said.

"Did you see the cat?" Bones asked.

"There's no way," Jeff countered. "They removed all the bobcats like three years ago."

"They could have come back," Bones said.

Kim set her can down. "Do they swim?"

"Probably. I dunno." Jeff took a toke. "Either way, no cat is dragging a cow into the falls. Maybe a bear. Even that's stretching it."

"We definitely don't have bears," Reaper said. "My dad is a deputy, and he'd know if there were any sightings."

"Wonder what it was?" Bones stared at the fire. The sun had started to set, and stars began to reveal themselves as the blue morphed to black.

"Maybe it was a person," Reaper whispered.

"A person?" I blurted.

"I'm telling you, Sarge is…" Bones began, and I interrupted.

"His name's Buzz," I told them.

"Buzz? Sounds made up too." Jeff tossed the roach into the flames. "He's a creepy dude."

I wanted to remind Jeff he wasn't any better, hanging out with people two decades younger than him. His hair was slicked into a ponytail, showcasing an expansive brow.

"I think we should pay him a visit," one of the other guys said. His steps swayed, his cup sloshing with keg beer.

"Just let it go," I said, not liking the direction this party was taking. "It's the Fourth. Let's enjoy ourselves."

Headlights shone from the parking lot, and soon more noise drifted across the reservoir as a group of people arrived.

"You have to be kidding me," I groaned.

Cooper and Bethany trailed behind the others. Paul carried a boom box, some song with far too much synthesizer blasting from the speakers.

"Who invited the greasers?" Paul asked.

Reaper stood, staring at the jocks as they flooded the reservoir. There had to be twenty-five of them. I knew most of the group, and had played sports with a few.

Bethany noticed me and stopped in her tracks, shoving Cooper's arm off her shoulders. The girl that had been with him earlier on the ferry was nowhere in sight. My ex-girlfriend's gaze drifted to settle on Kim, and I stepped closer to the waitress.

"What are you guys doing here?" Bones asked.

"Hank, you look like you stuck your finger in the electrical socket. Didn't your dad teach you… Oh wait, he's gone, isn't he?" Cooper laughed at his own joke, and only Paul joined him.

Bones' hands balled into fists, and I intervened.

"Cooper, where's Katie?" I asked innocently.

"Katie?" Bethany shoved him in the shoulder. "What's he talking about?"

"We saw them on the last ferry today, didn't we, Bones?"

"Sure did. They looked pretty friendly," Bones added. "What is she, a high school senior?"

"She's eighteen," Cooper said defensively.

"You're such a dweeb." Bethany stormed off, one of her girlfriends following her.

"Look what you did, Hoffman." Cooper was ready to throw down, and the entire group of Bones' new friends came to defend me. They were a tough bunch, all scars and leather.

"We're adults, aren't we? Why must you resort to violence?" I inquired.

"This is bull. We always come to the reservoir." Cooper pointed at the water.

"It's big enough to share," Reaper suggested. "Build a fire on the other side."

Cooper glanced at Paul, then at Bruce, who nodded in acceptance. I was glad to have one of them on my team. "Whatever. We're out of here."

Paul, not willing to make amends, walked to my cooler and grabbed a beer. He stood in front of me and opened the top, chugging the can. The brute burped and crushed it on his forehead before dropping the empty on the gravel near my feet.

I didn't react.

Then they left.

"What a zoo animal," Kim said. "I heard small towns are different, but this is next level."

The sound of engines starting carried from the

temporary parking lot, and headlights flashed on, cutting through the forest of trees. And then silence.

The fire crackled, and I felt the first raindrop of the night. The clouds had gathered, but they were still light gray, a wispy blanket above Bell Island.

Bones lifted a pack of wieners. "Who wants a dog?"

"Does he always eat this much?" Kim asked.

"This is a light day for him," I admitted. "Kim?"

"When in Rome." Kim jabbed one onto a metal stick, and we went to the fire. "I don't do this very often."

"Not much of a camping family?" Bones asked her.

"Nope. My dad was in commercial real estate and didn't take time off. My mom was a nurse."

I noticed how she'd said 'was,' but didn't press the subject. She was just a year or two older than me, so her parents couldn't be retired. "Bones and I used to go with my dad. Mostly on the mainland, because there aren't a lot of good spots on the Island. We'd fish in the mornings, play cards in the afternoons, and tell scary stories in the evenings."

Kim sat on a stump, and I rolled another beside her. "I like scary stories."

I pictured the stack of real horror in her motel room. The tales of true-life murderers and serial killers. That bothered me more than the idea of a ghost.

"If you're into scary stuff, I have one for you," Jeff said. He'd lit another joint, and the skunky scent blew upwards with the bonfire smoke.

"What's it about?" I rotated my stick, trying not to char the outer edge.

Jeff's face was illuminated by the flames, his eyes dark hollows. "Have you ever heard of the Bell Island Demon?"

Kim grinned and shook her head. "I just moved here."

"Then you're in for a treat, because this will knock your

socks off." Jeff cracked his neck and leaned closer, changing the pitch of his voice. "Bell Island was formed long before anyone lived on it. In the early 1900s, people would come from the mainland, docking in the very cove we use today for a marina. The waters are calm, making it the ideal location for fishing."

"I thought no one settled here until the war," Bones said.

"Common misconception," Jeff told him. "The community wasn't built until the mid-thirties, and when the war took all our resources, the plan was stalled. But things took place years before the first shovel dug into the old area."

"What happened?" Kim lifted her stick and blew on the end, where the wiener was burning. She shrugged and slid it into a bun with ketchup. A girl after my own heart.

"The Bell Island Demon waits for unsuspecting victims. A boy named Victor Koslov was with his father, a Russian immigrant and fisherman, in the cove one morning in 1903. The boat must have struck a rock too close to shore, and it began to sink. They escaped, getting to the island. Sounds like they lived on the land for a week before anyone returned, finding them on the beach. Victor was pale, his hands trembling. He saw something."

We were consumed by the tale, and I pulled my dog out, taking a bite before he continued.

"Victor described it as a ball of sun," Jeff said, flicking his lighter on. Everyone stared at him. Bones chewed loudly, finishing his first hot dog before sliding another on his roasting stick.

"It's like your grandmother said," I told Bones, who didn't seem to follow.

"Holy crap, you're right!"

"Are you guys juiced?" Reaper asked.

"She said she witnessed that exact thing, decades ago."

Jeff nodded. "Not surprising. It happened again with the building crews in the thirties." He lifted his finger. "Bob Smithers, framer from the Midwest, came out in search of a new life. Got a gig here nailing two by fours. One day, he was as right as rain, the next... he was someone else."

I pictured my Uncle Taylor. There were periods where he didn't seem like himself. Sometimes they'd last for days. My dad had told me he might have multiple personalities, but the doctors found no evidence of that.

"And again in 1949. Lillie Hanson, a retired teacher, was gardening in her backyard when the storm hit. She called it an angel sent from heaven. Her husband had died, and she thought it was there to escort him to the afterlife," Jeff proclaimed.

"Like the grim reaper," Reaper whispered, looking at her tattoo of the scythe. "How do you know all this?"

"I've been around all my life, and I listen. When I first heard about poor Victor, I had to know more."

"What happened to him?" I asked.

"Drowned... a week later," Jeff said.

I swallowed a lump in my throat and grabbed my beer, drinking deeply. Bones gazed at me with the news. Something gnarly was transpiring.

"Why doesn't anyone talk about this?" Kim asked.

"Not sure. It's our little island's dark secret."

I finished my hot dog and rested my elbows on my knees. "Jeff, were there any other sightings?"

"One other that I've heard of. A boy and a girl. Twins."

I froze, my vision narrowing as lights sparked in my eyesight. I rushed for the picnic table. Kim followed me, grabbing my arm. "Are you okay?"

"That's my mom and her brother. They saw the demon," I said.

"It's not real, Elliot. It can't be." But her expression contradicted her words.

I turned to the fire, confident I had the answer to my question. "Where did this occur? Was it near the drive-in theater?"

Jeff puffed on his joint, nodding. "How did you know?"

Bones clapped his hands, the loud noise startling in the looming silence. "Who's ready for a treasure hunt?"

───────────────

As the clock struck nine on the Fourth of July, I parked near the drive-in. Reaper was the only one of the group that joined us, the others preferring to enjoy the fire and keg they'd saved up for. Now it was a good thing I had the van, because it could accommodate everyone comfortably. Kim sat in the passenger seat, with Reaper and Bones in the back.

"What's the plan?" Kim asked.

Bones poked his head between the front seats. "You have the paper, Elliot?"

"Right here." I unfolded the note we'd discovered in the Camaro.

We got out, and I peered past the chain-link fence. ET was playing a double feature, and the theater was three-quarters full. The closest truck had two high schoolers making out in it, and I noticed Cindy and her friends watching from a bench. She ate popcorn and threw a kernel at Becky.

"We start at the intersection," Bones ordered, like he was in charge of a covert mission. He carried a flashlight and the shovel from earlier. Kim had thrown her jacket on and held the umbrella.

A moment later, we stood at the corner of Dawson and Royal. A light drizzle began to splatter our heads.

"Now what?" Reaper asked.

"We walk." I turned northeast, counting off my steps. That led us to the mini-mart parking lot, the store closed for the night. I stopped near a dumpster, smelling the day's unused food rotting away from the earlier heat. "Now northwest." I did the same, the others letting me go ahead. "One hundred."

"I think that was less," Bones said. "If we screw up each of the directions, we're not going to be on target."

He was right. Also, we didn't know if the 100 on the note meant paces, yards, feet, or some variation. I took another couple steps, and Bones seemed satisfied. "Fifty to the west." We were blocked by a tire shop. "So much for that."

"These were marked before any of this was developed. It'll be there," Bones said, circumventing the fence.

"What will?" Kim asked.

"I don't know. Maybe the Bell Island Demon," he muttered, holding the flashlight under his chin to make a scary face.

"You guys are a riot. But we should get out of here before it really comes down." Reaper clutched a flashlight.

"Nothing wrong with a little rain," Bones said, but she didn't seem to agree. For all her bravado, I thought Reaper was scared.

"Fifty paces would be right out back." I estimated this was the location, directly west of the tire yard. I lingered on a patch of grass and studied the scene. There was no one in sight, the alleyway streetlights dim and yellow.

Reaper leaned on the fence. "I don't like the vibe."

"It's fun. Let's summon the demon," Bones whispered.

"No way." Reaper shook her head. "I thought this was just a game. I'm not staying for this."

Bones tried to reason with her, but she jogged off, leaving us. My friend returned with his chin drooping. "What's her problem? We're just kidding around."

"Are we?" Kim asked.

I'd driven our group. "How's she going to get out of here?"

"Her car's parked at the arcade. She caught a ride earlier." Bones tapped the spaded shovel on the earth. "What a bummer. I was hoping to have some fun."

The rain began to douse us, and Kim flicked the umbrella open. "We should go."

"Where?" Bones asked. "This rain's ruining the night."

"Not necessarily," I said. "We could hit the bar."

Thunder boomed over Bell Island. The ground trembled slightly, and I glanced at Kim. "What was that?"

"Do you have earthquakes?"

"Some fault line tremors, but nothing serious," I told her.

Bones lifted the shovel, jamming it into the grass. "This blows."

I was almost shaken to the ground, and caught Kim when she tripped.

"Who's there?" someone shouted. "Elliot? Is that you?"

It was Cindy, trudging through the alley. Her hair was plastered to her head, and she shivered.

"What are you doing here?" I bellowed over the sound of the storm.

"Me? You're digging behind a tire yard!"

"Where are your friends?"

"We were leaving, and I saw Mom's van… then the flashlight beam." She glanced between us, as if she was striving to puzzle out the situation.

The earth rattled again, and Bones fell to his knees. Cindy slipped, landing in a puddle of water on the road. Kim held the fence, and I managed to stay up.

For a moment, I thought the flashlight had fallen and aimed at my eyes, but this was something different. The ball rose from the dirt, the size of a softball. It dimmed and shimmered with the light of the sun.

Cindy sat up and screamed so loud, it hurt my ears.

The light bobbed up and down, floating above us.

Kim's hand found mine, her grip tight enough to hurt. None of us could speak.

The glowing sphere shifted to Cindy, and a shriek caught in her throat. One second it was a foot from her face; the next it was gone. Her eyes shone bright, the light escaping her mouth and nostrils, and she went rigid, arms straight out.

"Cindy!" I shouted, running to her.

She let me hug her, her body going limp. She spoke just loud enough for me to hear. "He's coming. I can feel it. Don't let him get me."

"What? Who's coming?" I demanded, but she passed out.

I lowered her to the ground, Kim and Bones there to assist me as the rain intensified. Lightning penetrated the skies, and the streetlight blinked off, casting darkness all around us. The flashlight continued to work, and I took it, aiming the beam at Cindy as Kim held the umbrella over my sister.

"Cindy!" I shook her, but she didn't react. Her chest rose and fell in a smooth rhythm, indicating she was alive.

Bones peered down the alley. "What do we do?"

"Let's carry her into the van," I said. "Stay with her. I'll grab it."

With a final glance at Cindy, I darted off, splashing through the puddles until I reached the van. The headlights were excessively bright compared to my surroundings. The brakes screeched as I slammed them on, locking up the tires, and I didn't waste any time opening the back. We ushered Cindy in, laying her on the rear row. Her eyes rolled up in their sockets.

I slid the door closed, keeping the rain out, and heaved a deep breath. "Where do we take her?"

"The ferry isn't coming, and the medical clinic is closed. We could try calling Doctor Murphy," Bones suggested.

"Good idea."

"There's no hospital on the island?" Kim asked.

"We're not big enough."

"There are boats, though, right?"

"Yeah, but you don't want to be caught in the channel with a flimsy motorboat during a storm. Odds are you'll capsize before making land," I told her.

Kim stared at my sister, hugging herself. "I don't think I like living on an island."

"Little late for that," I said. "Let's find a phone."

The sky flashed, and I saw a person in the distance. He was big.

I jumped into the front seat, squinting as I gawked through the water-covered windshield. The wipers streaked it away, and when I focused on the figure's previous position, it had vanished.

I threw it into gear and raced off, ready to locate the nearest payphone. There was one a few blocks away at the grocery store's parking lot, but the moment I turned toward the drive-in, every car had escaped the movie. The screen was off, along with every streetlight. "Power must be out," I mumbled.

"That means…" Bones didn't finish.

"The phones will be too." I honked the horn, but no one budged. There was an accident ahead, and two hot-headed middle-aged men were shouting at each other. "Screw this." I drove onto the sidewalk, keeping two tires on the road, and pulled around them. The van bounced level as I cranked the wheel and sped to the store.

As expected, the payphone was dead. I even went as far as dropping coins in and tapped the receiver for good measure. I returned to the driver's seat wet and deflated.

"We can go to the Doc's house," Bones said.

"You know where he lives?" Kim asked.

"She. And it was on my old paper route." Bones offered directions. She was in Cooper's neighborhood… of course.

"Then that's our destination." I turned onto the main drag cutting through the island. At least Cooper probably wasn't home.

"What are we going to tell her? That a white light entered Cindy?" Bones let out a nervous laugh.

"We'll worry about that when we find Doctor Murphy." The roads were pitch black, but my lights kept me between the lines. The rain was relentless, and my wipers were on full, trying to improve my view. I almost skidded off at a sharp corner, but managed to lurch into the middle of the road.

Bones cursed at me, and I told him to put his seatbelt on if he wanted to complain.

"Any changes?" I spotted Cooper's block ahead, the entire area shrouded in darkness. I could only see the houses' outlines when the sky flashed.

"Nothing. She's the same," Kim informed me.

"Great." I slowed. "Bones, which one is it?"

"It's been a while since I slung papers from my bike

basket. Uhm…" He pointed past my face. "That big house on the right."

I pulled into the driveway, and leapt over drenched hydrangeas before racing to the door. Bang. Bang. Bang.

"Doctor Murphy! Are you home?" I rang the bell, and a sharp dog bark announced my arrival to the household. I could see the shadow of the beast growing agitated behind the glass.

I waited for a minute, but no one greeted me. Headlights shone in my direction, a vehicle coming directly for us. I thought it might be the Doc and walked to the street, waving my arms. Only it wasn't her.

The truck almost clipped me as it slid to a stop, and the man driving leaned over the console, cranking his window down. "You have to follow me!"

"Buzz? What the hell are you doing out here?" I asked.

"You saw it, didn't you?" His eyes were wide, his mouth almost curled into a smile.

"Saw what?"

"The Sphere," he said.

There was no point in denying it. "We did. It went into my sister."

He rubbed his chin and slapped his steering wheel with the ball of his hand. "It's worse than I thought. Is she…"

"She's alive but unresponsive," I told him.

"Good. Bring her to my place," he advised me.

"She needs a hospital."

"No. She requires protection." He raised a handgun, and I backed up. "Not from me, Elliot. From *them*."

I brushed water off my brow and glanced at Kim and Bones in the van. "Lead the way."

He grunted and spun his vehicle around, waiting for me to trail him.

Part Two
The Dark

1

9:15 P.M.
July 4th, 1984

The Reeve farm was one of the oldest homesteads on the island. The land hadn't been cultivated for two decades, which was probably the reason Buzz had been able to afford it in the first place. Mrs. Reeve, the eighty-seven-year-old widow, had moved to the city a couple years ago to live out her days in a retirement community, and her son had quickly listed the property. It had been empty since I'd first left for school.

Farmland on Bell Island was very rare, but no one wanted to grow crops out here, not when shipping to the mainland was such an inconvenience. The value wasn't there. I'd heard my father talk endlessly about the topic when she'd first packed her things and vacated the farmhouse. It had been a hit to the island's pride to see such a once pristine plot of land lose its long-time caretaker. I imagined that Buzz's arrival had caused deep resentment from the lifers.

"This is a bad idea," Bones suggested as I pulled beside his truck out front.

"I agree. Did you see his eyes?" Kim asked.

"They're just two different colors. It's called heterochromia," I told them. "It's a genetic thing."

"You're such a nerd," Bones muttered. "Can we all take a moment to remember the sphere of light that your sister ingested?" His mohawk had tilted from the rain.

My door opened before I could respond, and Buzz growled, "What are you waiting for?" He checked behind him, like someone might be following, but it was as dark as the rest of the island.

"Nothing." I hopped out, moving to the back of the van. With Buzz and Bones' assistance, we carried Cindy to the house. Buzz took a moment to unlock the door, which apparently was sealed tighter than Fort Knox. He used four different keys on various bolts, and held it wide, ushering us inside. He lingered on the front porch while the rain splattered against the awning, before joining us in the entrance.

The house was the opposite of what I'd expected. I'd imagined animal heads mounted above a stuffy fireplace, a ratty recliner with empties littering the floor, but this was anything but.

"Gimme a minute." He rushed from his living room into the kitchen and through the rear door. A few moments later, the lights hummed and flickered on. The sound of a generator burning fuel echoed in his walls. He returned and set his gun on the coffee table.

I placed Cindy on the couch, laying her end to end. It was a nice piece of furniture. Nicer than we'd ever afforded.

"Everything I tell you is going to sound… slightly

impossible, but it's all true." Buzz knelt at the fireplace, adding paper and kindling into the hearth. He started it with the flick of a butane lighter, and after a moment, added a couple of small logs. When he turned, his expression was grim.

"What happened to Cindy? Is it the demon?" Bones asked, his voice cracking.

"Demon? What are you talking about? There are no such things as demons. You've been listening to that church group too much. No, it's nothing like that." Buzz plopped into a leather chair, resting his hands on his lap.

"Then what?" Kim stayed near Cindy, despite only having met earlier while wearing a towel. It was nice to see how protective the new girl was of my sister. We'd experienced something unprecedented, and it had bonded us forever. I nodded when she glanced in my direction, and I sat by Cindy's feet.

"Your sister has been taken by an alien." Buzz said it with a straight face.

"Did you say *alien*?" Bones asked. He was pacing the floor, his boots dripping water on the antique hardwood. Buzz stared as the mess spread.

"Would you take those off and stop wandering?" I said, beating Buzz to it.

Bones stared at the water and muttered an apology. He unlaced them, tossing the pair of leather boots onto the mat near the entrance, and sank into a soft chair across from the couch. I noticed there was no TV.

"Start over, please, Buzz," I urged.

"Around the time the folks in the States were protesting our efforts, I was knee-deep in jungle swamps, working my way north. It was useless. No matter how much ground we gained, they continued to rally. We started out with twenty in my platoon, and every damned member of my

94

squad was dead within the first month. They sent reinforcements. At one point, I'd been promoted three times, and the only reason was because I hadn't been shot, or killed from whatever the hell everyone was catching. Don't even talk to me about the snakes." He shuddered, rubbing his arms.

We listened, and I tried to picture this man navigating the jungle with his gun raised above him, gaze darting around trying to spot the enemy.

"Afterwards, most of the guys that survived ended up dead anyways. Agent Orange seemed like a game-changer, at least to the people making decisions from behind a desk back home." He slowly shook his head.

"The aliens?" Bones prompted, and I shot him a look to shut him up. "Sorry, I thought that's what this was about."

"It is… exercise some patience, kid." Buzz gazed at the gun on the coffee table. "I was one week from being discharged. I'd been deployed for nearly two years. Can you believe it?"

When no one answered his rhetorical question, he continued. "His name was Private Hunt. Billy. Eighteen damned years old, sent to defend his country. I doubted he'd ever even shaved his face." Buzz scratched at his stubble. "When I saw the end coming, I did everything I could to ensure he survived. I took a bullet."

"That doesn't sound like fun," Bones mumbled.

Buzz lifted his shirt, showcasing a half-dozen scars on his gut and ribcage. "I'd rather forget that time entirely, but fate won't allow it."

"What happened to Billy?" Kim asked.

"It was dark, almost as black as Bell Island with the power off. The jungle was filled with swarms of these tiny flies. They were everywhere. In your eyes, nose, mouth.

Sometimes the elements were worse than the fear of attack. A monsoon came in the middle of the night, the rain relentless. Billy walked away from camp, and I watched his back as he took a piss. The light came from nowhere. A brilliant globe rising from the water. It drifted toward Billy, and I ran, attempting to stop it, but the sphere had other ideas. It sped into him, filling him with light."

"That's what happened to Cindy," I told him.

"I suspected so. Billy passed out as well. I brought him to his tent, and the medic assessed him. Said there was nothing wrong that he could see. Thought maybe a parasite had affected his brain function. Then we were attacked by the other side. We fought like hell, with Billy sleeping it off in his tent. Just when I thought we were about to lose, *he* came."

My skin crawled at the simple word. "Who?"

"It was unlike anything I'd ever seen. He tore through the enemies, then my allies. He went for Billy, and I fought to stop him. My bullets didn't seem to work. It knocked me aside, and I slammed into a tree before falling into the swamp while Billy was dragged away."

"Did you save him?" Kim sounded out of breath.

He glared at her. "No. When I chased after them, he was gone. I tracked their trail for a few miles. Found fragments of Billy's body scattered around the jungle floor. The other guy disappeared."

I stared at Cindy. "Are you suggesting that one of these… things is coming for her?"

"I think so. They usually appear with a storm. It hides their ships," he said.

Bones jumped to his feet. "Ships? Did you say *ships*!?"

"Calm yourself. Yes, they have spaceships. How else would they get here?" Buzz asked.

"You're telling us that there's an alien in my sister, and

that another alien is coming for her?" I looked at the window when another flash of lightning dazzled over his land.

"That's what I'm saying," Buzz grumbled.

"And what are we going to do about it?" I asked him. "Defend ourselves."

"This is nuts," I said. "We need to get her to a doctor."

"No doc is going to help her," Buzz whispered.

Thunder shook the roof, and Kim peered at the ceiling. "I think we listen to Buzz, Elliot."

We both looked at Bones, like he was the tie breaker. "A vote? We're doing that?" His socked feet slapped on the wood floor. "Fine. We stay."

Sirens sounded from somewhere, and I noticed them getting closer.

Buzz rushed to the entrance, peering through his drapes. "The cops are here."

"Why?" I asked.

"How the hell should I know? I haven't done anything," Buzz blurted.

The red and blue lights lit up the glass as a pair of cars arrived. They killed the sirens, and I saw Sheriff Parker exit his squad car. The deputy was a younger guy, and I didn't recognize him.

Before they arrived at his door, Buzz opened it. "Can I help you with something?"

"Where were you an hour ago, Buzz?" Parker asked. His hand lingered near his holster.

Buzz's gaze was on the man's weapon when he answered. "Is there a reason you're asking me this?"

The sheriff must have finally noticed us, because his frown eased up. "Hoffman? Larson? What are you doing with this man?" Parker pushed past Buzz and saw my sister on the couch. "Would someone tell me what in tarnation is going on?"

"Cindy was at the movies with her friends, and one of them stole some wine coolers from her mom. The storm came, and when I went to pick her up, she was drunk as a skunk. I started to drive home, but my mom's van was acting up. Buzz saw us stranded and offered us a place to wait it out."

"Radiator leak. I dumped some water in to get him here," Buzz said, and I had no idea if that was a plausible story or not.

"What happened an hour ago?" Kim asked, and Sheriff Parker blinked like he hadn't noted her presence earlier.

"You're the waitress, aren't you?"

She nodded.

The deputy smiled at her. "Her name's Uhura."

Kim let out a small laugh. "It's Kim, actually. I borrowed someone's name tag that day."

"There's nothing funny about a dead body, missy." Parker put his hands on his hips.

"Who's dead?" Bones muttered.

"We found Cameron Gains five blocks from downtown, his throat torn out." Parker stared at Buzz, as if searching for a tell.

"And what does that have to do with me?"

"You haven't said where you were."

"We already did, he was…"

"This was before the storm hit," the deputy added.

"I was at the celebration."

Sheriff Parker stepped closer, until they were nose to nose. "You came here with a checkered past. Don't think I haven't looked into you. Wandering around these here United States like a vagrant. Every time you leave a town, there are bodies in your wake. I've been waiting for you to strike."

"You have the wrong…" Buzz gasped when Parker

punched him in the stomach. The deputy rushed around him, handcuffing Buzz's left hand.

Only this man wasn't a pushover. He shoved the junior, knocking him to the floor, and I could see the moment where Buzz decided not to fight. He could have lunged for his gun, but that would have been the act of a guilty man. None of us knew Buzz well, but whatever the sheriff thought he'd done, I doubted it was true. Parker's revolver pointed at his chest.

Buzz put his hands behind his back and turned around. "You shouldn't be wasting your time here."

"You just assaulted an officer." Sheriff Parker directed him to the door.

"Wait here," Buzz told me. He took a final glance at Cindy. "I'll be out soon."

"Hold up!" Kim shouted as they left the porch.

"What is it?" Parker asked, without stopping.

"We found something. A dead cow at the falls. There might be someone camping out there. It felt strange. Maybe they killed this Cameron guy."

"The falls?" Parker glanced at his deputy. "I've heard a couple complaints. Deputy Bradshaw will take you to check it out."

"I will?" Bradshaw countered.

"See if there's any evidence. It's possible that Cameron's wounds were inflicted by an animal, but highly unlikely."

Buzz met my gaze before he was shoved into the back of Parker's car. The lights continued to flash as he sped down the length of the driveway from Buzz's farmhouse.

"Come with me," Bradshaw ordered.

"I can't leave my sister," I said.

"We'll stay with her and lock the doors," Kim promised.

If what Buzz said was true, there was an angry space alien on Bell Island searching for Cindy at this very moment. But that was too preposterous to consider. It wasn't just improbable, it was impossible. We'd seen the same thing as my mother and my uncle all those years earlier. Ball lightning. It was the sole explanation.

Cindy had passed out or been shocked when it touched her, and she'd wake up any minute, safe in Buzz's house. Everything would be fine. I lifted a hand, waving at them from near the squad car. "It'll be okay. I'll come right back."

I went into the car, watching them stare after us from the front porch.

"What a night," Bradshaw said. His uniform was ruffled, and he had beer on his breath. But at least he let me sit up front, not in the back like a criminal on his way to the jail cell. "What's your name?"

"Elliot."

"I'm Ben Bradshaw."

"Nice to meet you, Ben. You guys busy?" I asked in a vain attempt at small talk.

"The storm's making a lot of people antsy, but there's a chance it'll clear up before midnight."

"Really?"

He shrugged as he drove to the main road. "Guess so. Heard it on the radio before the power went out."

The deputy used his bright lights, leaving the siren and cherries off.

"You new to Bell Island?" I asked.

"Two years."

"Do you enjoy it?"

"It's fine. Miss the night life of the city. These people are good stock, though. Don't cause too much trouble. Just some local drunks, and a bit of domestic assault. Nothing too strenuous."

The casual way he spoke of spousal abuse was shocking, but I didn't have to deal with it every day. I was certain that you became hardened to countless offenses with a job like his.

"What about you?" he asked.

"Finance student. Going into my senior year," I told him.

"Seriously? What are you doing here?"

"My parents and... sister are still around. I'm working at the video store," I said.

"That's why you look familiar. Think I've seen you there." He turned toward the falls, and slowed when we encountered a fallen tree blocking the road. No one else would be stupid enough to drive in the middle of this, especially at night. It was dark and ominous. His headlights blared against the pine, and he sighed. "Give me a hand?"

"Sure."

We each grabbed a limb and managed to drag it far enough to squeeze by. I wiped my sap-covered hands on my pants. They were already ruined, so what did it matter? We returned to the car once again soaked, and he threw it into gear, rolling for the end of the parking lot.

"What were you doing at the falls tonight?" Bradshaw asked.

"I brought Kim. She'd never seen them."

"Kim. She's a doll." Bradshaw grinned, and I did my best not to feel a surge of jealousy. Kim didn't belong to me, and she was free to do whatever she wanted. I had a brief lapse, wondering where Bethany was at that moment.

"Take this." He shoved a spare flashlight at me. It was heavy and black, no doubt filled with D batteries. I flicked it on and followed him to the trail, which was waterlogged, so I stepped cautiously, trying to not become any filthier.

It seemed like the storm had finally relented, but the clouds were so low and dense, there was no visible sky in sight. The entire island was covered by a dome of darkness. The trip didn't take long, and the whole time, I worried about Cindy. If anything happened to her, I'd be to blame. My mother was locked in a room for her own safety, and my dad was out with his friends, in denial that his life was slipping away from him. She was my responsibility, which wasn't fair, but it was reality. We removed our shoes and socks before getting into the water.

"The sheriff told me about the bobcats. But you think it could be something else?" Bradshaw asked.

"I don't know. How could a cat bring a cow to a cave?"

"Not sure. They are pretty strong."

"Not that strong," I muttered. My flashlight beam caught the falls, strands of light pushing past the rushing water. I listened for any animal sounds, but there was nothing.

We rounded the outer edge and waded past the barrier. I was already drenched.

Bradshaw had his gun out, his flashlight on top of it. The beam settled on the carcass, and I half expected an alien to rush us, green claws scrabbling for our throats. Instead, we found a baby bobcat mewing. Now I saw it wasn't an entire cow, but just the head. There were also pieces of the deer I'd crashed into the previous night.

"It dragged the head, not the whole body. It's a cat. I'll call it in. Get animal control out here from the mainland on Monday," he said.

For some reason, I was disappointed. I glanced at the shivering cat and knew its parents would be nearby. "Let's go."

We hurried through the pond, quickly throwing our shoes on. We jogged as the rain intensified and rushed into the car, huffing our breaths. Water dripped from both of us, soaking his seats.

Bradshaw grabbed the radio. "Station, this is Car Three. The falls is a bust. The bobcats are back."

"*Roger that, Car Three. Sheriff wants you out at Cove Peak. Someone came to the station, claiming they found another body.*" The voice was a woman's, and it sounded tired.

"Copy." He placed the radio into its cradle and gave me an apologetic look. "Sorry, Elliot. Going to have to do a stop before I return to your sister."

Cove Peak, a place I was very familiar with. Bethany and I used to park there on hot summer nights, anticipating the future. Our future. At the time, everything seemed so possible, but with each passing year, the dreams were dampened by uncertainties. We grew apart faster than we even knew.

The trek was perilous, with Bradshaw driving much slower than he was probably used to. The storm progressed as he climbed the steep incline, his tires spinning a few times before catching on the asphalt.

Lightning forked across the black clouds, and I spotted a figure on the cliffside. It was huge.

"Did you see that?" I asked.

"No. See what?" Bradshaw's car crept along the short row of parking spots.

When his headlights struck the spot, the shape was gone. "Nothing. I must be losing my mind."

"It's the dark. My eyes are always playing tricks on me." Bradshaw reached for his radio, and the glass smashed. The sound was so sudden and sharp, I stared at the deputy, like he might have a reasonable explanation. He fumbled for his gun and dropped it near my feet when something struck him.

A blade sliced his neck, and he turned to face me when

his head drooped forward. He was pulled from the car through the driver's side window, and I heard his body land on the gravel. My heart almost exploded with panic, and white spots floated into my view. I had to get out of there.

Instead of waiting for my own death, I clambered into the newly vacated seat, and threw it in reverse. My tires squealed as I gunned it from Cove Peak. The lightning lit up the area, and I peered into the rear-view mirror, seeing the figure looming over Bradshaw's body, watching me leave.

2

I clutched the steering wheel as rain soaked me from the open window. Bits of glass jabbed into my legs, and I struggled to get a full breath. I'd just witnessed a murder. But by what? It used a knife, an obsidian blade of some kind. That implied it wasn't an animal, and it was clearly standing on two legs, but it looked to be almost ten feet tall.

The road to the Reeve farm was slick, and I splashed through puddles as I turned onto Buzz's property. I was in a stolen police car, and the deputy was dead.

He'd been kind to me as we'd investigated the falls, and now he was gone. I gawked around the car, seeing blood on the console and radio. I couldn't escape the vehicle soon enough. I parked near the house and fell out, leaving the door open and the car running.

Kimberly was at the entrance, sheltered from the cover of the porch. "Oh my God, Elliot!" She met me on the stairs, grabbing my shoulders. "Are you hurt?"

I peered at my shirt, seeing Bradshaw's blood. "No. It was…"

"Where's the deputy?" Bones called from the entrance.

"He… the thing killed him. Smashed the window. Dragged him out." I stood in the rain, unable to bring myself up the steps.

"Get in here!" Bones shouted, hauling me by the arm.

He slammed the door behind me, and I saw Cindy remained on the couch, eyes closed.

"Tell us," Kim pleaded.

And I did. I explained finding the bobcat at the falls, then the incident on Cove Peak.

"We have to make sure Bradshaw is really…" Kim stumbled for the exit, but I blocked her way.

"Not going to happen. His throat was ripped out." I glanced at my stained shirt.

"The radio! We call Sheriff Parker and explain what happened," Bones suggested.

"I should have thought of that," I whispered.

"You were messed up. Don't worry about it." Bones reached past me for the knob. "You coming?"

I nodded, returning outside. The lights were blinding as we rushed to the car, and I went into the passenger side, remembering there was a gun on the floor. I picked it up and handed the weapon to Bones. The radio was sticky with the deputy's blood, but I used it, attempting to contact the station.

"Come in, this is Elliot Hoffman. Deputy Bradshaw has been involved in an accident." I glanced at Bones, who shrugged.

"Anything?"

I released the button and only heard static. I tried a couple more times, with the same result. "Nothing."

Bones went around and cut the engine. "Let's go to the station."

As much as I didn't want to relocate Cindy, he was right. We returned to the house, and I peered at my sopping and stained clothes. "I better see what I can change into."

"Good call," Bones said.

I walked down the hallway, feeling like a trespasser in Buzz's house. I stripped from the clothing, tossing them into a garbage can in his bedroom. Then I checked the closet. It was mostly jeans and long-sleeved plaid shirts. I grabbed a pair of pants and rolled up the bottoms. I found a belt and cinched it, keeping them on my hips. I took a blue and black button-up and went to the bathroom, washing my hands and face before dressing. Streaks of red circled the drain.

There were no pictures in Buzz's home, nothing to suggest he had any family to speak of.

By the time I was in the living room, Bones and Kim had Cindy between them. We loaded her into the van, and I sat in the driver's seat for a moment, gawking blankly at the cop car.

"You want me to drive?" Kim asked.

I turned the key. "No. I can do it."

The police station was about six miles away, and it took a good fifteen minutes to get there. It was after ten, and I'd expected to find at least one car in the lot, but it was empty.

Thunder rumbled overhead, and I couldn't believe the tenacity of this storm. It wouldn't let up.

"Kim, can you stay with Cindy?" I asked, and the woman nodded.

"Be careful," she said, peering around the parking lot. It was completely black.

Bones and I ran to the entrance, and I opened it, finding the glass door unlocked. "Hello?"

A few candles were lit, flames flickering on the reception desk, but the seat was empty.

"Hello?" Bones called this time. "Where are they all?"

"No clue." I grabbed a tapered candle by the holder and thrust it out like a torch. Bones did the same, and we slowly traversed the police station, heading by offices and the staff lunchroom.

We finally reached the end of the building, where three jail cells sat. Only one was occupied.

"Buzz!" I called, and the man glanced up, his eyes wide.

"What are you doing here?" He lumbered to the bars.

"What do you know about these aliens?" I demanded.

"They're big. Dangerous. Deadly." He stared at me. "You saw him, didn't you?"

"Yeah. He killed Deputy Bradshaw."

"Dammit." Buzz shook the jail cell bars. "Find the keys."

"First you stole a cop car, and now you're breaking a prisoner out. This won't look good on your record, Elliot," Bones said.

"Neither will being slaughtered by this bastard," Buzz added.

That seemed to motivate Bones, and we split up to search the offices. "Hey, Buzz, where is everybody?" I shouted as I opened a drawer in Sheriff Parker's desk. The key ring was half-buried by old menus.

"More bodies piling up. They called everyone in, and I listened as Parker issued the orders. At least they know it wasn't me," Buzz said.

I set the candle down and tried the keys until I heard the lock click. With a tug to the side, Buzz was free.

"What do you think you're doing?" someone asked. A deputy reached for his gun, but struggled to remove it from the holster.

"Hey, Mr. Sadie. It's me," Bones said.

"I know you." The deputy relaxed slightly. "I thought you were with Mary." He rolled his eyes. "I mean Reaper."

"I was, but…" Bones glanced at Buzz.

"What the hell is happening to our island?" Mr. Sadie asked. "We've had reports of three bodies, throats torn out like they were attacked by an animal."

I stepped forward. "Sir, I have to tell you something."

"Get on with it," he urged.

"Deputy Bradshaw is dead. There's a monster loose on Bell Island, and it's big."

"A bear?" The man furrowed his large brow.

"This is no bear. It's not from around here," Buzz said. "You need to alert your friends and get word to the entire population. They have to go home and lock the doors. Stay inside."

"Then what?" the deputy asked.

"Then I kill it," Buzz muttered, walking past the dumbfounded man.

"You can't just leave," Mr. Sadie said.

"Don't worry, we'll keep an eye on him," Bones said, patting the deputy on the back. "If you see Reaper, tell her to hide somewhere safe."

"Will do."

"And the fireworks. See that they don't happen. It'll only attract his attention," Buzz told him as he neared the foyer.

"And who is he?"

"Your worst nightmare." Buzz exited into the storm.

He was already in the van when we emerged, and he spoke with Kim somberly.

"No, she's still unconscious."

"Damn it. I was hoping we could talk with it."

"It? That's my sister," I said.

"Not anymore."

I ignored the comment. "Where are we going?"

"Back to my place. If we're going to fight the Traveler, we do so on my terms," he said.

"Traveler?" Bones gulped.

"That's what I call them." He shrugged. "In my experience, it's easier to fight an enemy with a name."

"You've faced them since Vietnam?" Kim asked.

"Twice," he admitted.

"And killed them?" I stared at the man, trying to picture him in combat with that beast I'd encountered on Cove Peak.

"Not yet. But I've come close." He gestured at Cindy. "But I've never had one of the Spheres with me."

"And that'll help us?"

"They feed on them, so yeah, it's good. We can draw him out," Buzz said.

I shook my head emphatically. "You want to use Cindy as bait? I won't let you do that."

"Either way you shake it, he's coming for her. So if you'd rather wait for it in your parents' basement, be my guest. I'll be hunting the Traveler."

"Elliot, we should listen to him. He seems to know what he's talking about," Kim said.

"He's seen these things three times before, and he's never stopped them from killing people. Why should we think he'll succeed now?" I asked.

"Because I have a plan. I've been preparing for this moment," he whispered.

"Why? Why Bell Island?" Bones inquired.

I turned the van around.

"Because of the sightings. What you've heard of as the Bell Island Demon, I knew was actually the Sphere. They're all around the world," he said. "If you listen to the right story, you can determine their destination."

I wanted more information about the Spheres and Travelers, but I had to bring Cindy to safety. Was taking her to Buzz's the best idea? "Will you promise she'll be okay?"

"Kid, I'll do my best, but there's no guarantee this guy won't tear us all to shreds. He's already killed a few on the Island. He has a taste for violence. Some of them are nastier than others." Buzz spoke as if he had years of experience with them, rather than a few chance encounters.

"Fine. We'll go to your place." I pressed the gas pedal harder, speeding toward the Reeve farm. We arrived in one piece, and noticed the storm was briefly letting up. The drops came fewer and farther between, and I slowed the windshield wipers of my mom's van. Thinking about Mom finding this very Sphere floating near her and Taylor when they were kids made me feel terrible. She'd gone years repressing a memory, and when she'd finally admitted her experience, she'd been made to think she was crazy. Uncle Taylor too. And he was dead because of it.

"Don't stop at the house. I have something to show you," he said, indicating a giant red barn in the distance.

I continued on the gravel road, slowing as we approached the structure. The windsock attached to the roof was filled with air, pointing straight to the east.

Buzz jumped out and unlocked the doors, swinging them wide. He waved me inside, and I drove the van into the barn, parking beside the toughest vehicle I'd ever witnessed. Buzz sealed the barn up. We left Cindy in the van, and Bones rushed to the machine next to him.

"What is this? Looks like something from Mad Max!" Bones kicked one of the spiked tires.

"You have to fight fire with fire," Buzz said. He stalked across the room, which had the cleanest floor in the history of all barns. Everything was organized, with shelving and racks filled with neatly stacked gray crates. "What you're about to see might be a bit of a shock, so don't give me any grief, okay?"

"What could possibly scare us now?" Kim asked softly.

Buzz slid a crate from the closest shelf and unclasped the lid. It was loaded with TNT. Another had RPGs. And the last was filled with egg crates of grenades.

"We have enough ammo to fight a war," Bones said.

"That's what we're doing, my friends. There's been an ancient conflict between the Spheres and the Travelers. We're caught in the middle. And it's high time we stopped these freaks from treading on our planet." Buzz grabbed an assault rifle, slamming a magazine into it. He handed it to Bones, who rotated the weapon in his grip, grinning like he'd been given another cheeseburger.

"How do you know so much?" I asked.

"Because he's met one of us before," Cindy said from beside the van. Her voice sounded older.

"Cindy!" I rushed to her, but she didn't react.

"Cindy is here, Elliot, but I am not her," my sister said.

"Then who are you?"

"I do not remember." Cindy's head tilted slightly. "I knew your mother."

"You did?" I whispered.

"Yes. I lived within her for a while. But she couldn't help me leave," Cindy said.

I tried to make sense of the words, but was distracted when Buzz began loading his vehicle with armaments. "You guys gonna give me a hand or what?"

The three of us helped him, while Cindy observed silently. She appraised us with an innocent curiosity, her eyes rarely blinking.

"So what's your big plan?" Bones asked when we packed the final box.

Buzz crossed the room, removing a giant beige sheet from an object. He revealed a massive black box. He used a code on a numerical keypad and spun a huge wheel until it opened. "Bank-issued vault." Buzz knocked on it, the sound dull. "We trap him inside."

"Sounds like fun," I muttered.

"If we can't transport him here, I have a few other

tricks up my sleeve," Buzz informed us.

"Where to?" Kim was with Cindy, watching my sister closely.

"Cove Peak. Let's see if he's still around. Then we can lure him to the farm." Buzz hopped into the far-out black-painted 4X4. The back seat was tight with Cindy, Kim, and me cramped in, while Bones took the front. They each had their packs from my vehicle, and I knew Bones' held fireworks. I wasn't sure why he wanted to lug those around, but was too distracted to say anything.

It rumbled and shook as he fired it up, and the scent of diesel filled my nostrils. I hated to abandon my mom's van, but that was the least of my concerns. I recalled my father and everyone else on the Island. In the commotion, I'd forgotten that they were in danger.

Bones got out and shut the barn doors, and when he returned, Buzz tore from his property, heading for Cove Peak. I'd left the site of Bradshaw's murder an hour prior and hadn't intended to revisit the scene.

Now that the rain was lighter and the extreme light show had settled, the drive was much smoother up the steep slope. His vehicle was well-equipped for the trip, and it burned fuel quickly as it raced to the top of the road. Buzz kept pace as he reached his destination, and slammed on the brakes near the location of Deputy Bradshaw's body.

I got out, expecting to find the man's corpse where I'd left it, but all that remained was a pool of diluted blood.

"Where is he?" I crouched, struggling to see where he'd been taken.

"Over here." Buzz indicated a smear of blood on a tree trunk. "He dragged Bradshaw into the forest."

"Why?" Bones asked.

"That's a good question," Buzz said. He held an assault

rifle, his gaze drifting around the small parking lot. "He might be close."

Everything was silent for a moment, other than the gentle pitter-patter of the easing rain.

And the sky lit up with a thousand brilliant lights.

3

"*O*h no," Buzz whispered.

"What? It's just fireworks," Bones replied.

"They're going to lure him like moths to a flame." Buzz jumped into his armored vehicle and revved the engine, implying we join him.

He tore down the road. I grabbed for something to hold, but found nothing. The waist seatbelt dug into my gut as he rounded a corner sharply, and Kim clutched my arm as he sped faster.

"Hold up, Buzz. You'll kill us!" I shouted.

The fireworks continued to blast over downtown.

"They must have decided to use them early," Kim said. "With the break in the storm."

"He wants me," Cindy said mournfully. "Please don't let him."

Buzz's eyes flicked to the rearview mirror. "I'll do my best."

Cindy sat straight, her gaze lingering on the ditch as we drove past a couple neighborhood entrances. A few people were in the streets, teenagers with beer cans. They moved aside when Buzz's 4X4 ripped near them. A couple of them yelled and shook their fists, but we were already gone.

I hoped my dad had made it home safely, and that no one else would get hurt tonight. The power was still out, the streetlights off, making the trek all the more perilous, but we eventually made it to the Island's core. Buzz turned before Main Street, stopping at a parks and recreation crew gate near the edge of the park. The explosions continued in the skies above us, and I watched them through the window, wishing I could appreciate the display. Cindy flinched with each of the big detonations.

"What are you doing?" Bones asked.

Buzz held up a key ring, shaking it. "I have my own way in." He went outside, hastily unlocking the barricade. He shoved the gate, and it swung inward. Buzz left it open and returned to his seat before racing down the bumpy grass path. A few of the town trucks were parked there, along with a dump truck near a maintenance building.

He slowed, rocks crunching under his giant tires, and he killed his lights. Buzz circled the park, and I could spot Bell Island residents occupying the forest, all staring up at the remaining fireworks as they cracked and popped loudly.

Buzz pulled over and rushed to the rear of the vehicle, grabbing weapons. He shoved one at me, another at Kim. We stared at each other. "What if Sheriff Parker sees us walking around with guns?" I asked. I wondered if there was a chance I hadn't seen Bradshaw being murdered. His body was gone. Maybe it was just a tree branch that had shattered the window and cut him. He'd exited to investigate and fell on the uneven ground. When we returned, he was probably hiking back to the sheriff's office.

But that was a lie, and I knew it. Whoever this Traveler was, he was on Bell Island, intending to create more bloodshed.

"How do I use this?" Kim held the gun, and Buzz offered the basics.

"Brace it on your shoulder, because it has some kick to it." He carried an RPG in one hand, the assault rifle in the other. "If you see him, spread out. Make more than one target, and for the love of God, don't kill the bystanders. We'll direct him into the forest. I have something waiting about a half mile south."

"What is it?" Bones asked.

"A trap."

"Okay," I said, as if this all made sense. Cindy stood near Buzz, her fingers wiggling at the end of stretched-out arms.

"What is she doing?" Kim whispered to me.

"I don't know."

"He's close," Cindy said.

Buzz entered the forest in the direction of the park. We followed, trying to move quietly, but it probably didn't matter, given the racket from the fireworks. They ceased, and I sensed the end of the show was upon us.

Rock music played from speakers, and firepits glowed brightly with burning birch. Everyone looked so happy, and I spotted the sheriff walking behind them, his eyes narrow slits, his frown evident from this distance. He was searching for someone.

I scanned the area for an eight-foot-tall alien among them, but it all seemed so normal.

Buzz lifted a hand, stopping us. He pointed to the right, and I saw the shadow lurking in the trees. The area was dark except for the firepits. Rain started to drizzle again, and people groaned their discontent.

The fireworks resumed, the grand finale in effect. Blast after blast erupted, and the entire crowd watched with wide eyes. But I was staring at the silhouette. He grew even taller, and a man staggered back, trying to take a Polaroid of the sky. He looked drunk, his steps awkward. One moment, he was near the forest with the flash of his camera snapping; the next, he was dragged into the trees.

"Shit," Buzz groaned. He ran along the edge of the

woodland, and the four of us gawked at him.

"What do we do?" Kim asked.

"I'm not chasing that thing!" Bones complained.

"The show's over!" Sheriff Parker's voice carried across the park with the bullhorn. "Thanks for a great Fourth, but we have a situation. The power's out, and you need to go home this instant."

The crowd retorted, a bunch of them toasting beers to the sky.

"Bring on the storm!"

"We ain't going anywhere!"

"Parker, you're always ruining our fun!"

The protests failed to cease, and the moment the display ended, Parker strode into the group. I kept an eye on the last place I saw Buzz, while the sheriff raised the bullhorn to his mouth. "There's been a couple murders," he finally admitted. "Nothing to worry about if you go home and lock your doors."

"Murders?" Cooper was there, and I looked for Bethany. "What are you talking about, Sheriff?"

"Son, just bring your friends somewhere safe and secure the doors. We'll have this taken care of by daybreak."

Murmurs drifted through the crowd, but no one moved. Sheriff Parker handed a deputy his loudspeaker and pulled his revolver out. "It's time to leave!" He fired two rounds into the air, and it had the desired effect. They all ran toward Main Street, rushing to their cars. Soon the area was filled with headlights and brake lights. People honked and squealed their tires. The few remaining people were roughly escorted by Parker's two officers.

We stayed hidden in the forest and heard footsteps approaching behind us.

I spun around, aiming my rifle at the source, and Buzz slapped the barrel away. "Never aim that at me, kid."

"Where'd he go?" Kim's voice was shaky.

"He took the body and left. He's one fast SOB." Buzz stared at the park. "I see the sheriff finally did something." He looked at us. "Where's the Sphere?"

I glanced around our group. Cindy was gone. How had she vanished? "I don't know... she was right here."

"I didn't notice her leaving!" Bones proclaimed.

"Me neither," Kim said. "This is bad."

"We have to find her," Buzz told us.

The park was empty, and even the sheriff and his team were packing it up. Their squad cars flashed their lights once, and the last car sped off. We exited the forest and walked into the park. There was garbage everywhere, the cans overflowing with plastic forks and napkins. The barbecue's lid was up, and soaking-wet hot dogs sat on the grill. Bones plucked one and bit into it. He grimaced, but kept eating until he finished.

"Cindy's not here," I said.

"Where would she have disappeared to?" Kim walked onto the sidewalk and glanced at the diner across the street.

"The Spheres are terrified of the Travelers. They're constantly being hunted by them. I don't know the entire story, but I think the Spheres are a sort of trophy for the Travelers. Maybe a contest or a rite among their people."

"Why are they on Earth in the first place?" Kim asked Buzz.

"No idea, but Cindy ran because she saw him. It's instinctive in them."

"She probably caught a ride with someone. And that would mean a friend of Cindy's. They must have noticed her and dragged her along," I suggested.

"We need to split up," Buzz said.

"You have the only car," Bones told him as we walked to his 4X4.

Buzz dangled the key ring out again. "Not anymore." He tossed them to me. "Take the truck." He also gave me a walkie talkie. "Not much range on these things out here, but we should have a few miles' radius."

He pulled his own, pressing the talk button. "Testing."

His gruff voice echoed from the radio in my grip. "Read you loud and clear."

My voice sounded distant through the speaker.

"Wait, if we're splitting up..."

"You're with me, Spike."

"It's Bones," he muttered.

"You good with that?" Buzz asked me, as if I spoke for my friends.

Bones gave me a pleading look, but he knew full well that I couldn't leave Kim with this guy. "Yeah. He knows where her friends live. You check out Becky's. I'll hit Yolanda's."

"Got it. Stay in touch." Bones nodded at me.

"Good luck." I walked to the truck Buzz had indicated, and it was unlocked. Another stolen piece of property tonight. If I survived this, I was going to be in a world of trouble, but Cindy needed me. The vehicle was a newer model, with a series of tools in the box. It only had a single bench seat, and it smelled like cigars inside.

It fired up, and music blasted from the cassette deck. Kim and I exchanged glances when ABBA bellowed about being a dancing queen. I tapped the eject button and backed up, heading past the gate. Buzz went left, and I turned right.

"I'll check home first. It's on the way," I said.

"This is messed up, Elliot." Kim hugged herself in the passenger seat. Her bag sat on her lap, and she rested the assault rifle at her feet. "What are we doing? Stealing town property and running around with military-grade weapons?"

"I can bring you to the motel. You can stay behind," I said, wishing I'd thought of offering that earlier.

"Not even! I'm invested." She rolled the window down slightly, and the breeze blew her hair in her face. "I asked for a fun night, and so far, you're delivering."

I didn't think we were having much fun, but kept that to myself. Most of the island had returned home, and my neighbors' house was filled with vehicles out front. They were double-parked in the street, a few on their lawn. A group of them stood on the grass, talking loudly.

"If someone's murdering our people, it's our responsibility to protect the Island," Mr. Bellows slurred. He had a gun in his hand, and he shoved it to the sky with every word. "We'll find this sicko before Parker does."

The gathered crowd grunted in unison, and they started to walk east in the middle of the road.

"This is bad," I mumbled, then waited for the last of them to depart before getting out of the truck.

"Vigilante justice in the dark on an island? Someone's going to get hurt," Kim agreed.

My front door was slightly ajar, and I felt for the gun Deputy Bradshaw had dropped. It was in my pocket, and I pulled it free, entering quietly. "Stay here," I whispered to Kim as I heard her footsteps behind mine.

It was pitch black, but I knew my house well. I bypassed the living room and went for the hallway. Cindy's room was empty. A sliver of moonlight slipped through the clouds, illuminating her possessions. I grinned at the girly movie posters and pink bedding. Cindy was fifteen going on thirty, but she was still just a girl with big dreams. I picked up one of her blonde dolls and set it down. I needed to find her and convince the Sphere to leave. I didn't care if this Traveler ate the entity or not, as long as my sister was safe.

I checked my parents' room and saw my dad on his side of the bed. His arm was outstretched, like he was reaching for his wife. Only she was locked up on the mainland, because of this Sphere. The alien had admitted as much.

I closed his door and bolted the front on the way out. Kim didn't speak as she climbed in the truck.

"We'll bring her home." I drove the other direction so I didn't encounter the mob.

"I believe you," Kim said, placing a hand on my shoulder.

The clock read 10:47 as I sped toward Yolanda's. I passed the curve where I'd hit the deer last night, and slowed more than I needed to out of instinct. Had it only been one day? It felt like ages since Bethany had dumped me at the diner and I'd met Kimberly.

People were in front of Yolanda's house, and I recognized Bruce. I parked a few places down, trying not to raise any questions about the truck. *Bell Island Parks* was stenciled on the doors, and they all knew I didn't work for the municipality. I was a video store guy.

I hurried to the yard, with Kim keeping pace.

"Hoffman?" Bruce asked, peering at me, then Kim. "This is crazy. I heard from Carol's cousin that there's a serial killer on the loose. He's killed like ten people already."

"The guy's beheading them and drinking their blood," Yolanda added. "Maybe he's a vampire."

"Have you seen Cindy?" I asked.

Yolanda shook her head. "Not since she bailed at the movies. Didn't even tell us."

"Is Becky here?"

"No. She went home after the sheriff told us to,"

Yolanda said.

Bethany walked from the front door, pausing on the steps to stare. "Elliot?" She rushed down them, darting across the yard to hug me. She pulled me tight and buried her face into my neck like she hadn't just dumped me yesterday. "I'm scared."

"Then why didn't you go home?" I asked.

"Cooper was my ride." She broke apart and rolled her eyes. "They're still drinking. They want to confront the killer."

"They're not the only ones," I informed them. "Mr. Bellows has about twelve half-cut soldiers of his own."

"Great." Bethany seemed to notice Kim for the first time. "Hey."

"Hey." Kim mirrored the greeting.

"Can we talk?" Bethany asked, dragging me by my arm.

"Sure. Give me a minute," I told Kim.

We strolled down the street, and rain returned, gently drizzling on us. The streetlights flickered on for a second, and I had a moment of relief, but it was quickly shattered when the power went out again. "What's up?" I asked, trying to sound as casual as possible.

"What's up? That's all you have to say?" Bethany pursed her lips like she always did when she was upset.

"You want more? You dumped me a day ago, Beth," I said.

"I... I'm sorry."

"Whatever. I hope Cooper makes you happy." I started to leave.

"He's nothing. We're not even really dating. He's just been so... unavoidable. When you didn't come home in April, he was there. And you've been so distant. You don't call, write... and when we see each other, it's like you'd rather be anywhere but with me."

She wasn't wrong. "Then I should be apologizing. I never meant to drag it out."

"So it really is over?" Bethany wiped a tear from her eye.

"You don't want it to be?"

She shook her head. "I was impulsive, and instead of discussing it, I reacted. Maybe we can talk later. It had bad timing, with your mom and everything. I'm being selfish."

I glanced at Kim, and then at Bethany. "No."

"No?"

"I can't do it. I loved you, Beth, but we're just not at the same place. I can't be in a relationship that isn't fun. I'm twenty-two. If you choose to go out of state, then do it. I won't be this anchor keeping you on Bell Island any more than you want to hold me back," I said, feeling better for having said it.

She sniffled and took my hands. "You said you 'loved' me, as in past tense."

"That's right."

"I understand," she whispered. Cooper was in the yard with Paul, the pair of them observing us.

"Just do me a favor and don't end up with that guy. You deserve better, Bethany."

"I agree." She kissed me on the cheek and left. "Take me home."

Cooper looked pissed. "No way. We're about to…"

"Then give me the keys. I'm taking your car," she told him.

"We can use mine, Coop. Let her go," Bruce said.

Cooper fished them out of his pocket and reluctantly offered them to Bethany. "Be careful, and don't drive her over thirty-five. It's hard to see the road tonight."

Beth dashed off and sped down the street in his Mustang.

My radio crackled, and I moved aside, not wanting to be overheard. "Say that again."

"Meet us at Becky's... damage... fire..." Bones' voice was barely audible.

"We gotta run," I told Kim.

"Bruce, let it be. You'll just get yourself killed," I urged my old friend.

"Ignore the wimp," Cooper said.

"I mean it, Bruce. I saw him kill Deputy Bradshaw."

Yolanda paled. "Are you kidding?"

"Seriously?" Bruce asked.

"Yes. He's not what you think. Get indoors and barricade the entrance. Keep your family safe." I left them standing in the yard, gaping after me.

Kim slammed her door closed and sighed. "I have a bad feeling, Elliot."

The storm had returned, and a violent round of lightning arced over the cloud-covered skies. "So do I."

4

*B*ecky lived near Bethany. Only a handful of neighborhoods existed on Bell Island, and theirs was the farthest from Yolanda's. I used to ride my bike there, and in the summers, I'd be drenched in sweat before I made the halfway point. Bethany rarely came to my place, so we'd spent countless hours in her backyard. Her parents weren't rich, but they were well into the middle class, with a white picket fence and two nice cars. Her father put a pool in a year after we started dating, and I loved to veg out by the water and sneak glances at Bethany in a bikini.

I drove by her place, finding Cooper's car out front. A flashlight darted within the living room, and I suspected she was talking to her parents about what was transpiring across Bell Island.

Becky's was a couple blocks farther, and this area was extremely quiet. Most of the residents were older, retired folks, and I doubted many of them had made the trip downtown for the earlier event, especially considering how bad the storm was. I pictured the Hendersons, the old couple beside Bethany's, sitting with candles lit, drinking a bottle of wine while petting their cat.

"What the hell is that?" Kim exclaimed, pointing at the windshield.

I slammed the brakes, seeing half of Becky's house missing. There was a hole where it had sat a short time ago, with flames licking the remaining walls. I noticed someone across the street, peering through their window coverings. When they spotted me, they closed them.

I used the radio. "Where are you guys?"

"Out back. Bring the guns."

Part of the yard was still smoldering, smoke rising high. "We watch each other's backs, okay?"

Kim held her rifle and seemed to hesitate, but nodded instead.

The air smelled acrid, like melted metal. The phones were down, so no one could contact any emergency responders, and I had a feeling that Parker and his people were already overwhelmed. Kim took the lead around the house. There was a small crater where the steps used to be.

A gunshot rang out, and it sounded like it came from a block or two away.

"Don't shoot!" Bones called when Kim approached, raising her assault rifle.

"Where's Buzz?" I asked.

"He went ahead of us." Bones gestured at the open fence gate. It swung in the wind, bashing against the frame every few seconds.

"And Cindy?"

Bones didn't respond, and stared blankly.

"Bones!" I shook him. "Where's my sister?"

"She ran, and the Traveler gave chase," Bones said, barely loud enough for me to hear.

I went after them. The house backed onto a greenspace with a treeline bordering the tail end of Cove Peak. The grass was long and unkempt, with thick stalky weeds jutting from the earth every few feet. Kimberly shouted behind me, but I ignored her. I had to save my sister.

I slowed when the fences ended and glanced in both directions. They couldn't have gotten that far.

When I was planning to head left, I spotted a bright

flash. I could hear Bones and Kim huffing after me. It was good to have their assistance, but also too dangerous for any of us. The longer I trudged through the waist-high grass, the more I doubted our ability to stop this creature. I still hadn't seen more than its outline, but it was huge, far heavier than the three of us put together. Even Buzz, a well-trained ex-soldier, looked like a ragdoll compared to the beast.

He was an alien. How had he come to Bell Island? He must have a spacecraft.

I imagined a UFO descending through the clouds over the lighthouse, hovering toward the docking bay. Another boom struck a tree, and a giant limb melted at impact, falling between me and Kim. It hissed and burned into the ground.

"That's not fair," Bones said. "He's got ray guns!"

I finally spied the source of the blast. It was a tube-shaped weapon connected to the Traveler's arm. The pulse burst from the end, a strange bubble-like sound singing from the tip. He was even bigger now that I was closer. His head was wide and flat, his brow expansive above two apple-sized black eyes. They shimmered and glistened when he blinked.

Our gazes met, and his nostrils flared, mucus dripping from them. At first, I didn't think he wore clothing, but I realized it merely blended in with his green-gray skin. Everything about the Traveler was so obviously alien. His three-fingered hand flexed on a four-foot-long blade's grip, and he stepped into the open clearing, grass crumpling under his weight. He fired again, this time at the ground near Bones, who collapsed to the earth, his gun falling.

Kim's stance was set with determination.

We stood like this for only a second or two, but time slowed as I prepared for my death. I was one of the only humans to witness life from another world, and was about to be gutted because of it.

"Get down!" Buzz shouted from twenty yards away. I didn't hesitate as I dove at Kimberly, knocking her aside. The RPG's grenade flung across the hearty field at the alien. He tried to counter-fire, but the explosion rocked the Traveler.

I covered my ears, and Bones began to sit up. "Stay where you are," I urged him.

"What happened?" Bones asked.

"Buzz just killed the freak, that's what!" Kim jumped to her feet, running for Buzz.

Buzz crouched where the alien had been and surveyed the damage. "It might have injured him, but he's alive."

"You're telling me that a rocket launcher can't take this thing out?" I bellowed.

"Apparently not. I knew they were tough, but…" Buzz went quiet when a scream echoed across the field. "That's our cue."

I had no choice but to tag along, my rifle almost forgotten in my grip. If a rocket wasn't any good, what use was a gun?

The grass gave way to more trees, and the path became difficult to traverse. Big brush blocked the forest bed, making it almost impossible to navigate. It also made it obvious which direction the alien had taken. We slid between the broken branches and found him by the river. His body hadn't even fully turned when Buzz fired his gun. The burst of gunfire struck a tree. The Traveler was gone.

Buzz knelt at the water's edge, poking at the rocks. Green slime coated a few stones, and Buzz grinned in the darkness. "He's been hit. If it bleeds, it dies."

"You've never even shot one before?" Bones muttered.

"No. I said I've been close."

We continued to track it for twenty minutes and ended up at the road. Buzz stepped onto the asphalt, his boots scraping the surface. Thunder clapped, and the rain began to fall in earnest. "Lost him."

With those two simple words, my energy drained. I slunk to the street, depleted of any strength, but Cindy still needed me. Headlights shone from down the road, and someone slowed. It was Deputy Sadie. His daughter, Reaper, rushed from the passenger side to meet Bones.

"What have you guys been up to?" she asked Bones.

"Just a normal Wednesday night. Hunting an alien," he said.

I expected Deputy Sadie to laugh at the outrageous claim, but his jaw remained set with determination. "Hop in."

Buzz glared at him. "I ain't going to jail."

"Don't worry, I believe you. We've seen them too," Sadie said.

Buzz scanned the dark ditch. "Them?"

"So far, I've heard of three. But there could be more."

"Nah. It's the same one. He's fast," Buzz suggested.

Reaper thrust a photo at Bones. "Snapped this out by the reservoir. They got Jeff." It was a blurry picture, but the fact remained that two of the Travelers were within its white border. Jeff was in the air, the huge knife jabbed through his torso.

"No. This can't be happening," Buzz said.

The rain poured, dousing our group. "Why did you only expect one?" I dared to ask him.

"I thought they sent a single Traveler for each Sphere," he told me.

"Are you saying…" Bones left it unsaid.

"There must be two more Spheres on Bell Island."

Buzz checked his magazine and opened the cop car door. "We need backup."

———————

*T*hey'd had to drag me from the forest. Cindy was being tracked by that monster, and we were squished inside a police car, heading to Buzz's parked car. When we returned to Becky's home, Deputy Sadie got out first, revolver drawn.

"Stay here," he muttered, slamming his door.

We all disobeyed his order. Reaper stalked up the driveway, stopping where the concrete had been melted. "What kind of weapon could do this?" she asked.

"Something with high heat," Buzz said.

Sadie went to the spot where the door used to be and clambered past the wreckage. "Hello?"

I joined Buzz, and we entered the remaining half of the house. Becky's parents were on the floor, both dead.

"I hear something," I told them, but the deputy didn't seem to notice. He lingered over the corpses, blood soaking their pajamas. I walked to the hallway, seeing gashes in the walls. The alien had been inside.

"Hello?" I gripped the revolver from Bradshaw as I investigated the room at the end. My aim was shaky, but I kept it raised.

Cries could be heard from within the closet. "Cindy!"

I opened the door, but it wasn't my sister.

"Elliot?" Becky rushed out, barreling into me. "I thought he was back."

"You saw him?"

Becky was pale, her cheeks red and sticky with tears. "He killed my parents." This pushed her into another bout of sobbing.

"Where's Cindy?"

"She tried to stop him from hurting us, but he threw her out the back door. Dad chucked the TV remote at him, and he stabbed them both. I ran… like a coward," Becky cried.

I hugged her again. "You're not a coward. You did the right thing."

"House is clear," Deputy Sadie said, drifting into the room. "Looks like we have a survivor. You can join us at the station, dear."

Becky nodded and stared at me for approval. "Yeah. We'll get you somewhere safe."

Someone had placed a blanket over her parents, and I was grateful for it. Becky glanced at them, and I helped her outside. She barely seemed to notice her house was half gone.

"Where the hell did you get this?" Deputy Sadie asked, pointing at the Parks truck out front.

"I required a ride," I told him.

He didn't comment, just got into his car with Reaper and Becky. "Meet us at the station. We'll figure this out."

He drove off, leaving Kim and me with Bones and Buzz. A few people watched from their windows, but I didn't care. "Buzz, we have to find Cindy."

"I agree. There's two more Spheres," he whispered.

I shoved his right shoulder. "Buzz, did you hear me? Cindy needs me!"

"Right. We do what the deputy says. Station first." He climbed into his 4X4.

"Bones. Kim," I pleaded.

"He's not wrong, Elliot. What are we even going to do if we face this guy? Or his two friends? We aren't equipped for this," Bones said.

"And Cindy is?"

"That's not Cindy," Kim murmured. "It's the Sphere."

"And that's supposed to make me feel better?"

"No, but Buzz said they've been hunted by these Travelers forever. That means she knows how to hide," Kim added. It did little to ease my worry.

"Fine." Against my wishes, I returned to the borrowed vehicle, and we drove all the way up to the station. It was still raining when we arrived, and there were a couple other cars parked near the entrance. Kim stayed quiet for most of the trip, her gaze settled on the road ahead.

When I got out, I listened intently, as if I could hear my sister calling for me. It was silent except for the wind and booming thunder.

Everyone gathered in the sheriff's station, and I noticed a couple men in civilian clothes.

Sheriff Parker glared at us as we entered, hands on hips. "Deputy Sadie filled me in," he said. "I don't like having to do this, but desperate times call for desperate measures. I'll authorize you to wield guns tonight. Even you, Larson." He looked at Bones, who sheepishly grinned. "You're named temporary deputies." He walked up to Buzz, poking the bigger man in the chest. "That's *temporary*, stranger. After we figure this out, you're on your own."

"Loud and clear, sir," Buzz said. I almost expected him to snap off a salute, but he didn't. "Is there a safe place to talk?"

"This way." Parker led us to a room beside his office. The wall had a pegboard with a map of Bell Island pinned to it, and that was where Buzz went. Deputy Sadie brought in a couple of old propane lanterns, lighting them. They hissed as they fired on, and the added light was a vast improvement.

"This is Bell Island," Buzz said. "I thought there was

one of the Travelers…"

"Travelers?" Parker asked.

"Keep up, Sheriff. You've been invaded," Buzz said.

"By what?"

"Not what. Whom. They're aliens," Buzz whispered. "There are things happening around this world that would make you keep the blinds drawn, Parker. And they've set their sights on your safe little island. Sure, living offshore sounds like a good idea, until they cut the power and you have no way to the mainland. It's the perfect setting for an invasion."

"Are you telling me these… Travelers killed the grid?" Parker asked. He rubbed his handlebar mustache emphatically.

"I'd bet the farm on it," he said. "I was certain there was a Sphere nearby, and that's why I've been waiting and observing."

"What did you want the camera for?" I asked him, recalling him borrowing it from the video store.

"I figured the Sphere might be in someone at the Fourth of July fireworks. I assumed I'd watch over my footage and find the answer," he explained.

Parker crossed the room, pointing at the map. "Okay, the Traveler is the big baddie on a killing spree. What's a Sphere?"

Buzz nodded at me.

"It's a ball of light," I said. "We saw one enter my sister, Cindy. She's missing. We must help her."

"Kid's right. These Travelers are homed into these Spheres, like they can smell 'em." Buzz used a felt marker, making an X in red near Cove Peak. "Bradshaw was killed here."

Reaper lifted her hand. "Jeff at the reservoir."

Another X was drawn.

Buzz placed two where Becky's house sat. "Any others?"

Sheriff Parker grabbed another color and added three more around the map. "Those are the ones we're aware of."

"You can expect to find more," Buzz told him.

"Why do you know so much?"

"Earlier, you mentioned the bodies piling up behind me. I've spent the last fifteen years hunting the Travelers. I've encountered two. Both times, I failed to protect the Sphere," Buzz said.

Parker set the marker down. "Say I believe you for a minute. If there are three of these aliens on our island right now, how do we stop them?"

Buzz shook his head slowly. "I'd been planning on fighting one, not three."

"So it's hopeless?" Kim asked.

"Let's not go that far."

"We already locked the residents down. Most of them have no idea what's transpired, but they do think we have a killer on the loose. That should keep the population safe." Parker sat on the desk.

I'd almost forgotten about the mobs stalking the Island, and told him.

The sheriff clenched his jaw at the news. "We must protect our people. That's my priority. We also need to prepare a boat to send to the shore."

"Sir, the water's too choppy. It'll be nearly impossible to stay afloat," the deputy interjected.

"Be that as it may, give us the option." Parker gestured to the pair of men in jeans and short-sleeved plaid shirts. They looked about sixty, and I thought I recognized them. "Bob and Gerry are retired police from the city. They're good friends of mine, and part of my weekly poker game.

They'll work on the boat, won't you, gentlemen?"

"You bet," either Bob or Gerry said. They left in a hurry.

"You mentioned two mobs. I'll go with Hoffman and his girlfriend. Soldier, you head with Sadie and Larson. Tell them to get home," Parker said.

I grabbed Bones by the arm and dragged him closer. "Dude, be cautious. And if you see any sign of Cindy, radio us, okay?"

"Done deal." Bones glanced at Reaper. "I wanted a date, but not like this."

"I know, buddy." I patted his shoulder. "We'll get through the night. Once the storm passes, we can call reinforcements from the city."

He tried to crack a smile, but it fell flat. His mohawk was squished, and it drooped on both sides of his head, reminding me of my friend before he went punk.

"Keep your eye out for another Sphere," Buzz told us. "There are two more, and they're crucial to winning this battle."

Just when I thought the storm might finally be breaking, it grew worse as we stepped into the parking lot. Wind gusted, almost taking the breath from my lungs.

"With me, Elliot."

So he did know my first name. "Shouldn't we…" I motioned to the truck.

"Those things are too bulky and slow," Parker replied.

We grabbed our automatic rifles, and I offered Kim the front seat, sitting in the back of the sheriff's ride with a weapon resting on my lap. His headlights flashed on, brightening the waterlogged road.

Bones waved from inside Buzz's murder machine, and they tore off first.

I hoped I'd see my friend again.

5

There were a limited number of routes to take on Bell Island. The primary roads basically created a plus sign, with a handful of secondaries winding around Mount Alexander, Cove Peak, the bay, and the falls. As a kid, Bell Island had been a treasure trove of adventure.

Bones and I constantly got into trouble, riding our bikes where we had no business taking them. There were countless regions of the island you couldn't access by road, and that was to our detriment tonight. The Travelers weren't in cars or trucks. They were on foot, and the weather didn't seem to bother them.

Sheriff Parker huffed an exasperated exhale and turned around, craning his neck to see me. "What do you think, Elliot?" We faced the end of the street near the falls. "We've scoured this section of the Island, and there's been no sign of Cooper's gang."

"I wouldn't call them a gang, sir," I said.

"It's almost midnight, and they're looking for someone to fight," he said. "That's as close as you can get."

"Where would Cooper go?" Kim asked.

"I don't know him well enough." But that wasn't true. I knew his type. He was all show. Cooper would want to appear tough, but in reality, he'd go somewhere safe to avoid any real threat.

"The mines," I said.

"Mines?" Kim asked.

"The primary reason this area was populated. Prior to the war, and before the vision of a retirement community," Parker informed us. "They found traces of coal in the 1920s. The shafts were dug and braced, but it was only mined for about two decades. Was shut down before the war ended. There was no one to man it. Place has been closed for the last forty-five years. Don't think I've ever even been to the entrance, but I suspect someone like Elliot may know where it is."

I cleared my throat. "I can bring us."

I wondered if the Sphere would have the same idea. If she knew about the mines, it could keep her safe. I recalled my mother and uncle arguing about it when I was ten years old.

Bones and I had pedaled out there after hearing rumors of the shaft from a kid at school the day before. It was a hot August weekend, and we'd waited until our parents were asleep. I filled my pack full of soda and chips, and Bones brought the flashlights and licorice. We arrived just before midnight and stood at the entrance, panting from exertion from the ride.

We'd left our bikes and climbed into the opening. An hour later, we were both covered in grime, our faces black with soot, and we were lost. Thank God we had food and liquids, but I swore I'd never return. My parents had been so upset when we were finally discovered. The only reason they'd found us was because Horschel from class told his mom that he dared us to explore the mine. Turns out not even Horschel had ever been to the shaft.

Uncle Taylor had come over, and they'd quarreled in the living room while I lay in my bed, thankful Bones and I had been rescued.

We went as far as you could drive without bashing into a tree, and the sheriff parked, returning me to the present.

He pulled three yellow slickers from the trunk and tossed them at us. "This should help," he said.

I didn't suggest the bright color might make us stand out like a sore thumb. Kim and I slipped them on, and she flipped her hood up. I left mine down, not wanting to hinder my sight.

Sheriff Parker lifted his arm, as if he was making covert military signals. Kim and I shared a glance and shrugged, neither of us understanding his actions, so we just followed, holding our guns. Kim had her backpack slung over her shoulders.

The forest was wet, the ground soaked from the recent deluge. It had been a damp summer, and the water table was extremely high in this valley. Each step was soggy, soaking my socks within minutes.

Eventually, the sheriff slowed, letting me take the lead. I'd been reprimanded so badly after spending the night in the mines that I'd never returned. But I still recalled the path as if it was yesterday, not twelve years ago.

We found reprieve from the rain beneath the dense canopy of trees, and I slowed, trying to take in the surroundings. I assumed there had once been a trail, but it was long overgrown. You couldn't ride a bike in the current conditions. Even back then, I'd gotten scratches and claw marks from the tree branches.

"Over here!" I called through the gusting wind, and we tramped down a sloped decline. The barricade to the coal mine was ancient. There was no building, just a wooden barrier heading into the hillside.

A sign covered most of the entrance, and it read: *Caution: Closed Shaft. Do Not Enter.*

The corner was broken away, with barely enough space for an adult to navigate. I doubted one of the giant aliens could sneak past this obstacle, and that eased my mind a bit.

"I don't see anyone. Maybe we should leave." Sheriff Parker did a slow spin, gun raised.

I crouched, peering into the shaft. My memories threatened to freeze my body up. "There's light," I said.

"Must be Cooper," Parker said. "Good call, Elliot."

Before I could say anything, he was past the sign, working his way into the shaft.

"It's a mess. Stay close," I warned Kim.

She pulled my arm back. "We don't have to do this."

"It's okay. The alien isn't here," I said.

"That doesn't mean he won't come. If we're trapped in there when they arrive, we're screwed."

I didn't love the idea of being cornered by a Traveler, but Parker was already inside. "We'll be quick. I don't like Cooper, but they'll be safer at home."

Kim looked doubtful, but she followed me regardless. My flashlight beam struck the floor, and we used it to gain our footing as we descended. Old iron tracks lined the shaft, the wooden beams bent from years of misuse, and I cringed at the thought of the ceiling caving in, sealing us to our deaths.

"Where's the light?" Parker asked.

We'd all seen it a short while ago. "Let's keep going." I kept my rifle accessible while holding the flashlight, but for someone as inexperienced as me, it wasn't easy.

"Cooper!" I called, my voice echoing though the tunnel.

"Son, if you're down here, come out now. It's Sheriff Parker!"

No response. Maybe I'd been wrong about this. I suddenly wanted nothing more than to escape.

"There!" Kim pointed to a dim glow some distance away. She started to run, her steps kicking up dust. I almost bashed into an old wagon blocking the tracks, and jumped around it. There were another two, the wagons empty.

I found Kim at the end of the tunnel, her gun at her side.

We stared at the ball of light floating four feet above the ground.

"I'll be damned," Parker whispered. "Buzz was telling the truth."

The Sphere pulsed. The color remained unchanged, but the intensity shifted with each beat. Kim gasped, pressing against the wall as it floated by us. I wondered if this was the same entity that had invaded Cindy, but didn't think so. Buzz had guessed there were three Spheres on Bell Island, and hiding in the abandoned coal mine was as good a location as any.

It continued to Sheriff Parker, and he lifted a finger when it slowed near him. "What are you?" he mumbled.

It vibrated, the air shimmering around it, and it moved into Parker's mouth. Everything on his face filled with light before it subsided. His chin fell to his chest, and he let go of his flashlight and gun, then fell to the ground.

"Not again," I said.

"What are we going to do?" Kim crouched at his side, checking for a pulse. She seemed relieved, so that was a good sign.

"It took Cindy an hour or so to gain consciousness. I guess we wait," I suggested.

"I don't like it in here." Kim hugged herself after propping her gun against the tunnel wall.

"Me neither." I sat on the track, stretching my legs out. It smelled musty and damp, and a few drops fell from the ceiling about ten yards past our position. "Since we have the time, tell me about yourself."

Kim brushed some of her hair behind her ears and

laughed. "Now?"

"It'll be a good distraction, Kim... or should I say Leia, or Uhura? What's up with that?" I wanted to divert the tension filling the mines, and figured a light conversation would help with that. My eye twitched with any little noise carrying from outside.

"I've always loved science fiction. I'll never forget watching *Star Wars* for the first time with my older brother. I was sixteen, and while my friends were hitting the mall for deals on scrunchies, I was seeing history. Best movie ever."

"Until the sequel," I added.

"Not for me. The hero's journey. The laser sword. Romance. It had it all."

"Tell me again why you came to Bell Island," I said.

"I already mentioned..."

"Kim, no one moves to Bell Island after getting a degree and living elsewhere. Why did you want to disappear?" I thought about the true crime books she had piled in her motel room. "Was it a breakup?" That was what I'd assumed from our previous conversation, though she hadn't specifically said that.

Kim's hair was wet, her eyeliner running down her cheeks. "I haven't been entirely truthful."

I saw the trepidation in her expression.

"*Elliot... disaster... dead.*" It was Bones. I fumbled with the radio, nearly dropping it.

"Say again?"

"*Traveler... neighbor... killed.*" His voice was almost indiscernible.

I tapped the radio on my palm and tried to reach them. "Bones! I can't hear you. My neighbor is dead?"

Radio silence and static.

"They must have found the mob group," Kim said.

Sheriff Parker stirred, his left leg twitching, but he didn't wake.

"I don't know how long we—"

Something banged from the exit, and Kim and I jumped. I put my finger to my lips and aimed the flashlight down the tunnel. It hit the wagons and drifted to the ceiling. The shaft rounded, and I couldn't see past the curve in the wall. Another cracking noise, and I cut the beam.

"I think he's found us," Kim whispered.

"Who?"

"The Traveler."

I glanced at Parker's silhouette in the darkness, and then at Kim. "We have to hide."

"There's nowhere to go."

Wood groaned and snapped. "He's breaking in."

I'd said the hole wasn't big enough for the aliens to use, but he was changing that. Now the sounds made sense. The Traveler was tearing the barricade open one piece of lumber at a time. I could almost picture him tossing the large beams as if they were weightless.

The wagons were close, and I grabbed Parker's armpit. "Help me move him," I hissed.

Kim did so without questioning, and when she realized what I was thinking, she sped up.

The old transports were created to haul supplies and coal back to the entrance, but they hadn't been used in some time. They rotated on two hinges, allowing their contents to be dumped, but these were empty. I flipped the nearest one carefully, so the unlubricated joints didn't make too much noise. It barely covered Parker's body, but I made do by folding his legs at the knees. I hit a locking pin, and the wagon stayed upside down.

Kim went to the middle one, doing the same to hide herself, and I used the last. There were eight inches of clearance, and all I could hear was my own panicked panting. I took a deep breath and eased it out. Any sound would draw the alien to us. I was banking on the darkness, because I hadn't seen them with any lights, but they were aliens. Maybe their vision wasn't necessary. What if they utilized sonar like bats, or…

My head was on the gravel between the tracks, so I gazed to the far end of the tunnel and spotted him. The Traveler was shrouded in darkness, his bulk undeniable. There was enough light escaping from the open shaft, now that he'd torn it wide, to give me a sense of his position. His footsteps were heavy, and I thought I heard Kim whimper. I hoped the Sphere inside Parker would remain unconscious for the next few minutes, because it was our only chance at escape.

I didn't have a plan. Even if the Traveler walked by us, then what? I couldn't very well drag Parker out in time. We'd be dead within seconds.

Then I remembered the dripping ceiling where the tunnel stopped. The wood was rotting, the top buckling. I touched the rifle beside me and knew what I needed to do.

The Traveler was close, moving slowly. His feet planted right beside me, and he made a guttural sound, maybe a sniff of the musty air. I could smell him. It reminded me of a terrarium. Bones and I used to have a friend who was obsessed with his lizards.

The monster continued on, shuffling down the shaft.

When his footsteps were too far away to hear, I slowly rotated the wagon, sliding from under it. I grabbed my gun and crawled on my belly toward Kim. "I'm going to trap him. Get Parker outside when you hear the gunfire."

"You can't…"

I ignored her and quietly got to my knees, then feet. The Traveler wasn't visible. I snatched the flashlight. If previously asked, I never would have thought of myself as a brave man. I'd stood up for friends when necessary, but I usually stayed out of the limelight, letting others handle situations. I had no choice now, and a part of me considered running the opposite direction.

Aliens were on Bell Island. Why was it my job to defend our home?

I shoved the self-doubt aside and rested my finger near the trigger. I had one shot at this.

My movements were achingly slow, my hands trembling, but I was making progress. I heard him again. It was so black down here that I couldn't even see my own weapon. I guessed he must be at the end of the shaft by now.

I was about to flick on the flashlight when the radio clicked again.

"Elliot, it's a bloodbath…"

The Traveler bellowed at the sudden interruption, and I had no choice but to turn on the flashlight. I dropped it as he barrelled toward me, and I opened fire. The gun had a lot of kick to it, but I braced it on my shoulder like Buzz instructed and turned side to side. Bullets ricocheted off the Traveler, but a few struck. I focused on the ceiling and backed up as he approached. His huge gun whined, a yellow light shone on the tip.

"Die, you ugly son of a…!" I kept firing, and water rushed from above the alien.

Suddenly, Kim joined the attack, and she blasted the two support beams on the walls.

Water gushed from the gaping hole, and the shaft caved in. Rubble and dirt rained down on the Traveler, and he made eye contact with me, his big black pupils narrowing in anger. His shouts were cut short when he became buried, and I released the trigger, realizing my magazine was empty.

The Traveler's hand was extended out of the rock pile, the weapon still in his grip. It fell and fired, the pulse of light shooting past us to leave a giant hole in the tunnel ten yards behind us.

"Holy crap!" I yelled. The fingers clenched, and I thought he was going to burst from the rubble and kill us, but the digits relaxed again. He was dead.

Kim walked closer, gripping the fallen flashlight. She touched his hand without fear. "It's cold."

"I told you to stay with Parker!" I said accusingly.

"I'm not a damsel in distress, Elliot. I can help."

That much was clear. "Sorry, I didn't want anything to happen to you." My anger vanished with the spike of adrenaline. We'd killed one of the Travelers.

Kim bent to pick up the alien weapon. Her own gun was leaning on the wall, and I took it. "We have to leave. What if his friends are reading his vitals or something?"

"Right." Kim stared at the barrel and clutched it to her chest.

Sheriff Parker was still under the wagon, and I flipped it over, finding him sitting up. "What has transpired?" he asked, his voice even.

"A Traveler was hunting you. We killed him," Kim said.

"Why, thank you." He stood on his own.

"Let's not waste any more time." We raced for the exit, and as suspected, the wooden barricade was in pieces, the beams littered around the base of the hill. The lightning had stopped for the moment. It was growing colder, abnormally so, and I could even see my breath mist out when I exhaled. Kim cinched her duck-yellow slicker tighter, and I led them to the car. The vehicle was totally trashed. The Traveler must have done it. The tires were flat, the roof dented two feet down in the middle, the windshield smashed.

Parker offered the keys. "I do not know how to drive," he said, or the Sphere within him did. It was all very confusing.

"We're not using his car any time soon." I didn't take the keys, and he returned them to his pocket.

"The radio," Kim said.

I pulled it from my pocket. "Bones, are you there?"

"Where the hell have you been, man? We saw a Traveler. Buzz almost shot it!"

I glanced at Kim. "We killed one."

"There must be an issue with the reception. I thought you said you killed an alien," Bones said.

"We did. At the mines. Also… Sheriff Parker has been taken over by another Sphere," I told him.

Parker remained in a docile state.

"Where are you?" It was Buzz now.

"At the end of the road near the old hills. You know where that is?"

"No. But judging by the way your friend is nodding, he does."

"The Traveler trashed our car. We're stuck."

"Hang tight. And don't let the Sphere out of your sight," Buzz ordered.

"Not a problem." I slid the radio in my pocket and reached for the alien weapon Kim was holding. "Maybe we can survive the night after all."

6

"Show me," Buzz said when they pulled up.

"Dude, you don't need to waste your time," I informed him.

"You have no idea how strong these—"

"He was dead. I touched his hand. He was completely buried by mud and rocks," Kim told Buzz.

Buzz's gaze drifted to the weapon. "You're kidding me."

"Nope. Alien tech. Pretty cool, huh?" Kim passed it to him.

Buzz grinned, and he looked like a different man. "This might be a game changer."

"If we can find the others," I suggested.

Bones was with Sheriff Parker. "Do you have a name?"

"I do not recall," the Sphere said.

"Of course you don't." Buzz pushed something on the gun, and the tip began to glow yellow.

"What about my sister? Can you sense the other Spheres?"

He shook his head. "Not currently. I believe there might be a way, but I can't remember."

"Do you know why you came to Bell Island?" Kim asked.

"No."

"What *do* you know?" Bones quipped.

"That we are in danger," Parker said.

"Talk about stating the obvious," I muttered. "Buzz, what did you find?"

"That mob, the one with Mr. Bellows, your neighbor. They were…" Bones rubbed his forehead.

"The Traveler killed them all. Near the theater." Buzz turned the gun off. "I spotted him behind the tire shop."

"That's the same spot where the Sphere took Cindy over," Kim said.

"I thought so." Buzz looked at the sky. "There's a third Sphere on Bell Island, with two aliens hunting them. We have something that might actually kill them now, and one of the Spheres with us. We're in a better position than before. But we must gather the others."

"To lure them into your trap," I finished.

"That's right."

I turned my attention on Parker. "Do you know the man you've taken over?"

"Yes. I have his memories."

"If you were planning on hiding, where would you go?"

"Why is that relevant?" Buzz interjected.

"Just answer it," I pushed.

"Sheriff Parker has a safe room in his house. I would go there," he said.

I tried to think where Cindy might hide, and it became abundantly clear. "The school."

"School?" Bones asked.

"Cindy used to seclude herself in the slide when she was young. You know, the big twisty plastic one that always smelled funny on a hot day?"

"I remember that. You had to bribe her to leave it," he said.

Buzz opened the rear door. "Everyone in. We're going to the school."

"Where are the deputy and Reaper?" Kim asked from the middle seat.

"He stuck around. Said he couldn't leave such a dreadful crime scene." Bones rolled his window down when Buzz started to drive.

It was finally after midnight, so the fourth of July had now become the fifth, a day usually reserved for the entire adult population to recover from too many drinks. The kids all had gut aches from too many hot dogs and soda pops.

Even though we'd gained a slight advantage in the mines, reality was creeping past my borders. There were still two of the giant monsters terrorizing Bell Island, and my little sister had been invaded by a sphere of light.

I glanced at Parker, who stared blankly, hands on his lap.

"I can't believe you nailed one of the bastards," Buzz muttered from the driver's seat. "Been trying for years."

"You'll have your chance again tonight… or today." Kim reached over, taking my hand. It was cold, and my fingers intertwined with hers. The moment of contact helped keep my fears at bay.

I smiled at her, then realized she hadn't told me her secret. We'd been interrupted by the Traveler's arrival. Whatever it was could wait. We had more pressing matters to attend to.

Bell Island had three schools. One for elementary, one for middle grade, and the high school, which was in desperate need of renovations. This K-6 had a nice new coat of paint on the exterior, but the grounds were in disrepair. School had ended for the summer, and the grass was long, weeds poking up along the short chain-link fence surrounding the property.

Buzz rolled into the parking lot, finding it empty except

for three big yellow school buses. He avoided them, and killed his lights as he drove to the playground.

I was out first, running across the puddle-covered lot. I hopped the fence, pushing off with one hand, and raced for the playground. When I arrived, I slowed, worried I'd been too hasty. I couldn't go rushing into danger. Not tonight.

Instead of shouting her name, I went to the slide. "Cindy?" I whispered. "It's me, Elliot."

"Are they gone?" she asked with a small voice.

She was alive! I climbed into the exit and gripped the slide walls, ascending the curving plastic tube. Cindy was standing, her feet planted to keep her from slipping.

"Not yet, but we found another Sphere," I told her.

"What's a Sphere?" she asked.

"That's what we call you."

"Oh. It's not our name," she said plainly.

"Do you remember what you are?"

Cindy shook her head.

"Come out. We'll keep you safe," I promised.

Cindy looked dubious, but she let me lead her from the slide. She hesitated and looked to her previous resting place. "I want to stay here."

"You can't."

"Why not? They will eventually tire of this game and return home," she said.

"Wait, have they done this before?"

"I think so. Not on Bell Island, though. Maybe not this planet. My memories don't serve me well." Cindy stared at the sky.

"Get her over here," Buzz called.

Cindy froze in her steps. "There's too many people."

"Those are our friends. We can trust them."

Cindy noticed Sheriff Parker, who finally entered the

playground. She ran to him, setting her hands on his shoulders. Light slowly shot from their ears and mouths. It pulsed a few times, and waned.

"What are they doing?" Buzz whispered.

"Maybe communicating with one another," Kim suggested.

They turned and faced our group. "The Travelers are near. We must move," Cindy said.

"Which way?" Buzz grunted.

Cindy pointed to the north. "They come. And quickly."

"Good," Buzz said. "Let's go to my place. Draw them in."

I hated the idea of Cindy being used like bait, but at least he had supplies and a cage there. Instead of arguing with Buzz, I agreed. "That's the only choice."

It was a tight squeeze in the vehicle, but we managed with Kim pressed up close to me. We couldn't put on our seat belts, so I hoped Buzz didn't drive too erratically, but that was asking a lot. The moment he flicked the lights on, I thought I saw a Traveler across the school grounds. Then it was gone.

"Your brother killed one, Cindy," Bones said.

Cindy went rigid. "You did?"

"Yeah, well, Kim and I share the honors of our first alien kill," I said.

Cindy blinked rapidly. "They're going to be angry. It's not common for them to die."

"Well, too bad. They came to Bell Island and don't seem to have any problem hurting our people," Bones blurted. "I say to hell with them."

"You don't understand. It is a game to the Travelers. If they win, they leave. If they lose… they fight," Sheriff Parker said.

"Are you saying all we need to do is let them eat you,

and they'll fly home?" Bones asked.

Parker and Cindy took a second to make eye contact. "In a sense."

"Then what are we doing? People are dying in the streets. Give them the Spheres!" Bones shouted.

Buzz turned the wipers on high. "We can't."

"Why not?"

"Because they're stuck inside Elliot's sister and the sheriff," Buzz answered.

"Then leave!" Bones knelt on the front seat, watching the pair. "Take your little light bubble and get out of them."

"We will not," Parker said.

"You have to. It's the only way to save Bell Island." Bones was adamant, but I didn't love his suggestion.

"We can't let them eat the Spheres," I told my friend, and he sat down, facing the proper direction.

"I guess."

"What about the third one?" I asked Buzz.

"If they come for these two, then it doesn't matter. Not tonight."

"Will they send more?" I asked Cindy.

"I doubt it. Not for some time, but the game is now over. It is no longer just a hunt. The Travelers will do anything to end our lives, and if that means revealing themselves to your population, it's acceptable to them," she told me.

"Great." Bones rolled his window up as the rain pelted in sideways.

We were on the main road, heading for Reeve's farm, when I saw the flashlights near the turnoff to downtown. "Buzz, we should check that out."

He grumbled about it but listened to my suggestion. Almost all of the cars had vacated the area, and the park remained a disaster. Someone was near the diner. Buzz pulled up to the restaurant, shining his lights on the group.

"You have to be kidding me," I muttered. Cooper and Paul stood near the glass, baseball bats in their grips. I crossed the road to the sidewalk. "What are you doing? You're supposed to be at home."

Cooper seemed shocked when I approached him, and his lips were bleeding. "We found it."

"Found what?" Buzz asked from behind me.

"The thing that's been murdering everyone. It's not a serial killer, it's …"

"A big-ass alien?" Bones finished.

"I don't know about that, but it has claws," Paul said. Suddenly, the muscle-bound goon didn't seem so tough.

"Where is it?" Kim asked.

"In the kitchen. We trapped it inside and slammed the door." Paul's cheek was twitchy.

Buzz stared at me doubtfully. "And it stayed there?"

"Yes. How would it escape?" Cooper asked.

Buzz tested the door handle, which was unlocked. "Do they always leave this place open?" He directed the question at Kim.

"No. Someone probably grabbed extra buns for the barbecue," she said.

Buzz lifted the alien gun, and Cooper jumped away. "What in God's name is *that*?"

"A weapon. And it packs quite the punch." Buzz shoved Cooper aside.

I trailed after him, not sure why I felt the need to be a hero. Something made noises from the kitchen, and we darted past the empty tables, barely able to see. Kim and Cooper held flashlights from the doorway, guiding our path. I kicked a chair leg, and Buzz glared at me for announcing our presence.

The kitchen door was shut. We rounded the counter,

and Buzz reached for the handle.

"Let me," I whispered, staring at his gun. He nodded his understanding and braced himself with the alien weapon raised. He tapped the edge, bringing the yellow light on.

I touched the knob, turning it slowly, and shoved it in.

The animal scurried from its trap, bounding over the counter, and toward Cooper at the doors.

"It's just the bobcat!" I shouted, and Cooper tried to swing his bat. Kim blocked him, pushing my nemesis in the shoulder. The cat sped down the sidewalk.

"You let it get away!" Cooper yelled.

"You idiot. That's not what killed those people," Bones told him.

"Oh yeah, how do you know?" Paul defended his friend.

"Because that is." Bones pointed past him, to the park across the street.

A Traveler stood still, the clouds parting to allow the moonlight to illuminate him. He seemed even bigger from this distance. The picnic table only reached his knee, and the alien threw his head back, screeching in fury. I saw the long blade in his hand, and the gun strapped to him.

"How did he get here so fast?" I muttered.

"Take the SUV," Buzz whispered. "Bring the Spheres to my house. Keep them safe."

Paul stumbled off the sidewalk. "What is that thing?"

"Don't even think about it," Kim told him, but the big guy kept walking.

Paul didn't stop. "Is that a bear?"

I couldn't leave Buzz here alone. "Kim, you and Bones…"

"No way, Elliot. You're driving." She pushed me to the 4X4. Cindy and Parker were still inside.

"Sheriff Parker, is that you?" Cooper asked.

"Yes."

"Why are you sitting there?"

"Cooper, go home! If you see anyone, tell them to do the same. We've been invaded by aliens," I said, and Cooper cracked a grin.

"I see what this is. You're messing with us. Are we on TV? Pauly, did you hear that? There are aliens on Bell Island!" Cooper ran to join his friend in the park.

"I told you they were stupid," Bones mumbled.

"Boys, get away from there." Buzz's warning went unheeded. "Elliot, you heard me. I'll hold him off."

I wanted to stay, but seeing Cindy in the backseat made my mind up. This man had faced off against the Travelers before and survived, even a couple of times tonight.

I revved the engine, staring at the Traveler, who remained a hundred yards away. The moment I started to move, he did too. Paul was directly in his path.

Cooper and Paul jeered at the alien like it was a resident wearing a mask, pulling a prank on them. Then the blade carved through the air, slicing Paul's head clean off his shoulders, and the laughter turned to screams.

A pulse shot from Buzz's gun as I pushed the pedal, and I heard an explosion when I jolted to the left, racing from the scene.

"Your friend is brave," Parker said.

"You've got that right." I held the steering wheel tightly. "He better make it out of this."

The reprieve from the storm continued, and the moon gave me a better view of the roads than these dingy headlights. I almost missed the turn, but managed to make it in time, my tires slipping on the gravel. And we were at the Reeve farm once again, with not only Cindy and her Sphere, but a second alien entity.

Maybe Bones had been right in his suggestion. The Spheres were the ones causing all the trouble, but no one knew why they were hidden on Bell Island. Buzz thought they were scattered across our world, and that could mean pandemonium if the Travelers decided to hunt them in unison. It would resemble a full-scale alien invasion. And maybe they'd start out playing a game, like Cindy mentioned, but it would quickly transform into an all-out melee. I couldn't let that happen, yet I had no idea how to stop it.

I was just a twenty-two-year-old man, struggling to finish college and find my place in the world. My worries about grades and my future suddenly seemed irrelevant after tonight's events. Everything had changed.

Instead of going straight to the house, I chose the barn. Once inside, we all exited the car. "We have to defend this place." I glanced at the trap, trying to figure out how we could convince a Traveler to enter it so we could secure the latch behind him. I doubted that was possible. They were big, but that didn't mean they were dumb.

Bones took a rocket launcher from a crate, adding a couple of replacement grenades to his pack. "How hard can it be?"

I offered Parker a couple of guns, and he gawked at them like they were on fire. "You're the sheriff. Surely you know how to fire a weapon?"

"I do, but the Spheres are non-violent."

"Maybe that's why you're constantly being eaten by these guys." Kim shoved the assault rifle into his chest. "Take it. Point and shoot. You can do this."

He nodded, and I even gave Cindy a handgun. She didn't react as she accepted it, looking at the shiny chrome weapon.

"Where did Buzz get all this stuff?" Bones asked.

"I don't think we'd want to know. He must have friends in the military or something," I said.

I opened another crate, finding what I thought were Claymore mines. I'd seen enough war movies to understand what they did. I read the words embossed on it: FRONT TOWARD ENEMY. I hoped not to screw that one up. I took three of them and grabbed the blasting cap and tripwire.

"Shall we?" I headed outside, listening. It was deadly silent.

Bell Island had endured a lot, and the ground was still soaking wet. Leaves began to rustle in the breeze, but it was otherwise peaceful. Feathery clouds drifted in on the wind, blotting out the pale moon. It was almost possible to forget we were under attack, until I closed my eyes and pictured Paul literally losing his head.

I scanned the area, then the driveway, not seeing anything out of place. Buzz kept the property well preserved.

"What's this?" Kim pointed to a spot fifty yards from the house. There was a red flag in the ground. Being outside left me feeling targeted, like the Travelers might be watching us at that very moment. We knew there were two remaining, and Buzz had one downtown, indicating there was at least one more alien currently hunting these Spheres.

I set the Claymores down carefully and plucked the flag. "Maybe he has an issue with his utilities."

Bones poked at the ground with the rocket launcher. "Guys, this is sick." He lifted the corner of a tarp, revealing a hole beneath it. Long sharp wooden stakes jutted from the ten-foot drop. He returned it, brushing dirt and sod to blend it with the landscaping.

I strode to the front of the house, placing one of my explosives. The cable stuck into the back, and I looped the tripwire around two trees, hoping that it would detonate should the invader reach the porch.

"The other way," Kim said, rotating the Claymore. I read the simple three-word instructions.

"I was going to do that," I lied, trying to cover my mistake. She grinned at me rather than teasing.

Cindy and Parker were already in Buzz's home, and I heard the generator start up. A light within blinked on, and I was instantly relieved. It was amazing what the simple comfort of power could do to someone after a night in the dark, being chased by giant aliens.

When I had the second explosive positioned near the rear entrance, we joined the other two in the living room. The door had a few bolts, and I rotated every one of them, the locks snapping loudly into place.

"Bones, let's check out the situation on his roof."

"Roof?"

"I saw the widow's walk up there," I pointed up.

"What's a widow's walk?" Kim asked.

"Lots of old farmhouses had them during war times. It's usually a flat balcony with railings where the wife would sit every night, waiting for her husband to return from overseas, but they often didn't," I said, repeating something Uncle Taylor had once taught me.

"How sexist," Kim muttered. "As if they had time to just sit around, when they had mouths to feed and a household to maintain. Leave it to a man to—"

"The name isn't important," I told her as I jogged upstairs. The floorboards were ancient, and they creaked as I rushed up them. Bones was lighter, and his passage was quieter.

When I didn't find a second set of steps on this level, I searched for an attic. A rope hung at the end of the hallway, and I pulled it, sending a rickety ladder toward me.

"You expect me to climb that?" Bones asked,

shouldering the RPG.

"I'll give you a hand." I took the launcher from him, and he cautiously tested the first rung. When he realized it wouldn't collapse under his feet, he bounded up the rest. I passed the RPG to him and joined him.

The attic was organized, like everything Buzz touched. I wondered if he'd been the guy in Vietnam labeling their supplies, and folding blankets when the other soldiers left a mess. I couldn't picture Buzz doing anyone else's chores, but I could imagine him bossing them into it.

"This stuff is old," Bones said. He lifted a trunk lid, finding lacy baby clothing.

"Must be from Mrs. Reeve. Guess they didn't take all her things." The windows were easy enough to find with the flashlight, and I shut it off, not wanting the aliens to see the movement if they were nearby.

We found a second ladder, this one meeting up with a wooden hatch. I went up there, slid a latch sideways, and pushed it wide. Cool air blustered at me, almost sending me to the attic floor, but I managed to cling on.

The widow's walk was about eight feet across, and Buzz had left a chair. A set of binoculars rested beneath it. You could see for miles in each direction, and even more with the binoculars. I grabbed them, focusing the lenses as I found the mainland. Even though it was extremely late, the city was still bright with light pollution.

If only it was possible to contact them somehow. There had to be a way.

"That's it!" I shouted. My voice carried into the yard.

"What are you yelling for?" Bones' head poked through. "I'm not going up to the roof. Don't like heights."

"The lighthouse. He has a ham radio. Remember when we were on that class trip and old man McIlroy let me play with his dusty machine?"

"I do! Why didn't the sheriff think about that?"

"Probably a little frazzled with the body count," I said. "Maybe we should go."

"You heard Buzz. He said to come here and wait for him. Or the Traveler."

"Can you believe we're stuck in the middle of this?" I moved aside while Bones climbed the rest of the ladder. He gripped the railing, which shook at the touch. He instantly sat on the chair and held on to the seat.

"Aliens, Elliot. Real flesh and blood monsters from another planet. What does their ship look like? Do they have kids? Are they asexual? How far is their world from Earth?" He rattled off a flurry of questions, not giving me time to respond. "And what about the Spheres? They're not even flesh and blood. They're just a ball of light. It's pretty outrageous."

"You're not kidding."

"Everything good?" Kim called from the second story.

"Yeah, we're scoping it out," I told her.

"We're going to make something to eat. Grilled cheese okay?"

"Ask her if there's any bacon…"

I rolled my eyes and crouched. "Grilled cheese is perfect!"

"Bones, you stay put." I passed him another radio. I'd grabbed a fresh set from the barn and made sure we were on the same frequency.

"Me? What if I see something?" he asked.

"Then tell us, and proceed to blow them up. If Buzz arrives, shout a warning so my booby trap doesn't destroy him. Got it?"

He nodded and picked up the binoculars. "I'd been so excited to have a killer night because everything was about to change between us, but man… this wasn't what I had in mind."

I bumped his fist three times and gave a thumbs-up. "You and me both. We'll bring the food."

"Elliot," he said, stopping me when I landed in the attic.

"I'll check if there's any bacon."

He smirked from his perch atop the old farmhouse. "You know me so well."

7

The clock flipped to 1:01 A.M. It was the witching hour. Buzz had yet to respond to any of my radio messages, and I did my best to keep them discreet, on the off chance he was hiding from his opponent. I suspected he was smart enough to put it on silent mode if that were the case.

The stove ran off a propane tank connected to the house, and it still worked. Kim showed her culinary skills, making the best grilled cheese sandwich I'd ever eaten. I pecked at a slice of dill pickle and set the plate down, rubbing my stomach. "I thought you were just a waitress."

"*Just* a waitress?" she huffed. "It's a lot tougher than you'd think. My feet ache after every shift, and working for a cranky owner doesn't help."

"I didn't mean it like that. You can really cook. Maybe that's your calling."

"Thanks," she said shyly. It was uncharacteristic for her personality. The Spheres both ate without comment, not revealing if they even tasted the food. They sat in the living room, facing one another in silence. It was so strange to see my sister being controlled by the Sphere. "I'll be right back."

She went down the hall to the bathroom, and I saw her bag was open under the table. A journal was sticking out, the leather cover stained with a blue ink. For some reason, I grabbed it. The light was dim, but the contents were legible. I stared at a hand-drawn map from what appeared to be a cityscape. Xs and circles were marked in a different pen color. The next page had annotations.

August 21ˢᵗ, 1983 – Leads are dead in Omaha. Rumors of ball lightning dried up. Heading to the next town.

My heart raced, and I read the next missive.

Sept 2ⁿᵈ, 1983 – Back to St. Louis after studying an article in the National. Might have missed something.

"What do you think you're doing?" Kim asked from the hallway entrance.

"I…" I closed the book. "What is this?"

"Do you make a habit of snooping in other people's property?" she quipped, and yanked it from me.

"You knew about the Spheres," I whispered, and her expression gave her away. "Why didn't you say something?"

"It's not that simple," she muttered.

I was about to offer my rebuttal when the radio clacked. I thought Buzz might finally have made it out, but it was Bones, his voice frantic. "*Elliot, the bogey has landed.*"

"Just say it normal!" I returned.

"*There's an alien at the northwest corner of the Reeve farm. They're here.*"

I'd come in hopes of hiding out until daybreak, but these hunters were good. If they'd found us this quickly, there was no chance we could beat them tonight. Unless we managed to kill them all.

Kim gritted her teeth, grabbing an assault rifle. "How can we fight this thing?" she asked me.

"We defeated one already. What do you say we add another to our resume?" I smiled, but my recent betrayal of trust was too fresh. I had so many questions for Kim, but no time for an inquisition. The Traveler was coming.

"*Do I stay up here?*" Bones asked through the radio.

"Roger that. See if you can blast him around the oak

tree."

"Sheriff, you need to help us," I told him, fetching my rifle from the kitchen.

He hefted his revolver and nodded. "I will do my part."

"You don't have to fight him, just stand on the porch. When the bomb is triggered, jump through the door, okay?" I went to Cindy when he nodded. "We're going to the shelter."

She blinked once. "Okay, Elliot."

The entrance to the storm shelter was only accessible from the east end of the house, and I hurried out, careful of the tripwire. Buzz had left the door unlocked, and I swung it on oiled hinges, ushering my sister inside.

"Aren't you coming with me?" she asked, her eyes big.

"No. I'll be back for you."

A tear formed, and I didn't know if it was from my real sister or the Sphere controlling her.

"Cindy," I whispered.

"Yes?"

"I love you," I said.

"She loves you too, Elliot."

I closed the shelter, padlocking the latch. The Traveler wouldn't have an issue breaking through, but it might slow the alien enough to give us a chance to kill him.

The second I crested the side of the house, I saw the RPG detonation. The oak tree was on fire, but the Traveler continued stalking toward us, blade in one hand, gun in the other. It was obvious from his body language that he was pissed.

"Over here, you sack of...!" Bones called from the roof, and the enemy lowered to a knee, aiming his gun. The yellow tip shot a round blast, striking the widow's walk.

"Bones!" I bellowed. "You're going to pay for that!" I let loose, shooting the assault rifle with reckless abandon.

I rushed forward, goading the alien to the trap dug into the earth.

He swung his blade, and I assumed the gun took a moment to recharge, or he'd have used it.

"I'm right here!" I called, and his head cocked to the side, his eyes landing on me. "And I already killed your friend!"

The Traveler grunted, and his lips hideously curled into what could only be a smile. He was having fun. These were hunters, and they didn't murder just for fun, they loved what they did. It made me sick.

He crouched and leapt, landing across the trap. His feet lingered on the ground mere inches from the hidden spears, so I did the only thing I could think of. I started to run at him, but Kimberly raced past me, a roar escaping her mouth. He flew backwards, rupturing through the tarp and fake grass. Kim sank with him, her momentum too powerful to stop.

Everything was falling apart. Bones had been shot, and Kim had just skewered herself on…

She was alive, rolling off the Traveler. Her left arm had a bleeding gash, but otherwise looked uninjured. Unlike Kim, the Traveler was in deep trouble. Two wooden stakes had impaled him, one in the back, the second in his calf.

Kim was using him for balance, and any wrong move would possibly kill her. I rushed to the edge, offering my hand.

And the Traveler began to rise.

Kim screamed and kicked off from his hips, literally jumping into my arms. She knocked the wind from my lungs, and I struggled to sit up and find my weapon.

The alien managed to unpluck himself from the stakes and ascend from the trap. His blade was gone, as was his gun, but he was still a menace, green goop dripping from his wounds. He spoke, the words impossible to translate, but their meaning was clear. He wanted to tear us apart limb from limb.

Now we ran, this time away from him. Sheriff Parker still stood behind the Claymore tripwire, his gun nervously raised.

The Traveler groaned and sniffed the air, the smile returning. He slowly limped forward, reaching for the Sphere in the middle-aged man's body.

Then he stepped between the trees. I heard the click of the wire before diving onto the porch, dragging Kim and Parker with me. I didn't have time to shut the door, and the windows of Buzz's house shattered. I lay on my back for a moment, staring at the wooden ceiling, listening for sounds of pursuit.

"We did it," Kim murmured. She recovered before me, surveying the damage outside. "He's dead!"

I saw pieces of the alien littering the sidewalk leading from the driveway to his porch, and felt nothing but pride at the mess.

The victory celebration was short-lived.

"Bones is gone," I whispered, head hanging low. I put my arm around Kim's waist as we stood on the burning porch.

"What did I miss?" Bones asked from around the corner.

"You're alive!" I exclaimed.

"You didn't think I'd shoot a rocket at an alien and then stay put, did you? It's basic training 101, dude." Bones smirked and rested the loaded RPG on the ground.

"That's two," I told Kim. "One more to go."

---

*C*indy was so relieved to be released from the shelter that the Sphere hugged me. It was strange, because my sister hadn't done that in about five years.

"Now what?" Kim asked.

"Lighthouse. I think we can contact the mainland from it."

"Perfect," she said. "I wish we knew what happened to Buzz."

"He'll be fine." Not even I fully believed my own lie. We'd managed to kill a couple of the Travelers at that point, which was not only shocking, but altogether inconceivable.

"Kim, are you there?" We went to the front of Buzz's house, where Bones and Kim waited, their gazes set on the soldier's home. The steps were obliterated, and flames flickered near the living room window. I rushed over, removing my rain jacket, and bashed the soaking coat on the fire. It hissed out, and I returned to the yard.

"Elliot…" Bones pointed at the ground, and I followed his finger to the green ooze I'd stomped on. It clung to my heel and dripped. I wiped it on the grass and shuddered. Bits of the corpse were everywhere.

Kim clutched her arm to her chest, and I remembered that she'd been pierced by Buzz's sharp stakes. "Let's bring you inside."

She gawked at the end of the driveway. "What if the other one comes?"

The pair of Spheres stood closely, pulses of light emitting from their mouths.

"He's not dead," they said in unison. I'd never seen anything quite so disturbing as my sister and Sheriff Parker harmonizing their words.

"Buzz or the Traveler?" Bones asked them.

"We have no idea about the human. It's the hunter we fear," they told us.

"Can you two stop that?" Bones demanded. "It's creepy enough without you guys being so weird."

They separated, the light extinguishing. "My apologies," Parker said. "The Sphere is on the island, but their signal is muted. I haven't sensed this before."

"We should fix me up," Kim finally agreed.

Buzz had an assortment of first-aid items in his bathroom, and I cleaned her arm, then scrubbed the wound with rubbing alcohol. It was pungent, and she whimpered as I worked.

"You're tougher than me. I had this on a knee scrape once and almost passed out," I told her, trying to make her feel better.

"It hurts like hell," she muttered.

"It's not that deep." At least, I didn't think it was. The cut seemed shallow, the blood slowly leaking from the injury. I wrapped it with gauze, like I'd seen my mom do when Cindy hurt her hand climbing a tree. Then I used the little metal braces to keep it closed.

She rose, bending her arm at the elbow a few times before nodding. "Nice job, Elliot."

"Thank you. Let's hope I don't need to test these skills again tonight."

Kim's other hand touched my cheek, and she leaned in, kissing me gently on the lips. "I appreciate it."

"You guys done?" Bones asked from the living room. "We better leave. If that other alien comes and finds his friend spread out like jam on toast, he'll be upset."

Buzz's vehicle looked ridiculous, the tires huge, the spikes jutting a solid six inches from the wheels. The keys remained inside, and Kim came to the front with me, while Bones sat with Parker and Cindy. Despite his encouragement, Bones was terrified. It was evident in the way his voice lifted at the end of his sentences, and how his eyes were a constant blur as he scanned the surroundings. We were all scared.

It started easily enough, and I went in reverse, pressing the pedal as I shifted into drive. The bay was ten minutes away, as there was no direct line between the Reeve farm and the docks. I had to backtrack, and my eyelids began to droop. "Bones, anything to drink in that pack of yours?"

He searched his bag, retrieving a beer and a can of cola. "They're both warm."

"I need some caffeine." I grabbed the soda and cracked it, spray spilling from the top. I took a big drink and offered it to Kim, who shook her head.

I heard another tab pop, and watched Bones guzzle a beer through the mirror. "Seriously? Right now?"

"I almost died on that widow's walk. If ever there was a time." Bones finished it, wiping his lips.

The storm had broken, and the stars were visible. I paused at the main intersection, peering at the sky.

"We have more clouds to the west," Kim whispered. A distant flash of lightning reminded me we weren't out of this mess quite yet.

The bay was a couple miles to the left, making downtown about three miles on the right. I steered toward the water when the radio crackled.

"*Anyone there?*"

I didn't recognize the voice. Kim picked it up as I parked on the side of the road. "Yes. Who is this?"

"*Cooper,*" he said.

"Where did you get the radio, Cooper?" Kim asked.

"*That guy had it on him. He saved me, but I think he might be…*"

"Where are you?"

"Behind the record store," he said. *"In the alley."*

I didn't think. I just spun the tires, shooting Buzz's 4X4 in the opposite direction. The power was still off, but with the moon glistening above us, it suddenly seemed like Bell Island was under the safety of a spotlight, rather than shrouded in darkness. It gave me hope that we might actually survive the night. But we needed Buzz to accomplish that.

I bypassed some parked cars, one of them overturned in the ditch. It hadn't been there earlier, and I noticed the melted bumper. A few people were on the road, their guts hanging out. The Traveler was searching for prey, and obviously didn't care who obstructed his path. I nervously glanced at the pair of Spheres in the back seat. They were like a beacon for the monstrous aliens, and I had two of them in the car with me.

I passed the diner, spinning to the record shop. When we were closer, I killed the lights, crawling into the alleyway. It was a tight fit, and the spikes scratched the fence on my side before I tugged the steering wheel. The street was filled with puddles of rainwater, the gravel becoming mud in most parts, but the vehicle kept its pace. When I saw the dumpster behind Cliff's Records, I stopped and rushed out, finding Cooper next to Buzz's body. Cooper clutched a revolver, his eyes wide, his hand shaky.

"It's us!" I assured him. "You're going to be okay."

"What... was that thing?" he whispered.

"It's an alien. We tried to warn you," I said.

"Paul... he lost his head."

I pushed by Cooper to get near Buzz, but he stayed protectively draped over the soldier.

"Put the gun down, Coop," Bones said.

"Hank?" Cooper's brow furrowed, and he squinted at Bones. "I didn't know you were..."

A garbage can clanged to the ground farther in the alley. I strove to see what caused it, but couldn't make anything out.

"Let's get inside," I muttered. The video store was only a few doors down, and I had the keys. "Help me carry him."

"He saved my life," Cooper whispered.

"And it'll be for nothing if you don't snap to it and give me a hand." I touched the barrel of the revolver, and he finally crammed it into his pants.

"Got it." Cooper blinked repeatedly and hopped up.

"What happened to him?" I searched for wounds on Buzz, but didn't find any discernible injuries, short of a few scrapes and cuts to his clothing.

"Hit his noggin. That… freak clubbed him and collapsed into a hole."

I grinned. "Buzz is quite the character. If I didn't know better, he's placed traps all over this damned island."

"Lucky no one encountered it before," Bones said, grabbing a leg.

Buzz was heavy, and my six-foot, one-eighty frame needed help to carry him. Cooper gripped under his armpit, and he hefted the big man down the block, splashing through the alley.

He groaned as we neared the video store, and I set him on the road, searching the key ring to locate the proper one. The door was solid metal, painted bright red to match our company logo. I scanned in both directions, not seeing a Traveler in the vicinity, and clanked the lock open.

Mark would freak out if he knew we were using the store after hours, but I didn't care. It wasn't like we had a choice.

Once the Spheres were inside and the door secured, Bones flicked on a flashlight. The storeroom was modest, with a few unopened boxes of VHS movies near the wall, and a shrink-wrap station used to package previously viewed flicks to make them look new.

"Sheriff Parker, we have to call the army or something. You must have a way to contact them!" Cooper paced within the room, running his hands through his messy hair.

"There's something you should know," I told Cooper.

"What? Why isn't Parker answering? Did he hit his head too?" Cooper stepped closer to the man with the handlebar mustache.

"That's not Parker," I said. "In a sense. And Cindy isn't herself either."

"Elliot, what are you talking about?"

"You saw the big beast, right?"

Cooper nodded. "You know I did."

"We call them Travelers. They hunt these other entities, the Spheres. Little balls of light, and they can enter a person and control their bodies," I explained.

Cooper actually managed to grin. "You're telling me there's an alien in your sister right now?"

"That's correct."

"No way. This is impossible," Cooper said. "Bethany always said you were prone to delusions, but…"

I tried not to react to the comment. "Cindy, can you… do that thing?"

Cindy's face began to glow, light pouring from her ears, eyes, and nostrils. She opened her mouth, and the room almost became blinding.

"Holy…"

"Where…?" Buzz grimaced, attempting to sit up. He rubbed his crown, where a goose-egg had formed.

"My workplace," I told him. "You okay?"

"The bastard clubbed me." He touched the injury. "But I'll make it." He wobbled to his feet, and grabbed for the wall to steady himself.

"Let me find you something." I rushed into the lunch-room, which was really a converted office with a two-person table, a sink, and a microwave. It smelled like fish. I snatched a couple of pills from under the sink and brought a glass of water with me.

Buzz didn't even look at them, or ask what they were. Instead, he downed them, and swigged the water until it was gone. "Cooper, where did the Traveler go?"

"He was in that trap behind the maintenance shed. I dragged you here."

"That's quite a journey. Thank you," Buzz told Cooper.

"No sweat. I barely remember doing it," he admitted.

"We'd better check the trap. His friend might have assisted him," Buzz said.

Bones drummed his fingers on a box. "Nah, we took care of him."

Buzz's eyes blinked wide. "You did?"

"Sure. We wouldn't let you down." Bones laughed.

"What happened?"

"Bones shot at him with a bazooka from the roof, and he returned fire. You'll have to hire a contractor to fix that…" I paused when Buzz's jaw dropped. "Then he fell into the pit with Kim." I gestured at her bandages. "That didn't stop him. So we blew him up with a Claymore."

"And he's dead?" Buzz asked.

"Unless he can regenerate everything," Bones added.

"Nice work, gang," Buzz muttered under his breath. "All these years, and you've managed to kill two in one night. Maybe I just needed the ignorance of youth."

I wasn't sure how to take that. "Uhm, thank you?"

"That leaves one remaining, and he might be dead." Buzz went into the store, and light entered from the front windows. It was strange to be in here at two A.M. The cardboard cut-outs cast gloomy shadows across the aisles, and the posters looked portentous in the dark.

Bones took a chocolate bar, peeling the wrapper back, and shrugged when I glared at him. "Put it on my tab."

Cindy and Parker pointed past Buzz, toward the street. "He's here," they whispered.

The Traveler stalked from the park, his movements languid and calm.

"Maybe he's just looking for a good flick for the trip home," Bones suggested.

8

I'd watched Mark lock the entrance earlier, so I didn't bother to check if the bolt was flipped. The entire storefront was made of windows, posters, and promotions painted and taped to the surface to draw people inside.

"Where's your guns?" Buzz asked.

"In your 4X4," I said.

"Great." Buzz patted his chest and pulled a big chrome handgun from beneath his camouflage vest. I'd kept mine in my pocket, and yanked it free, checking the cylinder. It had five bullets.

Cooper was armed too, and he handed it to Buzz.

He evaluated it and gave it back. "Good."

"Here." Sheriff Parker had a holstered gun, and I knew the Sphere didn't want to use it. He offered it to Kim.

She accepted the weapon. "Me?"

The Traveler had stopped, his big black eyes assessing the store. Bones started to move, and I clasped a palm over the flashlight. "Turn it off," I hissed, and he did, muttering an apology.

The alien was huge, the biggest of the three, and I could spot subtle differences from the others. This one had a wider forehead, his eyes closer set. His mouth opened, and sharp teeth glinted in the starlight.

"He's injured," I whispered.

"I see that." Buzz grunted and limped forward. "His shoulder is bleeding."

"What can we do?" Cindy's voice was small.

"You two hide." Buzz glanced at me. "Any suggestions?"

"The safe. Mark keeps one concealed behind his wall."

"Get them into it," Buzz ordered and the Spheres followed me toward Mark's office. I half-expected the door to be bolted, but it wasn't. The wall had a tall picture on it, and I flipped it on hinges, revealing the safe's lock. I was one of the few that knew the code, according to Mark, but I hadn't opened it since last summer.

I tried to remember the numbers and heard the others moving around out front. "Come on, Elliot," I muttered. I finally recalled that he'd used his ex-wife's birthday, and wondered if he would have changed it since the divorce. Turned out he hadn't. The safe was barely big enough for Parker and Cindy to fit into, and they crammed in, both looking afraid.

"We'll let you out soon." It was the second time I'd promised this in the last couple of hours. I'd been good to my word so far.

I replaced the picture and heard the glass shattering as I entered the sales floor. The Traveler burst through the windows, dive-rolling to land on his feet. The weapon strapped to his wrist burned yellow, and the shot that erupted from it narrowly missed Cooper. He shouted as he jumped behind the counter.

"Over here, you ugly son of a…" Buzz fired at the alien, the bullets striking his chest.

The Traveler stilled, glancing at the wounds before pulling his lengthy blade from a gray scabbard. He bared his teeth and sniffed the air, likely sensing the Spheres in the other room.

Kim fired from beside him, and the Traveler lunged. The blade sliced through the air, and Kim was sent flying into the romantic comedies. She smashed into the shelving, knocking it over. Bones threw a video at him, and he batted it while I fired my revolver, hitting him in the neck. Bullets harmed him, but not in the way they would a human. I doubted we had enough firepower with us to take this beast down.

We spread out like Buzz had suggested, struggling to make as many targets as we could, but the Traveler only seemed interested in getting to Mark's office. Cooper shot until his gun clicked empty. The alien rushed to him, jabbing the blade, but Cooper was used to evasion as the high school football quarterback. He dodged the monster and kicked him in the knee, but showed his fury when his opponent clipped him with a thick arm. Cooper barreled into the popcorn display, crashing to the floor.

Buzz took the opportunity and tackled the much larger being. He managed to get him to the carpet, the knife clanging out from the alien's grip. I rushed to recover the sharp blade.

Buzz and the Traveler wrestled, the soldier giving it all he had. I aimed my gun, trying to get a clear shot, but they were too fast, and it was tough to discern who was who.

"Kill him!" Buzz yelled.

I pulled the trigger, targeting the alien's thick skull. When it hit, I pulled it again, and he went still.

Buzz rolled off, yanking the blade by the handle, and rammed it into the being's throat, leaving it sticking out upright. Buzz was on his knees, panting from exertion, when the sirens sounded, red and blue lights stopping on Main Street.

"Everyone all right?" a voice called.

"In here, Deputy Sadie!" Bones shouted, and the officer entered with his gun up.

He saw the dead alien and gawked at each of us, as if

trying to put the pieces together. "I'll be damned. You got him."

"Them. They're all gone. Three Travelers, three blasted corpses," Buzz managed to say.

Reaper trailed after her father, and when she saw Bones, she threw her arms around him, hugging him tight. "I'm so glad you're okay."

"Me too." Bones returned the embrace and smirked at me from ten feet away.

"Kim," I whispered, remembering she'd been tossed across the room. She was on the floor, splayed over the toppled shelving.

"No…" I supported her as she sat upright, gasping for air.

"Is he…?" She was almost on her feet, and I urged her to stay calm for a second.

"Dead. We did it," I said, and she relaxed.

"Thank God." Kim took her time, and gingerly limped to the rest of our group. "It's fine, just a charley horse."

"The sheriff sent those men to prepare a boat at the bay, and the lighthouse has a radio that should be able to reach the city. That was our destination before we heard from Buzz," I said.

Cooper slowly rose, dusting himself off like he had popcorn seasoning on his shirt. His eye was swollen, but his jaw was set firmly.

The deputy nodded. "Where's Parker?"

I led him to the office and opened the safe again. Cindy and Parker emerged, stretching their spines.

"Sheriff, what were you doing in there?" Deputy Sadie asked, and I realized he didn't know about the Sphere occupying his boss.

"We'll catch you up," I told him. "Let's go to the bay first."

Sadie looked dubious, but nodded regardless. "Whatever you say."

Cooper had drifted outside and started walking away from the store. "Where are you going?" I asked him. The gun he'd been holding dropped to the sidewalk.

He didn't glance back. "Home."

"One less hide to protect," Buzz grumbled.

The air was crisper, the wind blowing in a frigid ocean front. But the Travelers were gone, and that was something to celebrate. My arms began to ache, the energy sapped from my core. Three aliens, three bodies, and I'd had a part in ending each of their lives.

I'd killed something.

As a kid, I'd loathed the idea of hunting, not that I judged others for it, but it just wasn't for me. When Cooper's family rented a cabin a couple hours inland to hunt deer one particularly cold autumn, I'd gone, but refused to pull the trigger. But this was different. It was life or death, and I was proud that I'd had the strength to protect my sister and my fellow islanders when push came to shove.

I started for the driver's seat, and Buzz grabbed my arm. "I don't think so, kid."

Even after my heroism, this guy still treated me the same. I guess I preferred that to the alternative.

Bones hopped in with Reaper and Sadie, and when the deputy tried getting the sheriff into his car, I rejected the offer. "He'll be okay with us." I couldn't let the Spheres out of my sight, not until we found a way to detach them from our people.

"Have it your way. See you at the lighthouse." Sadie turned the strobing lights off and drove away.

"You sure you're fine?" I asked Kim.

"I've felt worse after a long shift at the diner. I'm cool."

Kim grunted as she settled into the back seat, and we left abruptly.

"They say the lighthouse is haunted," Buzz told me.

"Who does?"

"The locals. You haven't heard the stories?"

"Of course I have. I grew up here," I muttered. "Mr. McIlroy claims there's nothing strange about it."

"Mr. McIlroy might be hiding something," Buzz said.

"You mean…"

Buzz nodded. "I considered that he was holding a Sphere."

"For how long?"

"Years. Maybe most of his life," Buzz suggested.

The deputy's car was half a block ahead, and we followed him to the main road.

"Wait, are you implying someone could carry a Sphere forever?" I inquired.

"Why not?"

"I thought they hitched a ride for a while and then returned to hiding, or whatever they do." I glanced at Cindy, whose hands were folded on her lap. "Can you stay inside a person?"

"I haven't tried, but I think it can be accomplished."

"You took over my mother. What was it like?"

Cindy smiled slightly. "The twins. Taylor and Lorraine. They were my first memory of Bell Island. I don't know when I arrived, but I think I'd been hibernating, buried deep within the island. The storm came, and I woke at the presence of the Travelers."

"They were here?" Buzz barked. "Back then?"

"One. He came alone. I found Elliot and Cindy's mother and uncle. They were shocked to encounter a ball of light, and furious when I approached young Lorraine. I was more of a target in my natural form. The Travelers have a difficult time tracking us when we're shielded by an organic being. I knew that invading the local girl was a danger to her, but I didn't feel like I had a choice. I tried to convince her to uncover my ship, but she didn't know where it was."

"What happened to the Traveler?" Buzz asked.

"I have no clue. He never found me. Or the others, from the looks of it." Cindy stared at Parker beside her.

"And my uncle?"

"I don't believe he drowned," Cindy said.

"What?" I spun around. "Why do you say that?"

"Because he would come and visit me. Once a year, on the anniversary of our first encounter. He never knew I was there for certain, but he'd talk out loud, as if seeking my approval. He was searching for my ship, but it was a slow process. Three years ago, he came, and I showed myself, risking a lot. He said he figured it out, and that he was going to investigate the bay. He thought it was there."

"Uncle Taylor didn't kill himself," I whispered.

I recalled my dad's words, claiming he'd found my mom's van at the bay, with her swimming into the depths of the channel. They weren't mentally ill; they were trying to help the Spheres.

"This changes everything," I muttered.

"Kid, I don't know what you're thinking, but let's save it for another day." Buzz sped up to keep pace with Sadie.

"I have to talk to Mom about this," I said. Which would be tough, considering she'd bought in to the fact she suffered from delusions. But she didn't. I could tell her the truth. Show her Cindy and force the Sphere to remove itself.

"You'll have your chance, but for now, we should stick to the plan." Buzz tilted the rearview mirror. "Kim, you've been awfully quiet."

I thought about Kim's journal. She'd drawn maps and mentioned the Spheres. "I think you should tell him."

Kim sighed and leaned forward, head between the seats. "Elliot doesn't know what he's talking about."

"I saw it, Kim. You were on the search for the Spheres, just like Buzz was."

Buzz slammed on the brakes and jarred the 4X4 to the road's shoulder. "Kimberly, what's he saying?"

"Okay, I've been aware of the Spheres for a while."

"How?" he whispered.

"The Travelers killed my parents." Her chin sank to her chest. "They came into my house and tore them apart."

"Why would they do that?" Buzz murmured.

"Because they were looking for a Sphere," Kim said.

"Did they find it?" I asked impatiently.

Kim reached for my hand, touching it gently. "Yes. But they weren't able to kill it."

"Good. Where's the Sphere now?" Buzz asked.

Kim peered at Cindy and Parker, and her eyes began to glow white. Light escaped her face, and when she opened her mouth, the brilliance of a star emerged. "She's right here."

Part Three
The Finale

1

I paced the ditch, uncaring of the water drenching my shoes. My hair was a mess, but I managed to comb my fingers through it as I muttered under my breath, "Why didn't you tell me?"

Kim smirked, making this all the more difficult. "What was I supposed to say? I really like you, Elliot."

"But you're an alien!"

"In a sense."

Buzz and the other two stayed inside, watching our conversation with fascination.

"In a *sense*?" I bellowed. "You just made light shoot from your orifices!"

"Don't be bogus, Elliot. I'm still Kimberly."

"No, you aren't. Who's Kim? You hitchhiked a ride on some innocent girl, and now…"

"I've been Kimberly my entire life, or the part that I recall. I think the Sphere entered the baby when she was only an hour old. We were both born that day."

"For real?" I stopped stomping the puddles as if I was having a temper tantrum.

"Yeah. I spent the first ten years of my life unaware there was anything different about me. Then I had a revelation. Around the time I had my first..." She didn't say it, but I knew what she was implying. "My eyes glowed white, and I was too scared to tell anyone. I could control it for the most part, but every now and then, my true essence would reveal itself, and someone would see it. I had to pretend it was a trick, and I started carrying a flashlight and lighter with me just in case I needed to brush it off."

"You were really hunted?" Buzz was out now, leaning on the vehicle's front end.

"Twice." She glanced at the sky. "Three, if you count tonight."

"No wonder they found us so quickly," Buzz said. "We unknowingly had three Spheres with us. How have you survived this long?"

I recalled her diving into the alien at the Reeve farm, and understood the difference between Kim and the other Spheres. "She's not scared of violence. Kim fights back."

She smiled at me and nodded. "I think I'm unique. Or maybe it's the fact I've never lived outside of my human body. If I did, I don't remember it."

"Did you know she was one of you?" I asked Cindy, who was listening through the open window.

"I did not."

Parker lifted a hand. "I didn't either."

"Interesting," Buzz whispered. "There might be something important about this, but for now, can we climb into the car so we can continue on?"

"What are we going to tell the mainland when we radio them?" I asked.

"The truth," Buzz said. "That a wild animal attacked during the storm."

"What about all the witnesses?" Kim asked.

"Gas leak. Works every time." Buzz turned his key, and we hurried along the last mile toward the beach.

Cove Peak was high above us, and water flowed down the road. That was where I'd seen my first alien, and I was more than grateful to not have to face another.

Countless people had died tonight, including Paul and Deputy Bradshaw, and Bell Island wouldn't ever be the same. After this, residents would move away, fearful it might happen again, and if the Spheres lingered, it might. I didn't have enough information on the Travelers to make an informed hypothesis. If they failed, would they send more, or head to the next Sphere, restarting the sick game? Time would tell.

Buzz rolled through a foot of water as we hit level ground, and the lighthouse stood perched on the cliffside, shrouded in darkness.

"The beam isn't on."

"Power outage?" Buzz asked.

"No. It has a top-of-the-line backup generator. I remember from my trip there. McIlroy showed us how it operated and demonstrated a power failure by flipping the breaker. The light flickered but stayed on."

Deputy Sadie and Reaper stared at the water, where a boat was hung up on the sandy beach. "What happened here?" Kim asked them.

"These are the men Sheriff Parker sent to prepare the boat," Sadie said.

At first, I didn't follow; then I saw the heads sticking from the sand, like they'd been buried neck deep. I realized the bodies were piled a short distance away, limbs bent at odd angles.

Bones threw up.

"How could anyone do this?" Sadie mumbled.

"This had to be done before we killed them, right?" I

asked Buzz.

He gawked at the carnage, then the boat, and peered to the lighthouse. "I think so."

"Three Spheres and three Travelers. That's the rules," I reiterated.

"What did I say earlier about the rules?" Buzz strode to the boat. It was a big one, with a giant motor on the back, the propellers jammed into the sand. A mast rose from the middle, the sail cinched tight.

A metal ladder clung to the side, and Buzz jumped, catching the bottom. He pulled himself up, and I joined him, gripping the cold rungs and surveying the boat deck. A massive hole was burned into it, flames smothering on the surface.

"I can't tell how long ago this occurred," he said, then cursed under his breath.

Suddenly, the tension returned, and my chest tightened. Everywhere I looked, I saw another Traveler, and for a second, I thought they were surrounding us. But it was just shadows as more clouds rolled in, once again blotting out the moon.

The rain started up, causing the fire to extinguish.

"We'd better get to the lighthouse," he said, descending the ladder.

"Anything?" Sadie asked.

The sheriff stayed with Cindy, the pair of Spheres seeming frightened.

"Nothing definitive."

"I'll stay here with…" Deputy Sadie gestured at my sister. "Keep an eye on them for you."

As much as I didn't want to abandon Cindy on the beach, I also didn't want to be distracted as we climbed the cliffside staircase. The giant set of stairs was the one way to the lighthouse, since there was no paved road leading to it. Old Mr. McIlroy rarely left the grounds, and had his food delivered by the local grocer. As spectacular as the life of a lighthouse operator had seemed to a young me, I now understood how lonely it was.

Kim started forward, but I raised a palm. "I think you should stay with the others."

She frowned at me. "Don't lump me in with them. I'm coming with you."

"Let her," Buzz said. "We can fix the lighthouse beacon and radio the mainland. This shouldn't take more than an hour."

"Bones, what time is it?" I asked, and he checked his oversized leather-strapped watch, complete with metal studs.

"Two forty-five," he answered.

"And the sun rises at about five fifteen," Buzz added.

I wasn't sure why, but the idea of seeing another sunrise filled me with hope. We were close. But the aliens weren't vampires, and they wouldn't be fended off by the mere presence of the dawn.

I leaned toward my best friend. "Bones, make sure nothing happens to Cindy."

His eyes were red, and he rubbed them repeatedly. "Are they all gone?"

"Think so."

I offered him an assault rifle from the 4X4, and he shook his head, going to the box. He pulled out a second RPG, clicking a rocket into it. "I know what to do."

I clapped him on the shoulder. "Good man. See you soon."

We strode to the cliff and I turned around, finding Reaper with her dad. Bones rested the rocket launcher on his shoulder and stood beside Cindy and Parker. I waved, and only my sister returned the gesture.

The water splashed against the beach, and the sand gave way to rocks as we neared the edge of the cove. Within the bay, the channel stayed relatively peaceful, making it a great location to moor the locals' boats. The ferry dock was on the opposite edge of the cove, a half mile to our south. I wondered how many people would be leaving on it in the morning.

There were a number of residents that had gone on vacation for the holiday weekend. How would they react to the news about Bell Island's murder rampage? I suspected the entire place would be extremely chaotic for months to come.

The cliff was steep, rising a hundred and forty feet high. From this angle, the lighthouse was cut off from sight. I touched the stair rail, in awe of the elevation. The steps were slick with rainwater, and Kim zipped up her yellow jacket, flipping the hood over her hair. Our gazes met, and I still felt a spark, which couldn't work, considering she was an alien. I'd been dumped and had quickly fallen for another chick. Who, as it turned out, was being controlled by a ball of light. Classic Elliot.

The stairs proceeded in a switchback fashion, and we climbed wordlessly, getting to the first platform. I took a break, verifying our friends remained on the beach, awaiting our progress.

Buzz took the lead, his pace quickening as we neared the top.

"You seriously don't know anything about your people?" I asked Kim.

"Only what I've discerned talking to a couple of them," she admitted.

"So you have tracked some down?"

"Found one in Fairbanks, Alaska last year. She was living in an artist who called herself Watercolor. She'd been eccentric before the Sphere took her over, so no one noticed, but I saw the paintings online. The bright glowing ball, the silhouette of a Traveler on a dark night. I visited without contacting her first, assuming I could convince her to chat if I just showed up."

I kept climbing, but the effort was wearing on my thighs. "And?"

"She did. Actually, she was extremely chatty."

"Where are you from?"

"She didn't have the answer. But she'd been here for hundreds of years, and witnessed a dozen friends ingested by the Hunters. She called them that, not knowing their true name either. Watercolor would inhabit an elderly person, waiting until they died before relocating to do it all over again. Mostly, she invaded people with memory loss or dementia, and she claimed it was better for them and the family. When Watercolor was inside, she could cling to their memories, comforting the friends and family at a difficult time."

I didn't offer my opinion on controlling a human without their consent, because Kim was also doing the same. "That's all she knew?"

"Yep."

"Did you really finish college?"

"I was extremely diligent throughout school, and nothing changed when I went to college, even if I was distracted by my... research," she said.

"The Traveler really came and killed your parents?" I paused at the second platform, catching my breath. Buzz was farther ahead, but he slowed, shouting for us to hurry.

"I was seventeen years old. We lived in California. Dad was in commercial real estate, as I'd said before, and he did really well for himself. Mom was able to retire from her nursing job, and everything was going great. Until the cyclone hit. They called it the storm of the century, with manholes overflowing, and power outages for miles. We were on the coast, and I saw the damned Traveler lights as they descended from the skies, landing on the empty shore near our home."

Kim paused her story, wincing as she walked. "At seventeen, I had no idea what they were or that I'd be hunted. But the moment I spotted the alien striding up the sand, I knew he was there for me. My instincts took over, and I ran." She sniffled back a tear.

"You had no choice," I said.

"He killed them. So easily. I managed to escape, and hid in the safe room Daddy put in the summer prior. I only opened the door two days later when police officers banged on it, and the power returned. They thought it was a burglary gone wrong, and I was shipped to a foster home for four months until I turned of age. I inherited the family estate, which was far more than I'd expected."

"Hence affording a good college and all the traveling you did," I told her.

"Precisely." Kim slipped on a stair near the top, and I grabbed her wrist, keeping her upright. "Thank you." She clutched the railing. Our friends were now the size of ants below.

The ground trembled slightly, and we moved from the cliffside. "What was that?" Kim asked Buzz.

"Maybe all the water weakened something up here. Let's make this quick." Buzz had a strap on his shoulder, holding an assault rifle, and he pulled a revolver from his holster, checking the barrel. Under his influence, I did the same, and when I remembered I was empty, he handed me more bullets. Kim accepted a second magazine for her weapon, and secured it in her slicker's pocket.

"I don't anticipate any trouble, but let's be ready." Buzz

led us to the lighthouse. It really was a spectacle: tall and white, with horizontal red nautical stripes. The McIlroy house was attached, a small building with a front door and two windows. It may have been cloaked in solitude, but there was one hell of a view from up here.

I stared at the city, and for the first time ever, I felt the isolation of living on an Island. Twenty miles was a long distance from the mainland. When you grow up somewhere like Bell Island, it becomes second nature. You load up when you visit the big stores once a month, and make do the rest of the time. We're all dependent on the ferries, and we hope the supply chain keeps pace with the local businesses.

"It doesn't look like the invasion has spread," Buzz said.

"What?" I blinked, wondering if I'd heard him correctly.

"Spread. The mainland seems safe." Buzz pointed at the city.

"You thought they might be targeting other places?" Kim asked.

"I don't claim to be an expert. How do I know they're just here to play a game? Or a contest? A rite of passage, or whatever they do with you Spheres."

Until that moment, I hadn't considered a widespread invasion. Now my mind was reeling. "What would we do if a thousand of these things dropped at the same time?"

"Fight them, I suppose," Buzz replied.

"You don't think it'll happen?"

"It might. Depends how upset they are that we killed three of their own. Or this is the only ship on Earth, and the rest of the Travelers are none the wiser. We have no way of knowing." Buzz knocked on the lighthouse's door.

"But…"

"Relax, Elliot. The Travelers prefer a dark invasion."

"They do?"

"They come under the protection of a storm. There's a reason," he said.

"There's something I'm struggling with." I peered at McIlroy's home, and noticed the entrance was ajar.

"What's that?" Buzz spotted it too, and he unslung the rifle.

"The Spheres also emerge when there's a storm. Why?" I stared at Kim.

"I've always loved thunder and lightning. My parents used to have to force me not to walk out during the heaviest part. Once they found me naked in the yard when I was five, spinning around in the rain." She grinned at the recollection.

"That's it." I laughed out loud. "The Spheres are attracted to the energy of the lightning. That's why they emerge, and why the Travelers choose then to attack."

"That's a good hypothesis, Elliot." Buzz pushed the door inward with his military-grade boots. He flicked a flashlight on, holding it above his gun. The first room was a mess, furniture overturned, the kitchen table upended. The bedroom was the same, and a hole was burned through the rear wall. A picture with the Irish flag lay on the floor, the glass shattered.

I peered through the gaping opening, seeing the edge of the cliff.

It was tough to tell, but I thought I saw a body on the rocks below. Buzz aimed his light on the coastline, and nodded solemnly. "I'd bet that's McIlroy."

"Let's try the lighthouse," I said. The old man had lived here for decades, and for the last fourteen years since his wife's passing. The fact that he'd been killed by an alien throwing him over the very cliffs he protected was the ultimate irony.

We were trusting this had all occurred well before we'd slaughtered the Travelers, but we didn't have a way of knowing for certain.

Kim tested the handle between his residence and the lighthouse, and it was unlocked. The main space was filled with pamphlets for tourists, though I suspected those were few and far between these days. It seemed untouched, except for a speck of green ooze.

Buzz grazed it with a finger, glaring at the spiral staircase. "He was here. And he was hurt."

"Maybe it's the one we fought out behind Becky's house," Kim advised.

"Likely." Buzz checked the entire room before he was confident we could continue to the next floor.

This time, I let him go first, his gun raised; his steps were self-assured, as if he'd practiced clearing buildings with a big weapon on countless occasions. I wished we'd brought the alien blaster with us, but that was in the hands of our friends on the beach. They'd need it more, should trouble arise.

The metal staircase wobbled with the weight of all three of us, and I wondered when the last time was an engineer had given his stamp of approval on the thing. My foot slipped on the second to last step, and when I investigated why, there was another blob of Traveler blood penetrating the round cut-outs.

"Thank goodness." I rushed to the radio across from me, finding the lights on. Somewhere a generator was running, and I'd forgotten about the backup system. "Test the switch."

Kimberly flipped a lever near the staircase, and a dim bulb flickered on in the middle of the ceiling.

It was enough for Buzz to turn the flashlight off. "Let

me try." He grabbed the receiver and rolled a knob until he settled on a frequency. "This is Bell Island, over."

There was no response.

"How about …" Buzz's tongue stuck out as he attempted a second target. Same result. "Mainland, this is Bell Island. We've had an incident…"

The display hands vibrated and flipped to the right.

"Someone's listening," Buzz whispered.

We waited for a reply, and when it didn't come, he repeated his message.

Finally, we heard it. The voice was strange, the language unfamiliar.

"What is that, German?" I asked.

Kim was at the window, staring at the ocean. "It's them."

"Who?"

"The Travelers," Kim said.

"No way. How are they intercepting the radio waves?" I tapped the dials.

"It might be pre-recorded. They're spacefaring aliens. I bet they can disrupt any attempts at communication," Buzz said. "They want to keep Bell Island in the dark for as long as possible."

"But we killed them," I reminded him.

"Then it's their ship. We have to find it and shut it off." Buzz lowered his barrel and leaned on the wall. "I was hoping this was over."

"How the hell do we find their ship? We've already scoured the Island. Did you see anything resembling a UFO?" I barked.

"No, but we haven't tried one place," he said.

"You don't mean…"

Buzz smirked and went to a map of Bell Island, framed and slightly askew near a desk. "Ransom's Ridge."

"What's Ransom's Ridge?" Kim asked, nudging past me to get a better look at the ancient hand-drawn map.

"It's dangerous," I said. "Legend has it, you can make a wish atop Ransom's Ridge and it will come true. But it's a hundred-foot-tall wall of rock that's nearly impossible to climb, and even tougher to descend once you've arrived."

"Three people have died being foolish enough to make the trek," Buzz informed her. I was surprised he knew that, since no one spoke about it. It was just a no-go zone, and even Bones and I hadn't ventured to the top as kids. Sure, we'd ridden our bikes as far as we could, and traversed the dense forest to check out the base of the ridge, but that was as brave as we got.

"You think that's where they came from?" Kim asked.

"Could be. It's quiet, on the back end of the island. No one would see them coming from the west, and definitely not with that storm last night." Buzz looked antsy.

"So we locate this ship, then contact the mainland?" I asked.

"I have another idea," Buzz said.

I had a bad feeling, and braced myself. "Oh no, what is it?"

"Maybe we can learn something about these Travelers. Steal some of their tech. They're going to come to Earth, and not just for a quick meal—no offense," he said to Kim.

"None taken."

"But first, let's fix the lighthouse beacon." Buzz handed me his gun and started up the last section of stairs. The Traveler had smashed the bulb into a million pieces. "Looks like the wiring is intact. Couple of splices, and we should be good. The reflectors need replacing too, so let's find those."

I wasn't sure what he was talking about, but went along with it. The storage room was outside, secured with a padlock. While Buzz tampered with it, finally breaking in, I confirmed our friends were on the beach. They were still clumped together, safe as they could be.

"This is nuts," I told Kim as we hauled a chunk of glass up to Buzz.

"Are we sure this is a good plan?" she asked. "What if there are more?"

"You heard Buzz. One per Sphere."

Kim stopped in her tracks, locking gazes with me in the dimly lit space. "What if we're wrong? The Spheres can't sense me in here. Maybe the Travelers can't either, and I've connected with the entity long enough for it to go dormant."

"That means there would be another Sphere," I muttered.

"And another Traveler."

"Damn it." I set the end down. "We have to tell Buzz."

"Tell me what?" he asked from above. His hands were covered in grease, and he had a streak of it on his forehead.

We divulged our theory, and he laughed, only it wasn't a normal funny gesture. It sounded laced with anger and fear. "This is just great."

"What do you think?" I asked him.

"That you're probably right." He grabbed for the reflector, and we passed it to him.

Kim and I waited beneath the room while he put the finishing touches on the repair, and after a few minutes, he waved us up. "That should do it."

He taped off a wire nut and hit a red button. The beacon light shone brightly, almost blinding me until he spun it to face the channel. We observed as the powerful beam landed on the choppy waves, and I pumped an arm into the air. "Nice work, Buzz!"

It would only help if we found a way to contact the

powers that be across the channel, and without a working radio able to reach them, that wasn't possible. Not if the aliens were jamming the frequencies.

"It's a start," he said, rubbing his hands on his camo pants. "Let's move out."

It was still raining when we started the trip down the cliff, and the deputy had moved everyone into the parked cars by the time we got to the beach.

"What did you find?" Sadie asked from the driver's seat. The glass was down halfway.

"We fixed up the lighthouse. McIlroy is dead," Buzz said.

Sadie nodded soberly at the news. "He was a good man. Cranky, but diligent."

"The radio doesn't get to the mainland, and we think the Travelers are causing the interference," I told them. Cindy was in the back seat, and I smiled at her.

"I thought they were dealt with." Bones had jumped out, standing near me.

"That's where it becomes tricky." I glanced at Kim. "There could be another Sphere, since Kim's is different."

"Meaning there's more of the monsters loose on Bell Island," Bones mumbled. "What are we waiting for? Let's hunt the bastard!"

"Ease up, soldier," Buzz said. "We're heading to the ship first."

Sadie stared at Buzz. "And where is that?"

"Ransom's Ridge."

"You're kidding."

"Afraid not." Buzz motioned at the deputy's lap. "Mind if I take that?"

"Sure." Sadie shoved the heavy alien gun through the open window.

"Bring the Spheres to Parker's house. He mentioned a

safe room. Stay with them, and let no one in. Understood?" Buzz asked.

Deputy Sadie looked relieved to be ordered into hiding. "I can do that."

Reaper gave Bones a hug and slid into the passenger side with her father. "You sure you won't come?"

Bones gave her a firm smile. "I have to help my friends."

"Okay. See you later." Reaper stalled while Bones came to her. He touched her hand and kissed her on the cheek.

"We're going to be fine," he said.

I leaned toward the car, knocking on the back window. Cindy unrolled it. "Be safe, sis. I know you're in there somewhere, and I won't let anything happen to you. Love you."

Cindy's eyes welled with tears. "I love you too, Elliot."

"Was that her, or you?" I asked the Sphere.

"Both."

The car sped away, and it was the four of us again.

Kimberly studied the water as it bashed against the rocky cove. "The Sphere's have something hidden down there. I can sense it."

"We can't deal with that now," Buzz told her. "It's time to find this UFO and get on with our lives."

The 4X4 fired up, and we rolled from the bay with a seemingly impossible goal in mind. We had to track a UFO to the most deserted section of Bell Island in the middle of the never-ending storm.

After everything we'd encountered tonight, this might be the easiest task we'd faced.

2

I was in hell. If the afterlife was anything like this, I was about to resign myself to charity for the rest of my existence. Every step was worse, my wet shoes chafing my heels, where two painful blisters had formed. No one spoke as we wandered into the woods. If possible, I thought Kim was in an even worse mood than me.

Buzz was the only person maintaining silence. He'd seen far worse in Vietnam. Tonight, he just had to worry about a single enemy, not a platoon hiding in the trees. I admired his strength as we carried on.

"I wish the Traveler would put me out of my misery," Bones complained, and Buzz stopped, slapping a hand over Bones' mouth.

"Never say that again," he hissed. "This isn't a joke. The Travelers are capable of doing much more than playing games on Bell Island. If they wanted to, Earth would be a disaster within days."

"Okay. Relax." Bones tugged on his own collar, straightening his clothing. He shivered as we went, since he wasn't wearing a waterproof layer. I almost handed my jacket to him, but then I'd be in the same boat, and I knew he'd refuse. He hated yellow.

"Which way?" Buzz paused, and I attempted to gather my bearings.

Suddenly, the forest looked the same in each direction. Big oaks intermingled with half-dead birch trees. I listened to the wind, hearing the whistle as it carried through an outcropping on the peak of Ransom's Ridge. "To the right."

Buzz trusted my input and marched into the dense brush.

"What are you going to do if we succeed tonight?" I asked Kim as we trailed behind the other two.

"Keep searching for answers," she said.

"Like the bay?"

"For starters. If there's a Sphere vessel, I want to know."

"I'll help you," I said.

"You will?"

"Of course. We can hire a diver, or get trained ourselves."

"You'd do that for me?" Kim asked.

"Why wouldn't I?"

"Because I lied to you. And I'm not actually human." She whispered the last part.

"But you're still Kim, aren't you? And you don't know any different."

Kim picked up her pace, as if my words had spurred her on. "Thanks for saying that. It's been tough since I realized I was different. I haven't had many relationships. It took years to control the light within me, but even afterwards, I didn't know how to tell anyone. You're the first person I've told."

I smiled and put an arm around her shoulder. "I'm glad it was me."

"Same."

"What would happen if you had a baby?" Bones shouted from ahead. Clearly, he'd been eavesdropping.

"Don't be lame," I told him.

"I'm serious. She's in a human body. It would probably

work."

"Let it go," I warned him, and Bones shrugged.

"Whatever."

Buzz powered the alien technology on, the yellow light pulsing near the barrel. "We're here."

I glanced up as we exited the treeline, coming face to face with Ransom's Ridge. It was a huge ascent, something I didn't ever want to encounter, even in the middle of a comfortable day. It was far worse at three in the morning in the rain.

"There has to be a way around," Bones suggested.

"Let's try. I doubt any of us will climb that and survive," Buzz agreed.

We walked along the bottom, keeping our eyes peeled for signs of a UFO or the last remaining Traveler, but the area was paused in time. Not even the bobcats would be out in this. When we were certain no one was in the vicinity, we began to scale the handful of boulders leading to the edge of the ridge. I slipped, and my foot went sideways, slamming into another rock.

Bones offered a supportive hand. "You good?"

"Think so." I tested the ankle, and it was a little sore, but nothing that would hold me back.

The rain grew worse. Buzz stopped ten feet up and pointed at the water rolling down the hillside. "This is going to be tough. Maybe we should wait it out."

"We don't have time," Kim told him.

"Why? What if we're wrong, and the Travelers are dead?" Buzz asked.

"Then we still have to stop the shield and get the radio transmission open."

"Mr. Webb will be here with the ferry in the morning," Bones reminded us.

"But that's not for hours. If a Traveler is loose, he'll

create a lot more devastation in his wake. Bell Island is ripe for the picking, and I have a feeling the aliens no longer care about secrecy. They're angry, but not defeated. If he's still here, he'll assume we lucked out by killing his companions," I said.

"I'm committed regardless, but I had to know you three weren't just blindly following me. I can't be responsible for more deaths," Buzz muttered.

As if to punctuate his comment, thunder boomed above us.

"Not again," Bones whispered.

"Storm of the century." Kim flipped her hood on. "The sooner we get to the top, the better."

Now that I was older, Ransom's Ridge wasn't nearly as terrifying, but maybe that was because my mind was comparing it to being chased by an eight-foot-tall alien. We managed to move up about ten feet each minute, using the rocks as handholds. Everything was soaked, the boulders coated with a thin, slimy moss, making it all the more treacherous.

Thunder rolled through the edge of Bell Island, the sound echoing along the outer border of my home. From this point, the ocean was audible, waves crashing and slapping the shore. It was a far cry from the bay across the island, which seemed perfectly calm by comparison.

Whatever burst of energy I'd experienced after arriving at the ridge was gone twenty minutes into the ascent. My legs burned and shook, my hands aching with the cold and from gripping too tightly. Kim continued without protest, and Bones was the polar opposite, narrating every tiny annoyance that popped into his head. It was just how he processed things, so I didn't tell him to shut up.

But Buzz did. "If you say one more thing, I'm going to gag you and leave you dangling from a tree for the

Traveler."

That seemed to work.

"Could have asked nicely," Bones muttered, and stepped away when Buzz came closer. "Sorry."

Water gushed down the hill, nearly resembling a stream. If I wasn't wet before, I was now. I dreamt of drying off by a fireplace with a towel in my hand, and a cup of hot chocolate. Kim was there, wearing a bathrobe, her hair frizzy as she smiled at me…

"Elliot?" Kim tapped my shoulder, and I realized I was stuck in my daydream.

"Just taking a breather," I explained.

Kim walked past, leaving me to guard the rear of our group.

I checked behind me, and thought I spotted a shape below. I squinted as I stared at the base of Ransom's Ridge, but there was nothing. It must have been a figment of my over-active imagination. No one was crazy enough to be out in this.

Eventually, after what felt like an hour but was probably half of that, we found the top. Bones lay on the flat earth, rain striking his cheeks as he breathed heavily. "Remind me to stay home next Fourth. I'll rent a couple movies, maybe buy some comics… order a pizza. That would have been radical."

I agreed, but kept that to myself.

Buzz strode along the crown of the ridge, his footsteps sure. "Where did they park it?"

Buzz had a pair of binoculars, and he scanned the area with them. I doubted he could see much, not with the impenetrable clouds and black sky. From this part of the Island, the city wasn't visible, and all I could see for miles was the ocean. I felt vulnerable up here, as if the water might swallow Bell Island.

Buzz glanced at me and offered the binoculars. I took them while he lifted his rifle, using the scope. "Check east, I'll look west."

I nodded and did as he suggested.

The trees were thinner to the east, because it was more rock than dirt in that direction. The aliens would need a flat spot to touch down, but that was if they had a traditional spaceship. I didn't know what their vessel would resemble. All I had were science fiction movies to go by, and those were made up. There was even a chance that the Travelers had accessed a glowing portal.

"Nothing. This was a waste of time," Buzz groaned.

I kept searching, and after a quick once-over, I returned to any open areas. The second one caught my interest. "What about there?" I pointed, and he checked with his scope.

"I don't… there's enough space for a ship to land, but it's too dark to confirm."

A flash of lightning blazed over the ocean, revealing a brief reflection off something. "Did you…"

"I saw it." Buzz lowered his gun. "We have contact."

"How far is that?" Bones asked, his head poked forward as he tried to see what we did.

"A mile… perhaps further." Buzz didn't hesitate to leave. He was already trekking down the ridge in the opposite direction. What we thought was a ship was settled in a remote region, one we'd never explored before.

I recalled the legend of Ransom's Ridge and closed my eyes. The wind blew harder, the rain easing for the moment, and I made my wish.

When I opened them, my three allies were on the move.

I hurried to catch up. "Wait for me!"

If I thought the trip up the other side was bad, this

descent was worse. It took twice as long.

"We should have returned the route we came up," Bones told Buzz.

"It would have added two miles. There's no way to pass." Buzz slid down a boulder on his butt, landing with a splash. We all copied his efforts, and finally made it to the bottom of Ransom's Ridge in one piece.

My teeth chattered, and I rubbed my palms together. The storm had cooled the island off drastically, but we were forced to press on. It was quiet in this section, with the ridge blocking most of the wind. We lingered for a while, catching our breath and taking a rest.

"Won't do us any good to wear ourselves out if we encounter a fight," Buzz said. He gestured to my pocket. "Can you contact Sadie? See that they're secure?"

I tried to keep the radio from getting wet and bent over, pressing the button. "Deputy, it's Elliot. Everything good?"

After some clicks and static, it went quiet.

"Lots of interference around here," Buzz explained. "Nothing for us to worry about."

I didn't know him well enough to read, but I thought he might be lying for our benefit. I attempted a second time, and put the radio away when I didn't receive a response.

Buzz looked each of us in the eyes. "Is everyone ready?"

"Even if we find the ship, do you think we can access it?" Kim asked.

"That's to be seen, but I sure as hell hope so." Buzz shouldered the rifle and hefted the alien weapon with ease. "If you're all rested, let's move."

Now that we were on ground level, crossing the flat forest, my depleted energy began to resurface. We might be the very first people to see a real UFO, and that inspired my hurried steps. We made surprisingly quick work of the mile. It was simpler to rush over the smooth rocks than the deep forest brush.

When we neared the destination, Buzz took his time, leaning against a giant oak. I listened for anything out of place and scanned the region for signs of a Traveler, deeming it safe.

When we exited the tree cover, I saw it. "Is that a…"

"UFO," Kim whispered.

It was more compact than I'd expected, and round, with metallic edges. It was clearly sizeable enough to carry four or five Travelers comfortably, but I suspected that if they were anything like humans, they'd get on each other's nerves in short order.

"Thirty feet in diameter," Buzz said. "Twelve high. Not much headspace."

"Maybe they have beds. What if they're frozen for the duration of the flight?" Bones hugged himself.

"Only one way to find out." Buzz circled the entire ship, his hands searching for an entrance.

Kim stood near it, her eyes starting to glow. "I've seen this before."

"You have?"

"I think so. Not me, but… the Sphere," she said, as if they were two separate entities. She walked closer, grabbing the narrowest point. Kim released a lever, and a ladder dropped to the ground. She went to climb it, but Buzz held her back.

"Allow me." Buzz took her place, and slowly ascended the ten widespread rungs to the top of the vessel. Kim went after him, and Bones and I locked gazes.

"This is real, Elliot."

"I know." I went next, with Bones directly behind me.

A second later, we all stood atop the UFO.

Kim crouched near the center. "It should …" A hatch slid wide, giving a five-foot diameter access point.

Buzz aimed his gun into it. We waited, but nothing came to defend the vessel. I surveyed the area around the ship, expecting a Traveler to materialize from the forest, but it remained quiet.

"I'll scope it out." Buzz lowered himself into the opening.

I poked my head in, attempting to gain a view of the interior, and found it dim.

Buzz returned a couple tense minutes later and craned his neck up. "It's clear. You won't believe this."

Kim swung her legs through, and I helped her down. When it was Bones' turn, he seemed to hesitate. "I think someone should stay up here. Guard from a high position." He lifted the assault rifle. I didn't know if he was scared to be trapped in the UFO, or if he was being brave for our benefit.

"Thanks." I dropped into the Travelers' spacecraft.

The bulkheads were tall, rising almost twice my height, the ceiling rounded in congruence with the craft's shape. There were no corridors or halls, just a large open space. Screens lay at a forty-five-degree angle along the outer edge, a three-foot-wide desk circling the entire cabin. Their computers were at my neck level, which made sense, given their height.

"Bones was right," Kim said, motioning to the seats. They were almost like loungers, the frames heavy and light gray, the seats themselves cushioned and comfortable. "They do lie down."

Buzz didn't seem to care about any of the décor, but I was curious about the Travelers. They felt far less alien after being inside their ship. "How does it work?" He knocked on a screen, but it stayed dark.

I searched for something to stand on and found a crate near the third chair. I dragged it over, and it had enough surface area for all three of us.

"We don't even own a computer," I told them. My dad had been talking about getting one for a couple of years, but we didn't have the money for that kind of luxury.

"I do," Kim said. She looked around the desk. "Where do you put the floppy disk?"

"Don't think like a human." Buzz touched the desk. "They're extraterrestrials. They won't have plastic disks. Maybe they link to it with their minds." He tapped his temple.

I noticed the shimmer on the screen and waved a hand near it. I nearly fell from the crate when the light flickered on. Obscure text appeared, strange runes scrolling from right to left.

"There's no keyboard," Buzz said. His finger trembled as he touched the screen. One of the runes highlighted, zooming in as the others faded into oblivion.

The icon pulsed, and a map emerged.

"That's Bell Island," Kim proclaimed.

"And a perfectly depicted version too. The proportions are accurate," I said.

"Because they scanned it." Buzz pointed at Ransom's Ridge. The location of the ship was marked by an orange dot. "That's their vessel."

"Whoa." I pictured this craft hovering over the island, gathering intel before they settled to the surface.

Buzz touched the screen, rotating the map, and he zoomed on the bay. When he found nothing, he checked the other main regions. "I'd guess this is their only ship."

"Good," I muttered.

"What's that?" Kim rotated the image, and a blue

indicator light appeared. It was moving.

"I don't know," Buzz admitted. "If there's an icon for the vessel, then…"

"There might be one for the Travelers as well," I finished.

"Here's another. We were right," Buzz said. "We have to go."

"Not before we figure out this radio issue. The Traveler is changing trajectories." I pointed to the small dot.

"Why's he going that way?" Kim zoomed out, and I noticed he was a couple of miles from Bruce's neighborhood.

"Where does Parker live?" Buzz asked.

"About two blocks from Cindy's friend Yolanda," I told him.

Buzz hopped off the crate. "He's hunting them."

"The radio…"

"We don't have time."

Kim didn't listen to him. She poked a circle in the top corner of the display, and that returned her to the main menu. The runes continued to shuffle. She selected another, and after the third try, she found what she was looking for. Kim tapped one of the five displayed icons, and I heard Buzz's voice from earlier. *"Mainland, this is Bell Island. We've had an incident…"*

"This is it." Kim tested a couple others, and heard what must have been McIlroy's final message. *"Mainland, this is Earl McIlroy from the Bell Island Lighthouse. We've been invaded by aliens! He's trying to break in now. Send reinforcements. I'll hold him off for as long as I can. The bastard already busted out the beacon, so be careful. Over."* Before the recording ended, glass shattered in the background.

Mr. McIlroy had gone down fighting. He was a hero, and deserved a better end than what he'd gotten.

"I used computers at college, mostly to type articles for my senior year journalism classes. They were nothing like this. The instructors were clear that we weren't to touch the monitors," Kim said. "I can't imagine why anyone would want to control the program this way. It seems so… foreign. But, like Buzz said, I'm a basic human, so who's to say their system isn't superior?"

When we first met… all of thirty hours ago, she'd been carefree and funny. Then with tonight's events, she'd pushed into a protective shell. Now that she'd told her truth to me about being a Sphere trapped in a woman's body, grown with the real Kimberly since birth, she was starting to break out of the casing she'd woven around herself.

"Whatever it is, let's do it. That Traveler can't get to Sheriff Parker's," Buzz said.

I indicated the three dots on the lower left corner. "Try that."

Kim did as I'd suggested, and bright icons appeared. The purple was brighter, the orange and green dim. "Maybe this is the link."

Kim hit the purple icon, and it shut off. The other two blinked.

"It seems you have to have one of them connected," I said.

Kim's eyes went wide. "What if the orange or green draws their other ships?"

Buzz anxiously paced the deck. "We don't have time for this!"

"Buzz, there must be something useful around here." I hopped off the crate while Kim debated which icon to select.

"Maybe more guns?" Buzz seemed intrigued by the notion. He felt along the bulkhead, searching for more hidden levers, and he quickly discovered one. The foot-long latch fell when he tugged on it, and he turned it over, releasing a hatch. The storeroom was filled with supplies.

I entered the hole, wondering how the Travelers had fit inside, and slid a pack off the shelfing.

"Looks like an MRE to me."

"MRE?" I asked.

"Meal, Ready-To-Eat. Military thing." Buzz peeled a hard plastic cover off and sniffed it. "Whatever this is, it's not chicken."

I instantly regretted his decision. The food smelled rancid.

Buzz slipped the lid back on and dropped the container. There were numerous objects, most of which we didn't understand the function of, but the guns were blatantly obvious. These were smaller than the one we'd acquired in the mine.

"Take it." Buzz shoved the weapon into my hands, and I grabbed a second for Kim.

"You guys almost done?" Bones shouted from the roof.

"Be right there!" I replied.

Kim had the map up again. "I changed it to green. Green for go. Whatever that means."

"Where's the blue dot?" Buzz asked.

"He stopped," Kim said, zooming on the screen. She spun it around, and it gave a three dimensional image of the highway near Parker's neighborhood, the map complete with red lines to give the picture depth.

Buzz breathed heavily and scratched his chin. "What's he up to?"

The blue dot returned its' casual movement toward the sheriff's. "He's back on track." I went to the exit, taking a last peek inside the Travelers' vessel. I'd always read science fiction from the greats like Clarke and Asimov, and loved the movies, so witnessing a UFO was mind-blowing. I blinked and glanced up at Bones, who lowered an arm into the hatch.

Buzz helped me, almost throwing me through the opening, and Bones and I both lifted Kim from below us. Buzz passed the weapons over, then ran and jumped, hauling his own weight outside.

"According to the map, we're three miles as the crow flies to Sheriff Parker's house, but if we double back, it'll take us too long," Buzz said as we climbed down the rungs to the ground.

Bones smiled as he took one of the smaller alien weapons I'd brought. He clicked a button and it blasted from the barrel, melting a limb from a tree. Buzz shouted, his shirtsleeve singed and smoking. "You almost killed me!"

"Sorry, didn't know that was the trigger," Bones apologized.

Buzz normally would have exploded, but his mind seemed elsewhere. "It opens up after a mile. Then we can hit the road."

"Shouldn't someone go to the bay and radio for help?" Kim asked.

Buzz looked conflicted but shook his head. "We should stick together. If we stop this last Traveler, we'll be safe."

His logic was sound, and I nodded my agreement. I searched inward for the strength to continue tonight. My legs agreed and jogged behind Buzz, with Bones and Kim on my tail.

I could walk a mile in about sixteen minutes, but running at a decent pace through the forest was much harder than going for a stroll. When we emerged at the road, the ditch was wet, and we jumped across, trying to avoid another round of soaked shoes, but that ship had sailed hours ago.

The roads were black with the streetlights off. The minor amount of illumination we had from our flashlights reflected brightly on the wet roadway.

I predicted we might arrive at Parker's just before the Traveler, but only if we were lucky and he grew tired or encountered a distraction. From the indicator on the map, he wasn't rushing. I wished we could have brought the screen with us, but that wasn't possible. The concept of a portable computer was laughable, even for otherworldly beings.

We stepped onto the road, and all four of us instinctively came to a stop, peering in both directions. It was eerily quiet in the late hour. By now, all of Bell Island was aware of the murderer on the loose, and were likely waiting at home, the doors barred and baseball bats in their grips. Some might be peeking through drawn drapes, others braving the sidewalks to gossip with neighbors, but few would realize there were actual aliens inhabiting their forests. Those that had seen them were probably dead.

"We have to hurry," Buzz said.

"Agreed." With a last glance to my right, where my house was located a mile or so in the distance, I forced my body to follow him.

There was one more Traveler to deal with; then we could breathe easy. Or at least, that was what I told myself.

3

*T*he street was silent. If anyone watched our group stalk to Sheriff Parker's house, no one gave themselves away.

Bruce's house sat dark, and I recalled picking Cindy up there just yesterday. It had been the last time my Camaro's engine had rumbled. I missed her. The car… well, Cindy too.

"You here, Elliot?" Bones nudged me with an elbow. Buzz and Kim were off the road, crossing people's lawns to get to Parker's.

"Yes. What are we doing?" I asked.

"Currently, we're making ourselves big targets," he replied.

If the Traveler was in the vicinity, he'd see us coming for miles. I got his point and rushed to the house beside Parker's. The sheriff's property was well kept, the exterior crisp as if he'd recently painted it. The yard was perfectly manicured, and the garden was in full bloom, the scent of his azaleas filling the air. Parker wasn't married, and his only daughter was grown, with a new husband and a baby. My mom knew everything about the island residents, and would often regale me with their stories during our phone conversations.

There were no signs of a disturbance, but that didn't mean the alien wasn't nearby. One Traveler and three Spheres. He wouldn't let up, not until he was dead…or they were.

"Let's go to the back." Buzz tested the fence gate, but it was locked. He jumped it, releasing the latch to let us in. I secured it again, as if the simple barrier would stop a five-hundred-pound monster from breaking it down.

This yard was even nicer. The lot was large, and a playground sat behind his property. I used to come to Bruce's and spend countless hours on the swings, arguing about our favorite baseball players. He liked the Dodgers, and that alone was enough to stop being friends with him, yet we persevered somehow. Bones would join us on occasion, but he preferred the monkey bars.

I peered over the fence to find one of the swings jingling in the wind. Rain splattered on my head, but I left the hood off, not wanting it to impede my peripheral vision. Buzz was at the door, attempting to open it. He grabbed the radio. "It's us. Let me in."

Glass shattered from out front, and Buzz grunted. "Here we go again." He flipped the gun around and bashed into the patio doors with the butt end of it. The glass cracked but didn't smash. He succeeded on the second attempt.

He used his sleeve to clear the shards from the frame and ran in, gun raised.

Reaper stood in the kitchen with her hands up. "It's me!"

I glanced at the linoleum, seeing the broken water glass. She lowered her arms. "I dropped it."

I sighed in relief. "Where's Cindy?"

Reaper pointed to the basement. "Downstairs."

Buzz was already in the living room, checking through the curtains. "Get Kim into the safe room."

"I don't need to be coddled," she declared. "I can help you kill him."

"This is no place for—"

"Buzz, she's already proved she can throw down," Bones chipped in. "Hell, she's killed a couple of them. How many have you ended?"

Buzz stared at the smaller man, his mohawk still flat on his head. "It's your asses."

"That's right. It is." Kim hurried into the basement.

I stopped Buzz at the top of the stairs. "You sure it's a good idea to be trapped like this? There's no way out."

"I've already thought of that. But he's coming. We don't need to get out if we blow him up first." Buzz grinned.

"Lead the charge," I told him.

We joined Kim and shone our flashlights around the comfortable space. Parker had a big TV down here, and surprisingly, a bookcase with countless classics. I removed a Bradbury and flipped through the pages. "Good taste," I whispered.

"You can read when our enemies are dead." Kim patted my hand, making me grin.

"Where's the safe room?" I found no indication of one.

Buzz knocked on a wall, and now I saw the slight difference in the wallpaper. A door opened to reveal Cindy sitting on a wooden chair, with Sheriff Parker beside her. Deputy Sadie was with them, wearing a plaid shirt and jeans. They'd changed as well, and Cindy had on what I guessed were the remnants of Parker's daughter's closet. It said *Maui '76* on the front, with a giant white flower centering the pink t-shirt. Cindy would have hated it.

"Where is he?" Sadie asked.

"Close." Buzz leaned into the safe room, which had a shelf full of canned goods, a couple of flashlights, a candle and a plastic thing that looked like a toilet. I didn't want to be around when someone used it.

Sheriff Parker stood, knocking his chair aside. "He's

here."

I heard something hit the front door. "Everyone inside. Sadie, stay with them." I gave the orders, and shockingly, people listened. Reaper rushed into it, scooting up with Cindy on the chair.

"Don't get hurt," Sadie said. He lifted his revolver. "I'll do my part if necessary."

"It won't be," Buzz assured him. The safe room sealed, disappearing into the wallpaper, and the bolts audibly latched.

And it was Kim, Bones, Buzz, and me again.

"Bones, you and Kim stay here. If anything comes down those steps, you shoot it." He nodded at the smaller guns in their grips.

"Roger that, Captain," Bones said.

"Got it," Kim added.

I'd been called to join Buzz on the frontlines. I'd already faced off against three of them, but I felt my luck had run out. Each step up could have been my last, but we made it to the living room as the door blasted wide, the wood cracking and splintering around the jamb.

The Traveler wasted no time destroying it, and it didn't seem like he expected to meet any resistance. He was only ten yards from my position, his wide head turning to gawk in my direction. His large pupils shrank as he bared his yellow teeth.

Buzz shot him.

The blast struck a shield, and I noticed the metallic forearm guard glow white.

"He's got a shield!" I fired my gun, the pulse erupting from the bright tip. His guard activated, and my attack was rendered ineffectual.

The Traveler snorted, his nostrils dripping liquid. His shoulders shook, as if he was laughing at us.

"Bring it on, barf bag!" Buzz stayed near the kitchen entrance and threw a chair from the dining room table at him. The alien bashed it with a fist, shattering the furniture, then stepped closer.

His nostrils flared as he tilted his neck. He was searching for the Spheres. I stood near the doorway, which was closed, and he didn't bother with me. The Traveler aimed his gun at the floor and shot a perfect circle in front of him, the hardwood melting as the hole formed. And he plunged into it.

"Bones! Kim!" I called through the opening.

Buzz was already tearing down the stairs, and I took my chances, holding the edge of the hole before letting go. I landed in the basement, and Bones was on the ground, cradling his arm. His gun was across the room. The windows gave just enough light to see by, given the fact our eyes were now used to the utter darkness that Bell Island existed in tonight.

The monster was at the wall, and he punched through it, tearing the frame off the hinges. Sadie's gun popped three times, but the being's shield held. Sadie went flying as he was backhanded, and Buzz barreled past Kim and me, diving for the alien. They collided hard, and he managed to take the Traveler to the floor. I rushed to aid him, focusing on the guard strapped to the alien's forearm. I kicked it, then used the butt of my gun to bash into it while Buzz decked the Traveler in the face on repeat.

I knocked the guard loose, and he bellowed, throwing Buzz back ten feet. The Spheres were huddled in the corner of the safe room, Cindy protectively in front of Parker. The fact that my sister was protecting the grown man was inexplicable.

Both of their eyes glowed white, light escaping their ears and noses.

"Leave us alone!" Cindy shouted. Sadie was on the ground, with Reaper near him, but the Traveler ignored them.

Kim fired her gun, and the pulse lightened the dark basement, hitting the Traveler in the hip. He shrieked so loud I thought my eardrums might burst. She tried again, but it didn't work. The weapon needed a short recharge period.

But I still had mine. I aimed as he faced us and pulled the trigger as he began to run at me. It failed. I must have damaged it while bashing it like a hammer only thirty seconds earlier.

Buzz was groggily getting up, and he tried to intercept the alien, only to be shoved aside. When the monster hit me, it was like a freight truck struck my chest. The Traveler landed on me, and the breath shot from my lungs. Stars filled my vision, and everything hurt.

"Get off him!" I heard Cindy's voice.

The pain lessened for a second.

"Take me and leave," she said.

"Cindy, no…" I shuddered.

His bulky weight lifted from my body, and I attempted to sit up, but couldn't.

The Traveler grabbed Cindy's arm, dragging her with him toward the exit. She glanced at me, making eye contact, and was pulled away.

Buzz and Kim tried to chase them, but it was too late.

The Traveler had come, and now he had my sister.

Bones leaned against the wall, nursing his arm, and Reaper cried from the panic room. "He's dead."

Buzz's left eye was red, and I could instantly tell it would be a shiner by tomorrow. I rolled my shoulders and winced as I walked across the basement. One or more of my ribs were acting up. I wasn't sure if anything was broken, but it sure as hell felt like it.

Deputy Sadie was crumpled on the floor, his neck bent the wrong way. Buzz checked his pulse and swore so loudly, my heart raced at the sudden noise.

"We let him get away!" Buzz sat beside the Traveler's victim.

"He has Cindy. We have to track him," I said.

"Are you kidding me? Did you see what that guy just did?" Bones supported his right arm. "He was a one-man wrecking crew."

"He killed my dad." Reaper held the deputy's hand.

Sheriff Parker remained in the panic room, hiding in the corner. "You should be ashamed of yourself, Sphere," Kim told him. "You let a little girl go in your stead."

"They are older than me," he said unapologetically.

"The Sphere in her is your elder?" Buzz asked.

He nodded. "She's been here the longest. We came looking for her."

"So you do remember something," Kim whispered. "What else do you recall?"

"Home…" Sheriff Parker's gaze lingered on the flashlight in Kim's grip. He touched the end of it. "We live on a star."

"You live on a… never mind. I need you to track Cindy. Can you do that?" I asked.

He lifted his arms, extending his fingers, and he wiggled them. "I can."

"Great," Buzz muttered. "I'm sorry I failed you."

"It wasn't your fault."

"I've fought with them at least three times tonight, and I haven't managed to kill one."

"You know what they say?" Bones grinned. "Fourth time's a charm."

"That's not a thing," I told him. "How's the injury?"

"It's nothing. Just sore." He showed me the redness from his elbow crook past his bicep.

"He's invincible," Kim mumbled. "What's the new plan?"

I crouched near Sadie's body and picked up the shield guard I'd broken off the Traveler. I secured it to my wrist and felt the vibrations as it powered on. "We have this."

"You can't be serious? You want to risk your life? We don't even know if that works on a human!" Bones exclaimed.

"Then let's test it."

"How can we…" Bones stopped when it clicked.

Buzz didn't even hesitate. He took Kim's smaller gun and pointed it at me. "If this doesn't work, I'm sorry."

And he fired.

The guard buzzed on my forearm, and a pulse spilled around me, the protective bubble holding firmly. I laughed and hustled to the rest of them. "We need to hurry."

"What about Reaper?" Bones asked.

"He won't be back," Buzz said. "Sorry about your dad, kid."

She looked up, anger burning in her visage. "Do me a favor and kill that freak."

"Consider it done," Buzz promised.

"Parker, go outside and tell us where they went." I waited for him to leave.

The sheriff nodded, peering at the destruction in his ceiling. When we were upstairs, he gawked at the broken furniture and burning floor. Somewhere deep down, the real sheriff must have been processing what had just happened to his well-kept home.

We journeyed into the night, and Parker stepped to the sidewalk centering his front yard. His fingers were wriggling, and he turned to the west. "I sense the other of my kind. But there are two."

"Two? One's Kim, correct?" I glanced at the waitress who'd dropped a bomb on my life in the last day.

Parker wavered, his composure cracking. "She's different. There are two more Spheres present."

"We did guess there might be another Sphere, didn't we?" Bones asked.

"True. Can you tell which is Cindy?" I knew he couldn't by the slowness of his response.

"Uhh… no, that's not how it works."

"Where are they?" Buzz interjected.

"One west, the other south."

"South?" I stared in that direction. "The ship was north. That means he didn't take her to the UFO."

"We have a single choice. If we go west, it'll be easier to lure the Traveler to my farm. If we can trap him, we can learn so much about their people," Buzz said.

"That's why you haven't killed any." His real motives had become abundantly clear.

"What are you suggesting, Elliot?" he grunted.

"All these chances to end the threat, and you're trying to disarm them. You want to catch a Traveler alive! To poke and prod. Are you hoping to sell him to the highest bidder? You're not a hunter, you're a collector!" I tapped him in the chest, and he slapped my finger away.

"You better watch your tone, son."

But I wasn't in the mood to mince words. "No. You let him get my sister! You were supposed to be the big hero, mentoring us through an invasion."

Buzz's eyes darkened, his frown etching lines in his brow. "This isn't a movie, kid. It's real life. And these aliens will destroy our world if we don't learn how to defend against them. I only wanted to interrogate one so we could figure out how to stop an incursion."

"They don't care about us. Just the Spheres," Bones said.

"Exactly. We're expendable." Buzz huffed a deep breath. "Think what you want, but I'm on Earth's side, not yours. If they come back, we're doomed, and we have a chance to prevent that. I won't fail again."

I sensed the years of resignation and hardships he'd endured, starting with his time in Vietnam, and the anger I'd expressed at him melted away. I pictured hundreds of those UFOs littering the sky as the Travelers conquered our planet. We couldn't let that happen.

"Sorry for what I said, Buzz." I extended my hand.

He shook it, not making eye contact. "There's a choice to make. Which Sphere do we go after?"

"We could split up," Kim offered.

"No. Parker can only go with one group," Buzz said, making our decision on that front. "Let's head west."

"Fine." I glanced south, wondering if we were making the right call.

Buzz's vehicle was parked close by, and we filled it. Kim took the front seat, while Bones and I squished in with the Sphere. My body ached, my ribs barking at every movement, and the exhaustion took hold. Despite the adrenaline I'd had jolting through my body, I closed my eyes as the 4X4 rumbled to life, and fell asleep before we exited the neighborhood.

4

"You can do anything, Elliot Alexander Hoffman." My mother stroked my hair, sitting on the edge of my bed.

"Even fly to the moon?" I asked, grinning at the notion of becoming an astronaut.

"Why stop at the moon? There's an entire universe to explore," she said, making it seem as if that was possible.

I realized I wasn't awake, but this was a very real dream, a memory from my youth. I glanced at the bedspread, seeing the Flintstones adorning the fabric. I had to be about six years old.

"Where were you today?" I asked.

"Uncle Taylor and I went for a walk," she told me.

"What were you doing?"

"Looking for someone."

"Who?" My dad said I asked too many questions, but my mother always told me to be curious. I listened to her in this instance.

"An old friend." Her smile brightened the entire room, and I basked in the ambiance.

"Did you find them?"

She nodded, taking my hand. Hers was chilly, but comforting as only a mother's could be. I never felt safer than when she was around. "We did."

"Can I meet them?"

"Maybe one day." Mom stood and walked to the exit. She flicked the lights off, leaving the door open a crack. "Love you, Elli." No one else called me that.

"Love you," I replied, sinking into my pillow.

Through the open door, I heard the conversation between my parents.

"It's not healthy. You have to get help, Lorraine."

"I've told you, there's nothing to worry about."

"Honey, you and that damned brother of yours aren't right. There are no aliens on Bell Island!" He must have noticed he shouted, because the next words came much quieter. I missed the first part, but caught up on the second. "And I won't have you dragging my children into this."

"Your children? Since when do you do anything but complain about the mouths to feed?" Cindy cried from her crib down the hall. "Now look what you've done. You woke the baby," Mom said.

"Lorraine, I mean it… this ends today."

"Or what? You'll leave us?"

A sigh. "No. But I will call someone."

"You don't understand. I've seen them up close. They're scared. One of those… things is stuck on Bell Island. It's waiting for them to expose themselves, and it will call for reinforcements."

"Do you hear yourself? What things?"

"He's dangerous. Taylor saw him twice. He's missing an eye."

"Lorraine, you're delusional…"

"I know what I've seen, and neither you nor a shrink will take that from me! They're pure, don't you understand? The aliens feed on them. I can't let her be harmed." I heard my mother's footsteps stomp away, and she paused at my door, quietly closing it before heading to Cindy's nursery.

The conversation ended, and I stared at the ceiling, trying to make sense of everything.

"Elliot!" Bones shook my shoulder, jarring me from the dream.

"My mom knew about the Travelers and Spheres," I said.

"She did?" Bones asked.

"I just remembered. She had an argument with my dad

years ago. She said that one of them was here on Bell Island, waiting for the Spheres to reveal their locations. And that he would call others," I told them.

"That's impossible." Buzz turned the wipers lower as the rain slowed. "If there was a Traveler on Bell Island all these years, don't you think someone would have noticed?"

"She claimed my Uncle Taylor spotted him twice. Said he was missing an eye, but my dad never believed any of it."

"Have any of the Travelers we've encountered been missing an eye?" Kim asked. "I think we'd have spotted that."

Bones crossed his arms. "Well, we've been a little pre-occupied while battling them."

"If he's here, we haven't seen him," Buzz said. "How would something that big hide on Bell Island?"

"I don't know," I admitted. "But she seemed confident it was true."

"Can we talk to her? Your mom?"

"She's on the mainland."

"Went to visit family or something?" Buzz asked.

"No, she's at Pacific Northwest Hospital."

Buzz glanced at me through the rearview mirror. "Sorry, kid. Because of…"

"The alien stuff."

"There's a reason I don't mention it to anyone," he said.

"Speaking of mainland, shouldn't we be making a call to the authorities? We fixed the radio issue," Bones reminded us.

"We will once we have Cindy in our custody, and that Traveler's ugly mug on a stick." Buzz slowed at the intersection. "Which way, boss?"

Parker's eyes leaked white light for a moment, and he

pointed left. "There."

And for the millionth time tonight, we were heading back to Cooper's neighborhood. We drove by his house, and Parker urged us to the end of the block, indicating a home on the corner.

"Who lives here?" I asked Bones.

"I'm not certain. It used to be Mrs. White, but she passed away a few years ago," he answered.

Buzz parked the vehicle, cutting the engine with a turn of the key. It was dead quiet. A few drops fell on the windshield, but the storm had drifted away, heading past Bell Island into the channel.

There was light emitting from a bedroom upstairs. It was bright and made me wonder if they had a generator running. When we got outside, I didn't hear the sounds of one.

We all went, with Buzz in the lead, holding the larger of the alien weapons. We must have made quite the sight as we hobbled after him, with Bell Island's sheriff between us.

Buzz reached the house, searching for indications of a struggle, but there was no evidence on the home's exterior. It was a nice place, and probably cost a pretty penny, like everything in this section of the Island.

"What do we do?" I asked, and Kim reached past me to press the doorbell.

"See if anyone's home," she said with a grin.

After a minute, I heard footsteps, and with a glance upstairs, the light had gone out from the bedroom.

The door opened slowly, and Parker shivered when a figure stood in the darkness beyond the screen.

"Can I help you?" a man asked.

I squinted, recognizing the voice. "Mark?"

The screen flung wide, and Mark stared at the vehicle

on the street, then at the ragtag group of us. "Elliot, what are you doing here?"

"Is this the Sphere?" Buzz asked Parker.

"Yes."

"What's a sphere?" Mark asked, pushing his glasses farther up the bridge of his nose.

"Get in." Buzz shoved him lightly and entered the home. We went after them, Bones quickly locking up behind him.

"You can let the act go, Mark. We know everything," I said.

"Elliot, you almost bust down my door at three in morning with… what are those? Guns?" He reached for Buzz's weapon, and stopped when the soldier glared at him.

"Sheriff Parker has one of you inside him. So does Kimberly," I told Mark.

His entire demeanor changed, and his chin lowered. "I knew this day would come. I tried to hide it for years."

"So you admit it. You're a Sphere," Buzz said.

"I'm an Esol." His face glowed. "Why… oh, Parker was recently inhabited, wasn't he?"

"Tonight. In the mines."

"The mines… I should have known." Mark waved us in, and went to the bar to pour a drink. He offered to the rest of us, but we all declined. He downed the shot of brown liquor and refilled it. "I assume you're here for a reason."

"The Traveler has my sister," I told him.

"Traveler?" He lifted his hand, holding it well over his head. "Yea tall with an anger issue?"

He was far too calm. "That's them."

"I didn't think they'd ever come. We spent hundreds of years in hiding, and I grew tired of it. The others were too scared, but I decided to chance it. I took over this fine specimen twenty years ago. Mark was visiting for the summer holidays while attending school, and he was working at the video store. Much like you, Elliot." He smiled at me, and I realized that my boss of the past few summers wasn't even human. "I bought the business once the previous owner decided to sell, and the rest is history."

"What about Mark? The real one?" Bones asked him.

"He's fine with it. His life wasn't going very well. He's still with me. It's not really that different for him, to be honest," Mark said. He turned his attention on Kim.

"But you... this is unique." He touched her arm. "Why is the merge so... permanent?"

"I don't know. It's been with me since I was a baby." Kim's voice was soft.

"How very interesting. It appears you're no longer one of us," he said. "There were rumors of different Esol coming to Earth. They're supposed to guide us home."

"Guides?" Kim whispered.

"Cindy's out there. We have to find her." I started for the door.

"Wait, Elliot. Mark must be able to help us." Buzz grabbed the man by the collar. He was in silk pajamas, a fuzzy robe cinched tight around his waist. "How do we stop these... Travelers?"

"How many are here?" he asked.

"We've already killed three. The last is with my sister," I told him.

"You killed them?" His expression shifted in an instant. "This is bad."

"What were we supposed to do?" Buzz demanded.

"Sacrifice one of us. The youngest, usually." He glanced at Parker. "It's always been the way."

"What happens if we fight back?" I asked.

Mark brushed his robe off when Buzz let him go. "They become agitated."

"He has Cindy. Will he kill her?"

"Most likely."

"And why haven't they hunted you?" Kim poured herself a drink, chugging it.

"Because you and I have tricked them. We've found the ultimate hiding spot. The human vessel." He patted his chest with a palm.

"They don't sense us because we're merged with a human," she whispered.

"Mark, is there an old Traveler on Bell Island? One missing an eye?" I asked him.

"How did you hear about him?"

"My mother."

"I thought he was gone. Haven't seen him in ages."

"You know this Traveler?" Kim spoke softly, her voice calm.

"He showed up around forty years ago," Mark said.

"That's when my mother and Taylor would have seen the Sphere," I chimed in.

Mark nodded, like he understood. "We gave him someone… a friend."

Buzz cleared his throat. "You mean you sacrificed one of your people to the Traveler."

"You make it sound so evil," Mark coughed. "It's part of our understanding."

"Why are you on Earth?" Bones asked.

"I don't have those answers. The Esol struggle to remember their past. I only recall our name, and the sensation of being within the core of our star. The warmth… I woke here, as I mentioned, in the late 1700s. Not a single human came for nearly a century."

"Then they began fishing here, and you were known as

the Bell Island Demon," I murmured.

"It wasn't our fault. The first few humans we saw were so easy to enter. We spoke to them from inside their minds, and it drove them to do terrible things to themselves." Mark didn't seem fazed by it.

"What about a ship?" Kim asked him.

"Ship?"

"The Spheres… I mean… Esol. Do we have a starship in the bay?" Kim mustered.

Mark set his empty glass down. "I don't think that exists, or I'd have heard about it."

"Then how did you travel to Earth in the first place?" I lifted an eyebrow, curious about his theory.

"Who's to say?" Mark stared at the clock. "If you don't mind, it's late, and I have to get up and open the store tomorrow."

"The store?" I barked. "Bell Island is under attack. My sister is in their clutches, and you're worried about renting out cheap movies? No one cares, Mark!"

He pursed his lips, hands shoving into his robe pockets. "Are you saying you won't accept my promotion?"

"I'm saying you can go to—"

"Enough!" Buzz shouted. "Mark, you're not getting off so easily. What happened after you sacrificed your friend to the Traveler?"

Mark broke our eye contact. "He left. Or so we thought."

I struggled to picture it all. My uncle and mom meeting the Sphere that was currently occupying my sister during a storm forty years earlier. They must have had some details on the starship, because my uncle was trying to find its location. He'd drowned because of it.

"We're wasting time. Parker, where's the other Sphere?" I headed to the exit.

"Southern Bell Island." His glow brightened and dimmed until the light was gone.

"Mark, if you were leaving anything out… I *will* come back and expunge the Sphere from you." Buzz may not have known how, but the threat was enough to make Mark step to the far wall.

"If they're on Bell Island, give them a sacrifice. It's the only way to keep peace," Mark warned us.

"Thanks for the tip. We'll take it from here." Bones walked past him, moving to the door. "Can you believe this guy? Wait until he sees the dead alien in his store tomorrow."

"Dead… what did he say?" Mark called after us, but didn't follow.

"What's at the lowest point of Bell Island?" Buzz asked me.

"Nothing. Rocks and cliffs. It's dangerous."

"The perfect place for an old, one-eyed Traveler to live," Buzz added. "Time to face the music."

The rain had let up, and we marched for the 4X4 with Parker arriving first. Kim held me back, taking my hand. "Elliot, you aren't going to judge me, are you?"

"Did you realize what you were doing, invading the child?" I asked point-blank.

Kim shook her head emphatically. "Never. I have no memories prior to Kim. I don't feel like I'm a Sphere, just a woman."

"Interesting."

"My mother did tell me the doctors thought I wouldn't make it through that first night. Something about a congenital heart condition they didn't see before I was born."

"And after you entered the newborn?"

"She… I was fine. I don't know how to explain it."

"Perhaps the Sphere's intervention was necessary." I

held her door open, since Bones had jumped into the front passenger seat.

She smiled at me. "Thanks for being so kind."

"Let's save Cindy, then we can sleep on it."

Buzz ripped away from Mark's house. Twenty minutes later, he stopped when the road ended. A red metal gate blocked us from going any farther. Tire tracks flattened the grass, but it didn't look like it was used very often. I suspected the county parks department checked on the area a couple times a year, at best.

We clambered out of the vehicle, staring to the south. Parker confirmed we were still on track. "She is a half mile down this trail."

"Double check your weapons, and bring a revolver for the recharge moments. We can't be caught off-guard like before. Elliot, you have that device?" Buzz asked.

I lifted my sleeve up, revealing the shield generator. "Hell yeah."

And we were ready, or as prepared as five people could be after countless hours of exploring Bell Island in a storm, while fending off an invasion. We were an odd bunch, with Kim being a Sphere who didn't attract the Travelers because of her unusual connection. Sheriff Parker was still visible to the alien enemy, because he was only recently inhabited. Buzz, the Vietnam veteran, was our leader, but even he seemed hesitant for this final battle. Bones and I rounded off the group, with both of us in way over our heads.

My oldest friend glanced at me, swallowed nervously, and climbed past the gate. "I told you I wanted an epic night, didn't I?"

"One we could never forget." I gritted my teeth. Cindy might already be dead, but Parker claimed to know where the Sphere was. Could the Traveler extract it from my sister before eating the entity? I wasn't sure how it worked.

The clouds parted to reveal a perfect pre-dawn sky. The stars glittered brightly, their ambiance helpful on the rough terrain. The blanket of cover slipped from the moon, basking Bell Island in her glow. The darkness lifted off like a morning mist from a lake, and I was left feeling more optimistic.

Even my shoes had started to dry, which generally helped improve my mood. Everyone seemed lighter, their steps faster and more confident, while none of us commented on why. The moonlight brought hope.

The air was fresh, as this section of the island was near the ocean. I heard the waves crashing against the dense rocky beach a short distance away, and as we toured the tree-covered path, the view changed to reveal nothing for a hundred miles. It was beautiful and frightening all at once. Black waves rolled from the north, barreling into the craggy shore.

I searched for any signs of my sister, but it was bleak and silent, other than the sounds of nature. Sheriff Parker did his thing without any prompting this time, and pointed to the left. "Close. Down there."

The cliff ended twenty feet ahead. "How do you propose that?"

Buzz dropped his pack and tugged a rope from inside. He looped it around a tree, clipping a metal carabiner to keep it in place. Buzz yanked on it, satisfied it would hold. "He must have her in the caves along the cliff face."

"No one uses those," Bones muttered.

"Apparently, they do," I said. "Let me go first."

"You're not equipped for—"

I thrust my arm forward to show the alien shield connected to me. "This will protect me from any blasts."

"But not physical attacks," Buzz argued.

"Then keep close." I didn't wait for him to concede as I took the rope and tossed it over the edge.

"We'll stay here." Bones peered at the rocky shore. "Ready to shoot if anyone but you two emerge."

"Or Cindy," I reminded him.

"Her too."

Kim stood with me near the drop-off. "Be careful. Bring her back." She kissed me.

I rested my hands on her hips, returning the gesture. We didn't linger, but I could still feel the dampness of her lips on mine as she walked away.

"Focus, kid." Buzz went to his belly, overhanging the ledge. "It's twenty feet down. Can you hold that long?"

I nodded. "I used to be the fastest climber in my gym class."

"Did you have aliens chasing you?"

"Not unless you count Cooper," Bones joked.

"I'll be okay." And I started my descent. My rain jacket was filled with weapons, the weight of the revolver and alien gun wrenching on the lower half. But I did it, hand under hand, lowering toward the Traveler's hiding place.

It went fast, and I hung there, staring at the darkness of the cavern. The opening appeared, and I kicked off the cliff, swinging into the hole. I let go, almost stumbling to my demise. But I managed to grab the wall, steadying myself.

I could already hear Buzz climbing down, and stepped out of the entrance, not wanting to impede his arrival. It was quiet.

I waited for him, cautious not to shine my flashlight until he was with me. I inhaled, noticing the musky scent filling the cavern. It was animalistic. The smell of a hibernating bear, maybe, or… an old Traveler.

Buzz appeared in the opening, the ocean his only

backdrop. He tried to step in, but his foot slipped, and his left hand slid on the rope. I grabbed out in time, clutching his wrist, and yanked as hard as I could, forcing him inside. He fell to his knees, but he was safe.

"Thanks," he whispered. "Anything?"

I shook my head.

He was close, talking softly. "Let our eyes acclimate. I don't want to use the flashlights unless we absolutely have to." He sniffed and frowned.

In a couple of minutes, I could finally see the outline of the cavern, and noticed how deep it went. "There's a tunnel."

Buzz flung his gun around, aiming it at the opening, and went in front of me. "Stay close. Be cautious."

"I should go first. I have the—"

"Protect yourself if I die," he countered, and strode further inside.

My feet shuffled on the rock, pebbles scattering with each step. I lifted my legs more to avoid making the noise, and slowed when Buzz did. We'd reached the tunnel, and it went in two directions. "Parker didn't tell us enough information," Buzz said.

I listened, attempting to sense their presence. "Right. Head right."

Buzz did, taking it at a snail's pace. The corridor didn't go on long, and we made it to the end. I tripped on something, and Buzz finally used his flashlight, placing the beam against his palm, revealing a sliver of it to guide his path. The room was filled with bones.

I crouched, picking one up, and Buzz grabbed it. "Femur. Human."

Now I saw it. There were various animals within the nest, and the Traveler had placed their skulls along a ridge like trophies. I spotted a cow, a horse, a bobcat, and a human, along with an assortment of others that resembled dogs, cats, and birds.

It was revolting.

"He's hunted for some time, all right. And he's enjoying it," Buzz whispered.

"She's not here. We have to—"

The pulse blasted the corridor entrance, and debris rained down on my head. I shook the dust off and spun around, seeing the Traveler dragging Cindy behind him, her arms flung to the ground, her head lolling like she was unconscious.

"Cindy!" I shouted, firing back. My blast hit the beast in the leg, and he howled. When he shot at me, I surprised him. The explosion struck my invisible energy shield, and Buzz ran past me, shouting as he attacked the Traveler. He dove into the beast, and Cindy fell to the floor. I rushed to her, dragging her from the altercation.

"Cindy?" I cradled her face, and her cheek quivered. "You're going to be okay."

Sounds of an impressive battle carried from the cavern's entrance, and I left Cindy there to help Buzz defeat his enemy. When I arrived, the pair was locked in a wrestling move, their hands on each other's shoulders. Buzz was much smaller, but his grip looked as tight as the giant alien's. We'd injured the creature at Parker's earlier, and he seemed weaker because of it. He shrieked, the sound inhuman and pained.

I aimed my gun, but there was never a clean shot, so I bided my time.

"Where's your friend?" Buzz yelled.

The alien bellowed a response that neither of us could understand.

The Traveler kicked out, striking Buzz's shin, and he toppled over. The alien stood above him, arms outstretched, and he picked Buzz up. He threw my ally from the cavern.

"Noooooo!" I hollered, and he turned his attention to me. I fired, but the charge wasn't complete. I chucked the gun at him instead and fumbled for my revolver. The giant stalked toward me with a sadistic grin.

I heard something fall in the cave and saw a lasso. Buzz was inside, crouched near the exit, and he pulled with all his might as the Traveler stomped into the trap. He face-planted, scrambling for my leg as he clawed his fingers into the ground.

Buzz dragged him and the beast fell from the cave, his shrieks continuing. I rushed to Buzz, seeing the Traveler bashing into the cliff only ten feet below us. Buzz grabbed a knife, slicing the rope. It was easy, given the immense weight on the line, and it frayed, releasing quickly. We both watched as the Traveler plummeted to his death on the rocks below. He bent at an awkward angle, the waves drawing him into the abyss.

"That's for Mr. McIlroy," I said.

"Elliot?" Cindy's voice was gentle.

"Cindy!" I hurried to her and her face glowed bright. "It's still you."

"For now. I will leave. But we must find my way home," the Sphere said.

Buzz arrived, surveying the pair of us. "You heard her. To the bay."

I'd expected an argument, but he didn't bother.

"Buzz," I said.

"Yeah?" His shoulders slumped, and he looked half dead.

"You did it."

"Did what?"

"Killed an alien." I smiled, and he smirked in reply.

"Damn straight. If we're right, we might have one more to deal with before the sun rises. Come on." He'd never admit it, but I was sure I heard a waver in his voice.

5

"You're certain he's dead?" Bones didn't seem sold on the facts we'd delivered, but I was absolutely confident the Traveler was now swimming with the fishes, so to speak.

"Totally. It was gnarly," I said, and even Buzz cracked a smirk at that.

"Let's use the radio to warn the mainland, and sit tight until they arrive. If there's a final Traveler on the ground, someone else can deal with him. We did our job," Buzz told us.

"The Spheres are protected," Cindy added. "But we must find the…"

"Listen here… whatever you are." Buzz slammed on the brakes, jarring us in our seats. I almost hit the headrest in front of me, but managed to stick my arm out in time. "You come to our planet, infest our people, and make us defend you. What kind of sick—"

"They don't know what they're doing," Kim interjected.

"We."

"What?"

"*We*. You said *they*. You're one of them, don't forget." Bones' words struck a nerve.

"I don't feel any different than you. I didn't *ask* to start glowing." Kim broke down for the first time tonight. We'd all been through hell, and it hit us after Bones' comments. "I was doing just fine before they tracked me down and killed my parents. You think I *want* to be on Bell Island fighting aliens? I have a journalism degree. I want to travel the world, to feel the sun on my face as I write notes on the shores of Crete. I want to get married, have kids, sign a mortgage. I want to be *normal*."

Sheriff Parker took her hand. "You aren't a Sphere."

Kim paled, her tears still flowing. "What are you talking about?"

"I didn't know it earlier, but now I see. Every group of Esol is sent with a guide. That is what fell into you," he said. "They come much later, after centuries of our distribution on Earth. You were intended to track us and lead us home."

"Why didn't you say anything sooner?" I asked, feeling the sting of deceit.

"It is difficult for a Sphere within the complexities of a human brain. Other animals are much simpler."

"You can hide in different creatures?" Bones blurted.

"Yes. I spent some time in a bobcat. It was rewarding to hunt for food. It helped me understand the Travelers," Parker said.

"Do you recall why they seek you?"

"For sustenance," Parker claimed, but there had to be more to it. "We give them strength. It's a rite of passage among their warriors."

"So some of them aren't warriors?" Buzz asked him.

"Like any race. Are all humans soldiers?" Parker retorted, making Buzz grunt in acceptance.

Kim stared at the backs of her hands, as if they were no longer hers. "Can I rid myself of the guide?"

"It will leave at the proper time." Parker let go of Kim, while Buzz put the vehicle into drive again.

The first hints of dawn crept through the horizon, but it would be another hour or so before the sun was beyond the curvature of the planet.

"I wish he'd stop speaking in these cryptic riddles," Buzz muttered.

"I cannot explain more. Not yet." Parker faced the front. Cindy was half on my lap, and she didn't say much as we began the slow descent toward the bay.

"Everyone to the lighthouse this time," I ordered, hearing no resistance.

The climb was easier since the rain had ceased, but our energy was waning. Once we arrived at McIlroy's, we gathered inside, flicking on the lights. The generator was still running, giving us power.

"Anyone up for some food?" Bones rubbed his stomach.

"I'm starving," Kim said. "Let me help."

They went into the kitchen, scouring the cupboards. Cindy and Parker both glowed momentarily and settled to the couch, hands on laps. They closed their eyes and slumped into the cushions.

At least someone could sleep while we waited.

Buzz and I returned to the radio, and were pleased to see it worked when we tested it.

"*Roger that, Bell Island. What is your emergency? Did Old Benny blow another finger off lighting the crackers?*" The woman sounded like she'd smoked a half a pack in the last hour.

Buzz grimaced. "Contact the military. Police. Feds. Whatever you got."

"*Is this a joke? Where's McIlroy?*"

"What's your name?" Buzz asked her.

"*Penny.*"

"Penny, we have at least two dead deputies, along with over a dozen confirmed citizens. This is the farthest thing from a joke possible. Send reinforcements."

"*I've notified the Coast Guard…*"

"That's not enough. We require some Blackhawks…

the Marines. Don't fail me, Penny."

"*You haven't said what the issue is. How did they die? Flooding?*"

Buzz glanced at me, and I saw the cogs moving within his mind. "Terrorists. Ten of them. There are hostages everywhere, and they cut the power. I snuck away and managed to repair the radio. But…" He went quiet. "They're here now. Please hurry."

"*We… terrorists? Where are they from? I'm reaching out to my supervisor. We'll be there!*"

He turned the volume off and grinned. "It's not that far of a stretch, is it?"

"Nope." We took a moment to appreciate the lighthouse beam. It rotated in a steady pattern, casting a protective ambiance across the darkness of the bay.

"All we can do is wait," Buzz said.

"How long will it take them?" I asked.

"It's a bit of a hike, and given the fact that most of the reinforcements were probably getting drunk around a campfire until a couple hours ago, we might be an hour from seeing someone." Buzz stretched his back, and it popped. "Let's see what's cooking."

We rejoined our friends in McIlroy's place and smelled soup on the stovetop. Bones worked effortlessly on the grilled cheese, melting bits of cheddar on the outside of the bread like he always did. He called it Nana's specialty.

Buzz stayed by the front window, guarding the entrance with his assault rifle near him. The Traveler's weapon lay on the chair, and Buzz only broke his gaze when Kim offered him a serving of soup. He took it with a muttered 'thanks' and sipped it from the bowl rather than using the spoon.

I grabbed my own serving of tomato soup and devoured it, using half a sandwich to scoop up the last remaining drops. Saying it hit the spot would be an understatement.

Cindy remained unconscious, her eyes moving behind the lids, and Parker grunted in his sleep as if he was being chased.

I ate a second grilled cheese and sat at the oversized oak table, thinking how lonely McIlroy must have been the last few years. There were only two chairs, and Bones stood, letting Kim take the second.

"What a day," I said.

Bones picked at the crust of his sandwich. "I can't believe Mark was one of them."

"Twenty years he'd been hiding out. The Travelers chose to come now. I wonder why?" I set the last bite down, stuffed.

"It's because of her." Buzz peered at us from the door. "Kim's the guide."

"But they didn't seem able to track her," I reminded him.

"The oldest might be different. He stuck around for a reason."

Bones started to clear the plates. "Or his ship was lost."

Buzz stood rigid. "That would explain why he stayed."

"But how did he signal the others?" Kim asked.

"I don't think he did. They came because of the storm. The Spheres have become increasingly obvious. They're growing tired of hiding. The game is more about patience than the hunt. You heard what Mark said. He needed a change after they sacrificed one of their own to the last batch of Travelers. But one was left behind." Buzz paced in the living room, still clutching his gun. "I hate not seeing the big picture."

"There might be nothing to it," I said. "Forty years ago, my mom saw the Spheres, and they were attacked by the

Travelers. The one in Mark and these two gave up the youngest, whoever that was, and they thought it was over. Twenty years later, Mark was inhabited by a Sphere. Now my sister was. Then Parker. The guy with a missing eye must have missed his ride, or he chose to remain on Bell Island for another reason."

"Because the Spheres' ship is still here. He knew someone would attempt to use it. He's hungry."

"Then why didn't he go after them?" Bones washed the plates.

"Good question. I suppose we'll never know. Because if that son of a bitch shows up, I'll gut him before he can answer. You saw his nest. He's a monster, claiming skulls as prizes. We'll be doing this world a favor," Buzz said.

When I checked the time, only twenty minutes had gone by. "I'm going to keep an eye out for our reinforcements."

"I'll join you." Kim stood up and washed her hands, then followed me past the dozing Spheres.

"So you might not be one of them after all," I said.

"Maybe. I've never felt different, besides the occasional glowing eyes and mouth, that is." She managed a beautiful smile. It reminded me of our earlier kiss. It also made me want to do it again.

We climbed the spiral staircase, all the way to the top, and stared at the choppy waters down below. The storm was finished, but the channel continued to thrash against the outer bay. It calmed by the time it reached Bell Island's shore, but it was obviously still dangerous out there. Maybe help wasn't coming, not unless they heeded Buzz's suggestion of using a helicopter to bring soldiers.

"It's almost over," Kim whispered. "If I can release this guide and send the Spheres home, I can move on with my life. I've been so obsessed with this since the Travelers killed my parents. I have to let it go."

"Or fight them," I mumbled.

"Fight them?"

"Like Buzz. He's got a vendetta, and so far, we're winning."

"Are you suggesting we form some kind of alien lynch mob and travel the road searching for enemies?" Kim laughed, the sound refreshing.

"No, I suppose I'm not." That would be a good way to get myself killed. If I survived this night, I'd be the luckiest man alive. "You're going to leave Bell Island, aren't you?"

Kim leaned her head on my shoulder. "Probably. The diner isn't quite what I had in mind long-term."

What would I do? Could I go finish college after an experience like this? Pretend aliens didn't exist and wait for them to invade us in full force like Buzz predicted?

"Maybe you can stay in the city for a while. Just until I graduate."

Kim started to respond when her jaw dropped. "There's a boat."

I grabbed an old scope from the bench and searched the ocean. It was hard to discern, but I saw what she did. It was a large sailboat, the aft end half-sunken. Someone was on the deck wearing a bright orange vest.

"We have to help them!" I almost fell, rushing down the stairs. "Keep the beacon on the area. Don't move it."

Kim started to adjust the light. "I'll do it. Save her."

"There's a sinking boat coming to shore!" I shouted at Buzz and Bones, and the Spheres' eyes flicked open.

The boat was at least four hundred yards from the rocky beach, where the waters were still treacherous. All it needed was another hundred to bring it past the rough break. "Kim's manning the beacon. I can't do this alone."

Bones nodded at the Spheres. "Buzz, protect them. I'll

help Elliot."

My best friend joined me outside, and we descended the cliffside steps, energized from the brief pause and sustenance. Bones flew past me toward the docks and tried the door where the keys were kept. It was locked.

I shrugged and grabbed a rock from beneath the pier, bringing it to the boat house. With a quick toss, the glass shattered, and I undid the bolt.

The biggest boat belonged to Lawrence Banner, the proprietor of half the businesses on Bell Island. It was a small yacht, something I'd always dreamed of taking onto the water. Now I had my chance. I yanked the keys from the board and jogged to the proper section of the marina. The boats had calmed in the bay, no longer bashing into their docks like earlier. By the looks of it, Banner's yacht had been double secured, and there wasn't so much as a scratch on her hull.

"How do we free her?" I asked Bones.

He flicked a knife from his pocket and started sawing the thick nautical strapping.

"Any movement? Over," I asked into my handheld radio.

"*It's still coming. I think it'll be fully submerged in five minutes. Over,*" Kim replied.

"We better hurry. Cut the rest of them off and meet me on deck." I climbed the rungs along the side, landing hard on my feet. The steering room was above the common cabin, and I opened the door, appreciating the fine detail within. The white console was covered in screens and buttons I didn't understand, and I searched for somewhere to put the key. I found the ignition on the right and held my breath as I turned it. It didn't fire up.

"Anyone know how to start a boat?" I asked into the radio.

"*Should be a pushbutton. Make sure it's in neutral,*" Kim said. I didn't ask how she knew this.

There was just enough light through the windshield to go by. I found the engine button, a red disc with a wear pattern in the middle. The boat lurched, and I saw it was in gear. I quickly shifted it, hearing a grinding as I went too far to reverse.

Bones lurched into the cabin. "What the hell are you doing?"

"We're fine. Unstrapped from the dock?" I asked.

"Should be."

I put it in gear again and slowly urged the throttle forward, sending us to sea. The big boat bobbed up and down with the gentle waves, but I knew it would be much worse when we passed the break. The bay resembled a giant letter U, and once you crossed the threshold, the channel was far more dangerous under conditions like tonight's.

I thought of Kim's message and wondered how much of those five minutes we'd already eaten up. We had two or three at best. I gunned it, the front end lifting slightly. The bow slapped against the water as we went, and we flew by the remaining marina, our passage sending large ripples throughout the bay.

I searched for our destination, noticing the lighthouse beacon holding steady. I couldn't see much of the boat, just the top, and someone standing on it, waving their arms. "Grab me a lifejacket!"

"You can't swim out there. You'll be dragged under!" Bones shouted.

"Just do it." I slowed as we maneuvered the choppy ocean. The yacht lifted and dropped sideways. We stayed upright as the wave persisted. My full stomach lurched at the movements, but I'd taken the ferry enough times to deal with it, not to mention the countless summers boating around Bell Island, fishing when we were kids, and tubing as we got older. But we always took safety seriously, given the history of drownings around the place.

Bones returned with a lifejacket and slammed against the bulkhead when we were thrown a second time. I strapped it on and grabbed Bones by the shoulders. "Hold the ship steady. I'll bring them in."

He opened his mouth, but no words escaped.

I left him manning the helm. Wind buffeted me as I stepped outside. The sinking boat was close, only a few yards from our position, and I stood in disbelief as the ocean swallowed it. Long brown hair floated in the water before vanishing into its depths.

"I'm coming!" I called, and dove from the deck, splashing into the freezing water. It surrounded me, threatening to pull me under, but the life preserver did its job. I floated up and scanned the area.

A hand jutted from the chaotically stirring sea, and I swam for it, catching hold. The grip slipped, so I lunged, wrapping my arm around the woman. I kicked as hard as I could, dragging her through the waves to the yacht. It was violently bobbing, and I clutched the trailing dock straps dangling from the stern.

"Bones!" I shouted.

"What?" I finally heard after ten seconds of repeating myself.

"Bring us to the bay!" The strap was twenty feet long, and water churned violently as the propeller spun rapidly. I wrapped it around my bicep and clutched on to the woman for dear life, keeping her head exposed.

As the boat tugged us, I glanced behind me to find the massive wave coming at me. I gritted my teeth and held my breath. The water flowed over us, thrashing me down. The strap went taut, yanking on my shoulder, but it didn't break. We emerged in the safety of the bay, with Bones slowing the boat. He was on the rail, jumping to the lower deck. Bones pulled the strap in, offering his hand when I was close enough. I gripped the rungs, lifting the woman, who was spitting water from her mouth.

"Mrs. Hoffman?" Bones' question didn't make sense to me.

"Hi... Bones," my mom said. Her hair was plastered to her brow, and her teeth chattered.

I was in shock. "Mom? What are you doing here?"

"The moment I heard about the storm, I escaped the hospital. I expect they tried to call home to alert you, b-b-but by then, the power might have been out," she said shakily. We got to the deck, and she stared somberly at Bell Island.

I recalled the message left on the answering machine I didn't know how to operate. "Why did you come?"

Her eyes narrowed. "To stop them from hurting my family."

"We have a lot to catch you up on," I told her.

"*Is everyone okay?*" Kim asked through the radio I left on the deck. I reached for it, tapping the talk button.

"We're fine. My mom's here."

"*Your mom?*"

"We'll return soon." I was soaked, but put the radio into my pocket regardless.

"Bones, do you mind bringing us to shore?"

"I don't really know what I'm doing, but sure." He ran off.

"Mom. I believe you," I said.

"About what?" She stood, gripping the rails.

"Everything. The Spheres, the Travelers, all of it."

"Spheres? Travelers? Where did you come up with those names?"

"Buzz," I said.

"The soldier who bought the Reeve farm?"

"You've met?"

She nodded. "He was following me at the grocery store. I circled around him in the produce section and ambushed him. Considering he's a solider, it was easy. We went for coffee."

"I see."

"He had some very strange questions, without actually mentioning the aliens Taylor and I met."

"And the one-eyed Traveler?"

She shrugged. "It was so long ago. Taylor thought he was lurking around. Your uncle ventured into areas of Bell Island that he shouldn't have."

"And the ship near the bay?"

Her eyes went wide. "I… we weren't certain. But he finally told me he had its location. That's when we lost him. I searched for it everywhere, but never did find the coordinates."

"That's important," I said. "The monsters came. Tonight. We've already killed three of them."

She looked relieved, even with the dire news. "You… killed the aliens?"

"Had to. Kill or be killed."

Mom grabbed my arm, squeezing it. "Is your father okay?"

"He's at home. Don't think he really knows what's happening. The residents were told to stay inside, and that a serial killer was on the loose."

"Good. Cindy's with him?" The yacht bypassed the docks, and Bones drove it all the way up to the beach. The underside scraped against the rocks and tilted sideways.

"About that… you'll want to see this." I glanced at the lighthouse.

6

"Cindy!" My mom hugged her daughter, and the Sphere awkwardly returned the embrace.

"Hello."

"Mom, you've met the Sphere before," I told her, and Mom broke away.

"Hi, Lorraine," Cindy said. The brilliant white glow shone through her nostrils and ears, before shooting from her open mouth. "I've missed you."

"This can't be… Give me my girl back."

"All in due time. We must leave. The Sarc will be angry," Cindy said.

"The Sarc?" Buzz asked.

"I am remembering more. You call them Travelers." Cindy's lights dimmed, and she once again looked like my kid sister.

"How do you leave?" Mom demanded. "Cindy will stay with us, right?"

"We leave on our ship. Elliot thinks he can find it for us," she said. "And your daughter will be fine."

My mom looked dubious. "Just like I was fine?"

"You said Uncle Taylor had the location." I remembered the paper from earlier and grabbed it. The message was soaked, but the numbers he'd drawn remained. "What if he left directions in the car with this? We didn't look very hard."

"Taylor left this for you?" she asked, reaching for the

paper. Tears formed in her eyes. She clenched her jaw and glanced at Buzz. "I think we can expect the last Traveler to attack before dawn."

Buzz nodded. "I was predicting the same thing."

"We have to move these Spheres off the island. All of them." She peered at Sheriff Parker.

"There's another," Bones told her.

"Mark… my boss is an alien." I didn't anticipate her laughter. "I know it sounds like the name of a terrible B movie, but it's true."

"Okay, here's the plan. Buzz will gather Mark. Elliot, where's the Camaro?" Mom was in her element barking orders.

I swallowed and sighed. "It's in the shop. I hit a deer."

"Are you okay?"

"Yes. Cindy was with me. I picked her up in the storm last night," I said.

"See if your uncle left any other revelations in it. I'll stay with…"

"Kim," she said.

"Kim. And you are?"

"She's the guide," Cindy explained.

"It's complicated, Mom. Maybe Kim can fill you in while we're gone."

I hated to leave them, but knew it was our best option. I unclasped the shield from my arm and passed it to Kim. "Wear it. If he comes, protect them." It was a lot to ask of a girl I'd just met, but she nodded and touched my cheek.

"I won't let anything happen to them." She kissed me, and I heard my mom gasp.

"Where's Bethany?" she croaked.

"I have no idea." I left without further comment.

Another trek down the stairs, and I thought my legs might literally fall off. Buzz motioned to the parking lot, tossing me his keys. "Take my 4X4."

"What about you?" Bones asked.

"I'll manage." He started toward a couple of rusted old vans.

"Hot wire," Bones whispered. "Probably not his first time."

It was growing brighter by the minute, and that meant we didn't have long. The roads were mostly dry, and there were still no cars out. I wondered what the rest of the island thought was occurring. Were they all fast asleep, dreaming of barbecues and golf rounds, or were they huddled in their closets, awaiting a serial killer to stab them in the heart?

Bones' shop wasn't that far, and we screeched to the bay doors. Bones unlocked them, and we hurried in, using a flashlight to help our search. My damaged Camaro was where we left her, and the trunk was ajar. I reached in, searching for another note. The fabric lifted, and I removed the tire iron and jack. Just when I was about to give up, I spotted the corner of a business card. I dug it out.

"What is it?" Bones almost dropped the light trying to get a better view.

Smitty's Boat Repair. I flipped it around. "Coordinates. This has to be it. We're set."

"How do we even use that?" Bones asked.

"No clue, but someone will know." We locked up, and I stopped when I noticed the silhouette on the other side of the fence.

"I can't wait to see their ship… speaking of… what are we going to do with the one that's landed on our island? Those Travelers sure won't need it," he said, and I put a finger to my lips, trying to silence him.

The alien was massive, two feet taller than the others. He locked gazes with me from the across the chain link. "Bones…"

"Seriously, it'll be epic. We'll be in every newspaper from here to Tokyo." Bones reached for the handle.

"Bones... he's right there."

He must have picked up on the fear laced into my voice, and I realized I wasn't armed.

But we had an assortment of weapons in the vehicle. I backed up, my footsteps loud on the gravel, but I kept my eyes on him. It was growing lighter out, and I could see the scars on his face, the longest at his left socket, where the eyeball was missing. This was the Traveler living in the south cliff cavern.

The first crate had grenades in it, and I snatched one, trying to remember how they worked. Pull the pin. Throw it. How hard could it be? I passed a grenade to Bones, and his jaw dropped.

"I prefer a bazooka," he muttered.

The Traveler crouched, and I sensed what he was about to do. He leapt over the fence, landing lighter than should have been possible, given his bulky frame. His clothing was in tatters and barely hung on his waist. Everything was stained, mostly with blood, and it was a dried ruddy brown color. He was wild.

"Now!" I shouted, and plucked the pin. I held it for a second and used my best Little League pitch to toss it at One-Eye. Bones did the same, and we braced ourselves for the explosion. But the Traveler was faster. He kicked them both, sending them toward the shop. They exploded, leaving a crater near the bay door.

"Get inside!" I called, and jumped into the driver's seat. Bones didn't even have his door closed when I was halfway down the parking lot, racing for the street.

I checked the mirrors but didn't spot him.

"I think we're free," I said, grinning.

Just when I thought we'd made it, I heard him climbing

on the roof. He bellowed what could only be described as a war cry and slammed a fist into the metal. It left a dent right above Bones' head.

I smashed the brakes, and the Traveler shot forward, landing hard on the road. He rolled twice and came to a stop.

"Gun it!" Bones yelled, and I did, clipping the Traveler as I flew by.

When I glanced at the side mirror, I saw him rise and dust himself off. He stared at us as I continued further.

"He won't let up," I said.

"Then we'd better be fast."

We got to the beach at 4:55 A.M., and Buzz was shoving Mark toward the stairs. My mom was halfway down, with Kimberly, Parker, and Cindy in tow.

"Tell me you have something," Buzz told me.

"This is uncalled for! I just want to live my life in peace. I have a girlfriend. We're going to travel!" Mark called, and Buzz slapped a hand over his mouth.

"Keep it down. The guide is here, and you're all leaving. Understood?"

Mark's shoulders slouched, and he nodded when Buzz removed his palm. "Fine."

"I still don't know how to help," Kim said.

"You will," Parker told her.

"Where is their ship?" Mom asked me, and I handed her the paper.

"Any ideas on how to read these?" I looked around our group.

"Let me try," someone said, and I saw Mr. McIlroy emerge from the second van. He hobbled over, his cheeks almost as white as his shock of hair.

"You're… dead." Bones poked him in the chest, as if checking if he was a ghost.

"Me? Takes more than a giant monster to end Benson McIlroy, I'll tell you that."

"But we saw you on the rocks," I mumbled.

"My wife's old sewing mannequin. I couldn't bear to part with it after I lost her, God rest her lovely soul." He snatched the paper with gnarled fingers and made a sucking sound with his lips. "Yep. Know this very well. Great spot for fishing. Used to go there when I was younger. For some reason, they flocked to this exact location. I never told the guys about it. I actually warned them that the water had a terrible current to keep everyone away."

"I think we've discovered why the Spheres' ship was never found," Kim said.

"Sphere?" McIlroy asked.

"The balls of light living inside Sheriff Parker and my sister," I told him.

"Ah, yes, those. I've always wondered what they were," he said casually.

"You've seen us?" Cindy asked.

"Sure. I'm ninety and have lived here most of my life. I've seen a lot of things."

"Can you take us to this spot?" I tapped the paper.

"Let's use my boat," he said, and started to walk. Very slowly.

I kept peering over my shoulder, waiting for One-Eye to emerge on the beach.

I motioned to Buzz while we went. "He's real. Bones and I tried to kill him, but he got away. Or we did."

"Dammit," Buzz said, flipping the weapon in his grip.

"Where's our backup?" I asked, gazing at the city.

"Should be here soon."

The creature bellowed and I saw him at the end of the road, stalking toward us. "Hurry!" I called out. He'd arrived much faster than I'd anticipated.

They reached the pier, and half-carried McIlroy down the wooden planks.

A series of headlights flashed behind the alien, and I almost choked when I recognized the Mustang. "Cooper…"

Ten or so cars sped past the alien, honking their horns, and Cooper slid to the side, slamming the brakes near us. He hopped from his convertible, holding a baseball bat. "Let's kill this freak." Cooper's gaze drifted over the parking lot. The others came, and I recognized Bruce and Reaper, along with Bethany. They carried pistols, rifles, knifes, and bats.

"Where are they?" Bethany asked.

"What are you guys doing here?" I barked.

"We heard about the aliens from Cooper. He's spent the last few hours gathering reinforcements," Bethany said.

More cars appeared, and out came dozens of residents. When I glanced past their bright headlights, I could no longer see the Traveler. He'd vanished in the chaos. "Stay with them, Buzz. Make sure they don't shoot each other by accident."

"Where did he go?" Buzz asked. "Everyone spread out. There's a mean SOB on the prowl, and we have to distract him while our friends head out to sea. Reinforcements are on their way, but it's up to us, the residents of Bell Island, to defend it now."

"Roger that, Sarge," Cooper said.

"It's Buzz," I told him.

Cooper nodded and slapped the bat into his palm. "Let's find this sicko and give him what he deserves."

It was the first time in my life I didn't want to punch the guy.

"Elliot?" My dad climbed out of his truck, carrying a hammer.

I hugged him, knowing I didn't have time to explain. "Be careful. I'll be back soon."

He looked past me to the pier. "Is that Lorraine and Cindy?"

"I'll fill you in later."

"Elliot…"

I ran off, chasing my friends as they piled into McIlroy's fishing boat. It wasn't big, but had just enough room for us all.

Sheriff Parker's face began to glow, as did Cindy's, then Mark's. My boss was clearly not happy with the way his day was going. Neither was I, but maybe, just maybe, we could be done with this night soon.

My mom was quiet, her gaze on the waters. I could tell she was thinking about her twin.

Kim took the rudder to steer us after the engine started up.

The cove grew brighter as the sun began to ascend, the water changing from dark and mysterious to light and hopeful with the start of another morning. The clouds were all gone, the stars still gleaming from millions of light years away.

Was one of them the Spheres' home? Where did the Travelers hail from? There were so many questions we might never have the answers to, but at the end of the day, I wanted everyone I cared about to be safe. That was all that mattered.

The boat careened through the bay, the wind biting at my cheeks, and Bones met my gaze.

"How are we going to top this one next summer?" he asked.

"Hopefully by staying in and watching a movie marathon," I said with a laugh.

"Someone's coming!" Kim shouted, pointing toward

the mainland.

The Coast Guard search and rescue boat's lights flashed, and I guessed it would intercept us before we reached the Spheres' ship. I fell back as Kim gunned it, and old man McIlroy shouted with excitement. I bet he didn't experience a thrill like this very often.

"How did you escape the Traveler?" I asked him.

"They're big, but easy to fool. I placed the mannequin in the window out back. The alien went for it, throwing the thing over the cliff, but I was already gone. He probably didn't even notice it was inanimate." McIlroy grinned, his dentures stained yellow.

The waters north of the bay were calmer than before, the waves long and wide, causing far less disruption than I'd anticipated.

Gunfire sounded from the beach, and I spied an alien pulse. Considering One-Eye didn't appear to be armed, I guessed that Buzz had opened fire.

"Over here," McIlroy said, and Kim slowed. I watched as her Sphere began to brighten, until it was almost impossible to gaze at.

"This is so strange," Mom whispered.

"Kim's different," I said. "Special."

"Stay where you are!" a voice called through a bullhorn.

The Coast Guard had arrived, their boat fifty feet away. The red light flashed as it spun around atop the cabin.

"We're okay. They need help at the beach!" I called.

"I repeat, stay where you are!" he said.

"How are we going to do this?" Bones peered at my mom, then at Kim.

"We can't stop now. We're so close." Kim's face still glowed, and it wouldn't be long before the Coast Guard realized something was amiss.

The air crackled, and my fingertips tingled with energy.

A crash of lightning shot over the bay, despite a cloudless sky, and there it was. Another UFO.

"No, no, no, no," Mark uttered. "They sent a second craft."

"I guess someone called for reinforcements," Bones muttered.

"Stay where…" The Coast Guard stopped, and they all stared at the floating alien vessel. A bright white light shone from the underside, and it centered on the rescue boat. "Turn your lights off, and land on the shore. That's an order from the US…"

The Coast Guard officer lifted from the deck, his arms flailing. The bullhorn fell into the water, and his head tilted up as he screamed. Something snapped and he dropped into the water, splashing loudly. His counterparts stood there, mouths agape, until one of them fired at the UFO. The bullets clanged off the metallic hull, but they continued at it.

"While they're distracted," Cindy said. She slipped from the boat, diving into the ocean with a minimal splash.

"Cindy!" I scanned the murky waters, but she was gone.

"I feel it," Kim murmured. The light in her pulsed, as did Parker's and Mark's. They all went to their feet, unsteady in the fishing boat, and the two Spheres jumped in. Kim stared at me. "I can help." And with that, she joined them below.

It was just my mother and McIlroy left.

"We can't let them go alone. If they leave their human vessels behind, they'll drown."

My mom perked up, like she couldn't stand the thought of losing someone else to the ocean. "McIlroy, do not leave us behind."

He nodded, staring at the UFO as it hovered directly

above the search and rescue boat. Their vessel began to shake and crack, the roof of the cabin tearing from the frame. There were four people on board, and they lifted into the bright beam, each about to share the fate of their superior.

There wasn't much time.

I dove, feeling the chill of the water surrounding me. I sank deeper and blinked my eyes open. They stung from the salt, but I made out the glowing orb twenty feet below. All four Spheres managed to stand on the ocean bed, seaweed darting around their waists.

The object was the size of a beach ball. It was no wonder it remained hiding among the reeds. They all touched it, the lights escaping their human carriers. My mom arrived, her hair floating above her.

Kimberly's light shone the brightest, and it exited through her mouth, entering the craft first. The others kept close to their hosts, as if patiently waiting their turn. They plunked into the Sphere vessel one by one, adding to the brilliance.

My lungs began to ache, my head reeling from the pressure, but I had to witness this. The pulses quickened, the ship moving off the ground. It rose in the water, and Kim floated back, watching it leave.

And it shot upwards, darting from the ocean.

My mom tugged on my arm, but I needed to ensure Cindy and Kim made it to the surface. They seemed in shock for a second, but broke from it as Sheriff Parker began to release bubbles as he exhaled. Mark kicked, swimming away, and they trailed after him.

We breached, and I took a giant inhale, my chest burning. I looked around to find that what remained of the Coast Guard boat was on fire. McIlroy's fishing boat was upside down, the bottom singed black. The UFO was near the shore.

"Everyone here?" I called, and we met at the upended ship.

McIlroy spat a mouthful of water. "They thought they could get me, but I'll show those SOBs!" He clung to the engine. Bones was near him, unable to break his gaze from the UFO a short distance away.

Cindy hugged my mom as they held tight. "I remember everything. It was surreal."

"You saw it all?" I asked.

She nodded, wiping hair from her face. "You guys were so brave."

"I wanted to slap myself," Parker grumbled. "He was such a pacifist. Didn't sit well with me."

"We made it," Mark added. "I'll miss hosting him."

"How do we get to shore?" Bones asked.

"The dinghies." I pointed at the rescue ship. "They must have at least one."

"Who's the strongest swimmer?" Mom asked.

Kim lifted a hand. "I'm pretty good."

"Me too." I grinned at her, despite the circumstances.

We both pushed off, breast stroking to the wreckage. I bumped into something, and realized it was the first dead Coast Guard officer. I tried not to think about it and touched a large floating piece of debris. As expected, there was a standard dinghy attached, and we fought with the ropes to undo it. The flames were expanding, and I smelled fuel. "It's going to blow," I told Kim.

We unraveled the final tie, and it fell to the water. Kim unceremoniously jumped onto it, and I did the same, using the paddles to push off the hull. The fire spread, and just when we were out of range, it exploded, sending shrapnel raining over us.

I tossed a piece of burning fabric into the water using

my oar and headed to our friends.

"This is going to be tight," Bones said, flopping inside. Once Parker was in, we quickly helped Cindy, my mom, and old McIlroy to safety.

"Look!" Kim pointed to the ship rushing to shore.

"What are they doing?" Bones muttered.

"They should leave," Kim said.

The beach was frantic with activity and noise, and when we reached the middle of the bay, we noticed the UFO had landed near the marina. Something was on fire, and the sound of gunshots rang out as dawn rose over Bell Island.

As if straight out of a nightmare, three Travelers exited the UFO, each fully armed, and they didn't look like they were here for the hunt. They wanted revenge.
Buzz was the closest person, standing before the locals that had assisted the fight. The tip of his gun shone yellow, and the battle was on.

7

I paddled with all my strength, the muscles bunching in my shoulders and back. My arms were weak by the time we hit the sand, and we hopped out. The aliens hadn't engaged, and Buzz's first shot vanished on a shield surrounding their ship.

"Cowards," Buzz grumbled.

We weren't equipped for this. The aliens clearly had the upper hand. They were fresh, their weapons charged.

"You did it," he told me as we approached.

There were open crates from his 4X4 behind the group, and he gestured at it. "Take something. This ends now."

Bones hefted the RPG again, clicking a rocket into place. Kim and I grabbed the alien guns we'd had earlier, and a couple of grenades for good measure. Bones pulled something from his backpack, and I saw him test his lighter.

"What kind of fight is this?" Bones asked, staring at the trio of Travelers standing on the pier. The lighthouse beacon moved again, cutting across the bay with a bright beam.

Cooper pushed past us, a rifle in his hands. "It's BS. What are they waiting for?"

"Yeah," an older man said. I think he owned the dive bar near the diner. "Let's kick their asses!" He went ahead, staggering onto the rocky beach.

One second he was wearing jeans and a plaid shirt, his farmer's hat askew on his sweaty head; the next he was a pile of goo, hissing from the heat on the shore. The hat remained, melting into his ooze.

Cooper instantly lost his boldness and slunk behind Buzz.

"Where's One-Eye?" I asked.

"He ran off. Guess he met his match," Buzz said.

I searched the beach, but didn't spot him.

The Spheres remained in the sky, their ball of light glowing brightly.

"They're trying to help," I whispered.

Their craft lowered, speeding by the UFO. The Travelers finally broke from the protection of their shield, firing at the Spheres.

"Now!" Buzz yelled, destroying the pier out from under them. Two of the aliens stayed on the steady side of the dock, but one plunged into the shallow water.

"Bones, get him!" I called, and my friend took a knee, lifting the bazooka to his shoulder. I heard his exhale as he fired, the rocket hissing through the air. It detonated, and we rushed toward the location. The Traveler was still alive. He blasted at us with his massive weapon, and I dove, taking Kim with me. We swept up in a heap on the beach, and I pulled the stubby gun, shooting the monster in the chest. He thrashed, losing his gun in the water.

Bethany was behind me, and she shot him in the forehead. "For good measure," she said, turning her aim at the remaining two.

These ones seemed shocked by our resistance. They were used to hunting Spheres, who usually offered a sacrifice rather than opposition. It was about as one-sided a conflict as you could experience. Well, that was no longer the case.

The Spheres hummed by, nearly hitting the Travelers. Kim dragged the big gun from the water, shaking it off, and checked the charge. It was almost ready for another shot.

The pair retreated along the beachfront, from the marina to the far cliffside.

Buzz tracked them at the front of our mounted defenses, everyone taking pot shots and yelling threats at the aliens. It was clear they weren't going down without a fight. One of them yanked a blinking disc from his back and threw it at the crowd.

"Look out, everyone!" I shouted, and Kim blasted it like she was an expert at destroying clay pigeons. It detonated, rocking the entire beach.

One of our people cried out, and my mom tended to their injuries. I saw my father linger, running to his wife, and they hugged.

Cindy stuck close to the sheriff, who had a pair of revolvers like he was heading to the OK Corral for a gunfight.

After five more minutes, we had the duo cornered. Buzz grimaced as he raised his gun.

The left alien lifted his arm, tapping a glowing screen on his wrist, and the UFO took off, flying overhead. The light shone from the underside, and I knew what they were planning. We'd seen it already in the water.

"We have to stop them!" I yelled, and everyone fired. He had another of those shields on him, and their assaults were ineffectual.

Bones knelt, tugging fireworks from his bag. "Here goes nothing." He lit the ends, darting away as the fuses sparked. The Travelers were momentarily distracted, the UFO wavering through the air.

One-Eye chose this moment to drop from a ledge on

the cliff. This side was facing west, so the sunlight hadn't reached this point of the bay. He'd been hiding. Waiting.

I expected him to join his brothers in the attack, but instead, he lashed out at the alien controlling the UFO. They wrestled, and it allowed us time to strike his counterpart while the coconut firework erupted in the air. The UFO wobbled in the sky, dipping and rising as One-Eye attempted to stop the Traveler.

The energy shield held as we barraged the other alien, but it eventually gave out with endless rounds of bullets and alien pulses striking him. Bones had reloaded, and Buzz took the RPG, ending that threat. The Traveler was a mess of guts on the beach.

"Then there were two," Kim whispered.

One-Eye continued to battle his enemy, their arms locked in struggle. He hefted the smaller alien, bashing him into the cliffside until his neck cracked, and One-Eye hurled his body to the rocks. He threw his head back and shrieked, the sound horrible yet victorious.

The older alien staggered toward us, his good eye rheumy and red. He called out again, yet it wasn't menacing. The UFO crashed into the water, but it was shallow, and half of it jutted out as the lights flashed off.

The Sphere ship gently lowered to One-Eye, and all our attention was on the interaction. They pulsed three times, and he nodded, lowering his chin. Then they scattered, darting higher in a spiral pattern, until we could no longer see them.

The sky filled with a brilliant burst of light, and they were gone.

"Look out!" Kim shouted at One-Eye, but it was too late. The Traveler he'd been in combat with shot him in the back, melting a hole into the ancient being. He fell face-first, and I sighted the injured Traveler at the base of the cliff, pulling the trigger. The last alien died like the others.

Kim rushed to One-Eye, taking his hand. His breathing was labored, his chest heaving as Buzz rolled him over. His stench was almost unbearable, but he'd sacrificed himself to help us.

"Why?" I asked, crouching at his side.

"Friend," he croaked.

"Who? Who was your friend?"

"Ta—" He coughed, spilling green blood. "Taylor." His eye glazed over, and his chest stopped moving.

I stared at the beast as sounds of a helicopter's rotors echoed throughout the bay.

Part Four
Aftermath

1

"Just what in the hell happened?" Captain Miller asked. "We got a call about a terrorist gang, and there's a goldarn UFO stuck in your beach!"

"How much time do you have?" Buzz asked him.

"Who are you?" Miller asked.

"First Sergeant Ethan Scott. But you can call me Buzz." He snapped a salute.

Miller nodded, patting Buzz on the shoulder. "Then it's a good thing you were here. What are we talking about? Foreign military test craft? Did they come with it?"

"Something like that," Buzz said.

The beach was a flurry of activity. More boats arrived, along with four helicopters. Apparently, the terrorist threat had touched home, and they'd taken the radio message seriously.

My family stuck close together a short distance away,

but Kim was beside me and Bones.

"How many did they kill?" Miller asked.

"Tough to say. Twenty. Maybe thirty. Could be more," Buzz said.

Miller rubbed his forehead. "We'll have to…"

"Sir, there's a call for you," a younger man said, handing him a radio. This one was huge, probably with a lot of range. The antenna alone was two feet long.

"What… Yes, sir. Understood. But… Yes, sir." Miller watched Buzz and handed him the radio. "He wants to speak with you."

"Who is it?" Buzz asked.

"The President," Miller told him, and Bones gasped.

"Of the United States? Radical," Bones yipped.

Buzz took the radio, separating from our group. "Hello, Mr. President…" He wandered out of earshot.

"How do you feel?" I asked Kim when Captain Miller left with his junior.

"No different. The guide departed." She smiled, and I'd never seen such a gorgeous sight.

Seeing Bell Island filled with armed soldiers was strange, but it was nothing compared with the last twenty-four hours. I'd woken up yesterday morning with my car trashed, and my mother in a psychiatric hospital. But it had turned out she was anything but crazy.

"There are so many unanswered questions," I said. "Where did they come from? And why were they on Earth in the first place?"

"Maybe we don't need to know. I, for one, would be happy to never see another Traveler or Sphere again for as long as I live."

"I'm with you," Bones said. "But we won. When push came to shove, we didn't back down." He stuck his fist out, and I bumped it three times, giving the thumbs-up.

"No, we didn't."

Cooper and Bethany were arguing a short distance away, and I glanced at the stack of weapons they'd all been carrying. It must have been quite the sight for the soldiers on arrival. I wondered how the story would be told, and how much the rest of the world would hear.

Buzz returned with the radio and offered it back to Miller.

"What did he say?" Miller asked.

"That's between the president and me. Pack it up. You're heading home."

"But we just…"

"That's the order. It was wild animals, a clutter of bobcats. Apparently, they'd ingested a bacteria-riddled cow, and it drove them nuts," Buzz told him.

"Bobcats? That's the official story?" Miller asked, and Sheriff Parker arrived.

"You have a problem with that?" Parker asked, his chest puffed up.

"Nope. Come on, Randy, let's get out of here," Miller said to his subordinate, who started barking orders at the soldiers.

"Thanks for everything, guys," Parker told our group. "Bell Island is lucky to have residents who care so much. Even you, Buzz. I take back all the things I said behind your back."

"And in front of me. It was nothing," Buzz said.

"Still. It wasn't fair." Parker offered his hand, and they shook. "You sticking around?"

"For now. I could use a break after this," Buzz admitted.

"I could use something to eat," Bones added. "Kim, can we hit the diner? Maybe I could fry up some bacon and eggs?" He wiggled his eyebrows. His mohawk looked like a deflated balloon, and he swept it aside.

"Food? Now?" I laughed.

"Why not. What's the worst that can happen? They fire me?" Kim put her arm through mine and leaned her head on my shoulder. "You give any thought to your future?"

I glanced at my friends and family. "No, but I have a feeling it's going to be better than I'd expected two days ago."

There was a lot to clean up, but Buzz told everyone to leave the mess. The president was sending his own men, an elite forces team, to investigate. Bell Island would be under lockdown for the next week or so.

"That's for the best," the sheriff said. "It'll give us time to formulate our story. Only a handful of us saw the aliens, so it should be easy to corroborate."

"What about all the damage? Like Becky's house?" I asked.

"Gas leak explosion. Could happen to anyone in a lightning storm." Parker nodded. "It's a shame about my deputies. Bradshaw and Sadie were good men."

My family looked exhausted, and I told them we were off to the diner.

"Honey, we're going home. I think we all need some sleep." Mom smiled at me. I had a feeling she'd be far happier now that she'd been validated.

Cindy hugged me so tight, I thought my head might pop off. "Thanks, Elliot."

"Anyone would have done the same," I told her.

"No, they wouldn't. You never gave up on me, and… I love you so much."

This was a rare comment from my sister. "Right back at you, kiddo."

"See you at home," she said, and they walked off. Cooper and the others were transporting those without rides across the island.

"Buzz, you coming?" Bones asked our illustrious leader.

He seemed shocked. "You want me to join you for breakfast?"

"Of course. Sheriff, you in?" I asked.

"I have some work to do, but you go ahead. Enjoy your freedom." Parker stood with McIlroy, waiting as the remaining rescue teams evacuated Bell Island.

Buzz stuck out his palm. "Can I have my keys back?"

"Sorry. It has a few dents. You know, old One-Eye did a number on the roof." I gave them over.

"Why was he so hostile toward us?" Bones asked.

"Maybe because we threw grenades at him." I shrugged as we climbed into the 4X4.

Kim held my hand in the backseat and nuzzled in close. July fourth had ended, but I sensed some fireworks in my future.

2

The door's chimes jingled, announcing another customer. The blond boys rushed in, screaming and pushing each other.

"Mom, Brad hurt me!"

"Did not!"

"Would you two stop it!" Their mother gave me an apologetic smile and went to the drama section.

Mark had been more forgiving about the dead alien on the store floor than I'd initially expected. At the time, I hadn't known he was hosting a Sphere.

The cleanup crew took all evidence of the aliens, except for two of the guns that Buzz stashed in his barn, 'just in case.' After they'd departed with the alien corpses, we hadn't heard from anyone again, and I was cool with that.

All I wanted was for Bell Island to be left alone.

I rented the family three movies and cringed at their selections. But who was I to judge? I had a romantic comedy in my pack to watch with Kim later.

Bones held the door for them and walked in, his mohawk freshly dyed blue. It was pointed straight up, and he had a smirk. "Hey, Elliot."

"Bones. To what do I owe the pleasure?" I glanced at

Mark's office, and the blinds were closed. His girlfriend had come an hour ago, and their conversation was definitely heated.

Bones adjusted the cardboard cut-out of Molly Ringwald. We'd needed to replace the Stallone one after an alien bled on it. "I'm leaving to meet Reaper… I mean Mary. She's decided to go back to her given name, seeing how her dad always preferred it, and…"

"He's dead."

"Yeah."

"How's she doing?" I asked.

"Not great, but she'll survive. She's resilient."

"She'd have to be, to date you," I joked.

"As if you're one to talk." Bones strolled to the counter, patting his pocket. He found a cigarette and slid it behind his ear. "What about you? Still working at the store, I see."

"I figured I may as well earn some cash this summer before heading to school," I said. "Better than digging ditches."

"Ain't that the truth." Bones looked nervous.

"What is it?"

He opened his vest and took a folded envelope out. "I got the response."

"From the tattoo place?"

Bones nodded in long, accentuated motions. "This determines the rest of my life."

"That's not true. If they reject you, we move on, okay?"

"Think they'll turn me down?"

"If they do, they're crazy." I'd seen Bones' artwork, and it was great. I'd told him he should be working in the comic industry, but he refused to hear me out.

Bones handed it to me. "I can't do it."

"I shouldn't open it."

"You're my best friend, Elliot. Just be kind if it's a no." Bones turned to face the exit.

The letter looked extremely professional. I'd been expecting an envelope with his name and address handwritten. Their logo was clean and concise, the address in Henderson, Nevada, which may as well have been Las Vegas.

I used a knife from under the counter and sliced through the glued top, tugging the letter free. I slowly unfolded it for dramatics, and Bones huffed. "Would you hurry up!"

I laughed and read the first line before repeating it out loud. "Dear Hank 'Bones' Larson, we are pleased to inform you that you've been accepted into this fall's program…"

He snatched it from me and spun in a circle, his chain rattling loudly. The letter crumpled in his fist as he pumped it into the air, and he realized what he'd done. "Whoops." Bones set it to the counter and tried to straighten it out. "Nana might want to frame that."

Mark's office door opened, and a bleary-eyed woman appeared, her makeup smudged. She glanced at us and sped through the store, leaving without a word.

"She's gone, Elliot. Sharon left me." Mark came out, his voice low and sad.

"Sorry, sir."

Mark waved a hand dismissively. "Maybe I'm better off. It was the Sphere she was in love with, not me. I miss him."

"You miss the Sphere?" Bones asked.

"You don't understand. We were one. I relished in the company. I suppose now it's time to find myself."

"So you're still taking that trip to Europe?" I asked, knowing it meant I'd be working more hours this summer. Which meant I could pay for my repairs and a few dates with Kimberly.

"You bet I am. I'm heading home to pack my bags now." He came around the sales desk and clutched my shoulders. "Thank you, Elliot."

"For what?"

"Killing them, and for helping the Spheres. Also for accepting the role."

"You know it's temporary, right?"

"Sure. But the job is always here for you, should you need it. That's a guarantee."

I wanted to remind him of the store's mantra, and how their promise rarely paid out, but I refrained. "Thanks, Mark."

We closed up, with Bones puffing on his cigarette outside. I locked the doors, said goodnight to Mark, and Bones walked me to the diner.

"What about Reaper… or Mary. Now that you're enrolled, will it work?"

He stubbed the smoke with his boot. "Who knows? I'm game for trying."

I knew how long distance went, given my past with Bethany, but didn't mention that. "You'll figure it out."

"I have some news on the car," he said.

"Really."

"Fender is fixed, the door's the issue. It's a lot of work, and the new windshield is on order. It's not easy finding parts for these things, but we're on it. And we're doing it all for cost plus ten percent. And half labor. Of course, that means I have to work harder to earn the difference," he said.

I put an arm around his shoulder. "You're the best, buddy." We broke apart near the diner, and I bumped his fist three times.

His thumb stuck up, and he smiled again. "Just remember that you owe me, okay?"

"Where you off to?"

Bones continued down the sidewalk. "Meeting Mary at the arcade. Peace." He lifted two fingers.

I glanced into the diner to find Kim breezing through the place, carrying plates in both hands. She almost dropped one as she saw me, but managed to slide them onto a table with an infectious grin.

Her co-worker, Nadine, refilled someone's coffee and nodded at me. They were used to this routine. I'd get off work, and Kim would still be trying to serve her last customers. I sat at the counter, fidgeting with a coffee cup.

"You want any?" Nadine asked, and I shrugged.

"Thank you." I remembered a minor detail from that first night, when Nadine had shown up late crying. "Can I ask you something personal?"

"Sure, hon. It's better than talking to the Creasal brothers." She pointed at the two greasy men by the bathroom. Their plates were full of steaming meat. I cringed and put on my most sincere expression.

"You were crying on the Fourth. Why?" I asked.

She blinked a few times, her smile fading. "I can't tell you."

"Why?"

"We're not supposed to talk about that night. Sheriff Parker's orders."

"I'm friends with him. I won't tell anyone," I promised.

"Well, the storm was coming in, but not quite here, and I asked my oldest son to grab the laundry, on account of it being outside on the clothesline. He argued about it, trying to continue playing that stupid Atari of his, but I demanded he go. He finally did, as I was in the kitchen cleaning the dinner dishes. Then I saw it."

"What?" I leaned forward and sipped from my cup.

"The light."

Goosebumps rose on my arms, and I looked around, checking if anyone was eavesdropping. "What kind of light?"

"It was a ball…" She made a fist. "About this size. Brighter than the sun it was. My boy… he swallowed it."

I gulped. "Nadine, where's your son now?"

"He's probably at the quarry, or fishing in the pond near the falls. He goes there with his friends on Friday nights. He thinks I don't know he smokes grass, but I do."

"And this light… have you seen it again?" I whispered.

"I thought I did, the other morning. But he claimed it was just his lamp. Trick of the… light." Someone shouted her name, and she stared at me. "Do I have anything to be worried about?"

"No. Not at all."

She sauntered to the Creasals' table, bringing two more beers with her.

"You okay?" Kim asked from behind me.

"We have to talk."

"I don't like the sounds of that." Kim removed her smock and went to the back to change.

"See you later, honey!" Nadine called, and the owner waved Kim over, handing her a stack of bills.

We went outside, and she shoved the cash in her purse. "You get paid that every night?"

"Those are just my tips," she said.

"Jeez, maybe you can treat me to a steak some time."

My van was parked closer to her job, making it easier to pick her up. My mom had been gracious enough to lend her to me while my wheels were in the shop. She was at home, working on the garden and her relationship with my dad, who'd found work rebuilding the destroyed homes and structures from the aftermath of our island's invasion. He seemed happier, full of energy again.

"What do you have to tell me?" Kim asked as I started the drive down Main Street.

"Can we put a pin in it until we reach Buzz's?"

"I thought we were watching that movie. I've been looking forward to it all day."

"We will."

"Okay, I'll trust that whatever this is about is more important than…" She stopped and winked.

The sun had set by the time I reached the Reeve farm, which I now actually thought of as Buzz's farm. In the last couple of weeks, we'd stayed in touch, even becoming friends. It was strange having a relationship with someone old enough to be your dad, but he was cool, and we all found common ground. He had an endless stream of stories, most of which sounded too unreal to be true, but he swore up and down he wasn't exaggerating on any of them.

Floodlights shone over the driveway when I passed the trip, and I braked, letting him see it was me. The lights flashed off, and the porch light came on instead. Buzz appeared from the doorway, stepping down the stairs while we got out.

"Elliot. Kim," he said. "I wasn't expecting you."

I felt bad not picking Bones up, but the last thing I wanted was to drag Reaper into our mess again, not after her father had been killed by one of the Travelers.

"Sorry, Buzz. I have news."

"Come inside."

The living room was dimly lit, the fireplace crackling with wood despite it being in the mid-seventies. His window was open, and a breeze blew the curtains. Buzz had a beer sweating onto a coaster, and he offered us one.

"No, thanks," I said.

Buzz took his seat, facing the fire, and we occupied the couch. "Go on. But this better not be something I have to deal with tonight. I spent all afternoon chopping wood."

"There's another Sphere," I said, and Buzz spit out a mouthful of beer.

"What?" Kim snapped.

"I thought we were done with this mess," Buzz complained.

"Nadine… that night when she came in late, crying. It was her son. She saw the Sphere enter him, and it sounds like it never left," I told them.

Buzz cursed under his breath. "Does that mean what I think it means?"

"There might be another Traveler on Bell Island," Kim whispered.

As if to accentuate her comment, thunder boomed overhead.

"A storm. Really?" Buzz rose and closed the glass on his fireplace.

"Where do we look?" I asked.

"The kid first. We have to confirm things. Otherwise, we're wasting our time." Buzz snatched a rifle from near the front door and gestured to his 4X4. "There's a few surprises in there. Just in case."

We left my mom's van and hit the road. Kim took the passenger side, and I sat in the middle of the back seat. "Do you know where Nadine lives?" Buzz signaled and turned onto the main road.

"Trailer behind the motel. We carpooled sometimes," Kim said.

Buzz didn't need to be told where that was. Ten minutes later, he rolled past the motel, and I saw Kim's car parked near her suite. A few people lingered near the rear of the building, cigarettes burning. "You should move."

"Where do I go?"

"You have money," I reminded her.

"Stay in the barn," Buzz said. "Mrs. Reeve had a loft built for company. There's a whole empty suite."

"Seriously? You'd let me stay?"

"Sure. It's just gathering dust." Buzz slowed near the trailer park, which consisted of ten single units, each crammed in too close to one another.

"You have no idea how happy that makes me," Kim said. "Thank you."

"Glad to help. I should have offered it sooner. That place you're staying in is a dump."

"Nadine's is the last one," Kim pointed out.

The lights were on, and I peered at the storm as the clouds rolled in, bringing fat raindrops with it. Lightning snapped in the distance, the thunder a few seconds after.

"She's still at work," Kim said. "Maybe we should wait for her."

"We do this now."

Buzz was the first out, and already at the door before we reached the ground. *Knock. Knock. Knock.* "What's his name, Kim?"

"Uhm… Neil."

"Neil, are you home?" Buzz asked.

"I'm sure there's a better way to do this. I doubt anyone is going to open the door for a man banging on it in the storm." Kim walked past him. "Neil, it's Kimberly from the diner. Can you let us in?"

I heard footsteps, and the bolt slid free. He appeared, but there was a screen between us. "What?"

He was about sixteen, with a face full of acne and a mane of brown hair.

"We know about the Sphere," she whispered.

"Bogus. I wanted to keep this quiet…" His eyes glowed, the brilliance escaping his mouth. "Fine. Come in." He unlocked the screen and shoved it.

"Do you remember anything?" Buzz asked him.

"I missed my ride."

"You saw the Sphere ship leaving?"

He nodded. "I tried to contact them, but I wasn't supposed to be here in the first place."

"What do you mean?" I asked.

He sighed and slumped like he'd been working on a factory floor for a twelve-hour shift, the action looking too old for his teenage body. "The Esol were dropped off in groups, each having their own guide. I came to Bell Island later, hitching a ride on a family member visiting from Boston. They didn't know I was here."

"But the Travelers might," I suggested.

He nodded. "It's possible."

Thunder boomed louder, and Neil shivered.

"How could we have missed one?" Buzz paced the trailer.

"If the cleanup crew had left something, maybe they'd return to it, but they were thorough," Kim said.

Buzz paused and laughed. "That's it. The UFO."

"I thought they took everything." I stared through the kitchen window, seeing sheets fluttering in the wind.

"I didn't tell them about the second UFO. They only have the one from the beach," Buzz admitted.

"Why?"

Buzz gave me a look. "Because once the government is involved, we're not. I want to know more about the Travelers."

Neil was obviously petrified. "They're coming for me? Jeez, I knew I shouldn't have left Boston. Museums. Great sports teams. What was I thinking?"

"Then leave the body and get the hell out of here. Maybe you'll bring the Traveler to you," Buzz told him.

"No. I won't." Neil shook his head, his cheeks

bouncing with the rapid movement.

Lightning flashed, and I saw a figure beyond the trailer park, in the field. It was facing the house. I ducked and waved the others to copy. "He found you."

Buzz quickly turned the lights off. "So soon. The guns are in my vehicle."

"Go get them!" I hissed.

Buzz went quietly, slinking out the front. I dared a peek through the window again, but saw nothing.

"I don't want to be absorbed," Neil said.

I thought about the comment. "You didn't say *die*."

"Huh?" Buzz lifted an eyebrow.

"*Die*. You said 'I don't want to be *absorbed*.' Do they not kill you?" I asked him.

"They… okay, the Esol are more than a prize, as you may think. We fuel the Sarc. They devour our kind and won't let us go. We're held captive within them, destined to be mere observers as they desecrate worlds."

"Don't the Spheres occupy humans without their consent? Why is it so different?" Kim asked Neil.

"Because…"

Buzz was back in a flash, and he tossed Kim and me each a handheld alien gun. He kept the big one and told us to join him outside.

"Shouldn't someone stay with the Sphere?" Kim asked. Of course she was empathetic to him. She'd held the guide in her since birth. But that was a different entity, one that didn't stifle her personality; rather, it sat silently within her body, waiting for the moment to emerge.

"I'll do it," I said, but Buzz disagreed.

"Kim stays. We'll finish this freak and force the Sphere to leave young Neil alone."

The Sphere didn't speak, just sat on the couch with his head in his hands.

"We'll be…" Thunder rocked the roof, and for a second, I thought we were under attack, but it was only the storm. The trailer didn't seem built well, and water dripped from the ceiling, landing on a discolored patch of carpet.

I closed the door and heard Kim locking it.

Buzz moved along the right edge of the trailer and rounded the corner to pause at the back. We peered into the field, and the laundry whipped around like a gaggle of ghosts on Halloween. And I spotted him again.

"There!" I called loud enough for Buzz to hear.

"We've got him." Buzz pressed the button on the gun, his weapon powering on. "Give it up, you…"

We sped past the clothesline and found a man, not a Traveler beyond the fence. "Please don't point that at me!" Sheriff Parker bellowed over the wind.

"Parker, what the hell are you doing out here?" Buzz inquired.

Parker tipped his head, letting water gush from his hat's brim. "Had a report of a huge animal stalking these parts. Since I'm low on manpower, I came myself."

"Animal. It has to be the Traveler," I told them.

"I thought we were done with those." Parker rubbed his palms together, leaving them in a prayer gesture.

We explained what we'd encountered, and he gawked at the trailer. "Just what we needed. Okay, you two interested in being deputized again?"

"No," I answered truthfully.

"We want to kill the SOB and be done."

The lightning was unrelenting, the rain pouring so hard it hurt. Thunder surrounded the entire island, rumbling endlessly.

Glass shattered, and I heard Kim scream. We rushed past the laundry in time to see the Traveler exiting by a hole carved into the trailer.

Neil was already outside, and I caught sight of Kim entering Buzz's 4X4. She revved the engine, drawing the beast through the front door. I almost slipped as I ran in the mud, and Parker barrelled into the Traveler, trying to tackle him. The alien was too strong, and tossed the sheriff into a puddle. His revolver was out, and two bullets struck his opponent, slowing him. But the Traveler persevered and landed on the hood as Kim backed up.

Buzz hesitated, probably not wanting to accidentally shoot my girlfriend. She slammed on the brakes, and the giant tumbled over the roof, landing on the dirt road. I was there, firing at him, but he rolled away in the nick of time. Kim jumped out, her blast hitting it in the leg.

The Traveler twisted his head, screaming in fury. His dark uniform was torn, and green ooze dripped from the injury.

The beast aimed, moving his target from Buzz to me in the last instant, and he pulled the trigger on his massive gun. I prepared for the worst, seeing my end as the pulse expanded. And felt Kim's arms around me as she took my place, shoving me to the ground. The blast hit Kim, a bright light sparking all around her.

"Noooooooo!" I watched as Kim fell face-first into the street.

Buzz finished the alien, one more shot to the thing's head, and he slid the blade from the Traveler's scabbard, stabbing it into the creature's neck. It lay there unmoving as the deluge washed his blood away.

"Kim…" I panicked, helping her to her side, and she coughed, sitting up with a smile. "How?"

She rolled up her sleeve, displaying the alien shield guard clamped around her forearm. "Figured it was better to be safe than sorry."

I hugged her, splashing in the mud as we laughed. It

was almost enough to forget the attack we'd endured.

Neil started to run, and I glanced at Buzz. "Race you," he said.

We caught up to the Sphere a few minutes later, struggling to hop a fence, and Buzz grabbed him. "Time to bail."

"I don't…"

"I told you we'd take care of the Traveler. Now it's your end of the bargain. Exit Neil, and leave Bell Island," I ordered.

"You have no idea what you've done. All these dead Sarc. It'll attract them like flies to manure." The boy's face lit up, the ball of light pushing out of his mouth. Neil fell to his knees, gasping for air as the Sphere lifted and sped to the east side of the island. The bay. He was leaving.

"How are you feeling, Neil?" I asked, helping the kid to his feet.

"That was so cool," he said, staring after the Sphere. "My friends won't believe this."

"That's right, because you're not going to tell them," Buzz said.

"Oh yeah, why not?" Neil stood up, frowning.

Buzz clutched the alien weapon, and it began glowing yellow. "Because I said so."

Neil lost his defiance and stared at the road. "Yes, sir."

Headlights shone on the street, and we blocked the driver's path. Nadine observed us, and rushed out, hugging her son. "Is it… are you…"

"Yes, Mom, it's me. They got rid of our problem."

Her gaze drifted to the dead alien, and she fainted.

"Carry her inside. I have some tools in the back." Kim and I escorted Nadine into the trailer, and watched in astonishment as Parker and Buzz brought in an assortment of saws and drills.

"You have stuff to fix a leaking roof?" I asked Buzz.

"And the hole in the wall. I was going to patch the secondary barn at home, but she needs it more than my hay bales." They set to work, with a dead Traveler in the driveway.

3

8:06 A.M.
August 31st, 1984

"Elliot, can you pass the syrup?" Cindy asked.

"Sure thing, sis." I slid it across the table.

"It's a big day," Mom said, smiling at my dad.

"The biggest. My son is a senior." Dad lifted his coffee cup. "To Elliot. Without you, we wouldn't all be here together, enjoying your last breakfast at home."

"Until next summer," Mom added.

"Maybe," I said, getting a frown.

"What about you, Hank?" Cindy asked Bones. "You ready for Vegas life?"

Bones shrugged with a sausage in his mouth. He chewed it a couple times before answering. "I'm pretty stoked. Nana is going to miss me, but she'll get by. Buzz promised he'd check on her. I've arranged to have her groceries delivered, and the kid down the street is cutting the yard."

"Sounds like you have it all figured out," Dad told him.

"Thanks, Mr. H. Hope so."

The doorbell rang, and I rushed to answer it. My heart beat faster when I saw her. "Kimberly. You're late."

"Sorry. I had something to do."

I glanced at the car and spied the suitcase in her

backseat. "You don't mean…"

"I'm moving to the city."

"Seriously?" I kissed her, blissfully uncaring if my family was watching us.

"I found a cute little place near campus, and the local paper liked my sample enough to hire me." She squealed and spun around, her striped dress flitting behind her.

"Congrats," I said, finding my entire family huddled in the living room, eavesdropping.

"Well done, Kim," my mom said. "Just make sure not to take up all my son's time, or he won't finish his degree."

"Don't worry about that. I'll make him study every night." Kim came inside.

I peered down the street, checking for clouds, but the day was clear, the sky pristine and cerulean blue.

The last month and a half, we'd seen no signs of the Travelers or Spheres. Life had slowly begun to return to normal on Bell Island. We'd left wooden crosses on the sides of the road where our residents had been killed during that tragic night, and none would soon forget the event that changed our island forever. But we were robust, like you had to be when you were separated from the rest of society. I almost felt guilt leaving them all behind, but I'd visit for the holidays. Knowing that Bones was going too eased my conscience.

We finished our meal, and Cindy took me aside before I could leave. "Thanks again."

"You're welcome."

"I realized I was wasting my time chasing boys and worrying about makeup. I'm going to crush this junior year."

"Thinking about college? Going to take finance like your big brother?"

"Gag me with a spoon. No way. I want to be a doctor,"

she said, as if I should have guessed it.

"That's cool too. In a more traditional sense." I softly nudged her shoulder with a fist. "I believe in you."

She beamed with pride.

"Time to go. We just need to make one stop," Bones said.

They left me with my parents, and my dad went to the kitchen to clean up. My mom looked great, her health improving now that her experiences as a child had been substantiated. She no longer felt like she had done something wrong or was lying to herself about encountering aliens. Uncle Taylor's death still hurt, but that wouldn't vanish so quickly.

"They never recovered his body. Did you know that?" she asked quietly when we were alone.

"What?" I asked, not cluing in.

"Taylor. They combed the ocean, but all they found was the note in his car. The one explaining that he couldn't take it anymore." She made a sad smile, and tears formed in her eyes.

"And you don't think he's gone?"

"Oh, I do. But maybe not dead."

"Mom…"

"Just remember him, okay? I shouldn't have said anything about it," she said.

"If they didn't find a body, how did everything get through probate so quickly?" I'd gotten the car within a month.

"It was a special case. And someone else washed ashore three weeks later. Since no one could place the corpse, the M.E. and the sheriff signed off on it. And the note… that helped their decision."

I felt like I'd been slapped in the face. "He's not coming back, Mom. Even if he found the ship…"

"I agree. But I wanted you to know. No more secrets," she said, and kissed my cheek. "Don't forget to visit."

"And call," I assured her.

"Yes. I'd like that."

Dad came in with a tea towel slung over his shoulder, and they held hands while I left the house. Bell Island had been a great home for me, but it was time I ventured on to the mainland to forge my own path. I rolled my luggage down the sidewalk, placing it into the massive trunk.

Kim had her car out front, and Bones slid into the back seat. "What's going on?" I asked them.

"Don't ruin this, Elliot," Bones quipped through the open window.

Instead of driving toward the ferry in the bay, we proceeded to a familiar location. We parked at the body shop, and I saw the car cover on the vehicle with a giant red bow tied to it. "You said it wasn't done for a couple more months."

"I lied," Bones said, hopping out. His boss handed him the keys, and nodded at me before entering his shop.

I waved at him and ran a hand over the heavy sheet. "Can I…"

"It's all yours." Bones stepped away.

I slowly tugged the cover off, letting it fall to the ground. The Camaro shone like it was freshly waxed.

"It's beautiful," Kim whispered.

"Start her up," Bones said, tossing me the keys.

I did, and the engine purred like a kitten. A big strong one.

The owner came out with paperwork, and walked to Kim's car while she spoke to him.

"What's that about?" I asked Bones.

"She's selling it."

Her car was old, with rust spots and balding tires, but

the guy handed her a few bills and she signed the paper.

"Give me a hand?" Kim opened the trunk, and we transferred the suitcases into my car.

"You mind stopping at Buzz's quick?" Bones asked.

"Sure. What for?"

"Just want to say goodbye."

"We did at dinner the other day."

Bones stared at me, and I nodded, knowing I wouldn't refuse any request from my best friend, not after getting the Camaro back in such cherry shape. I pressed the cassette tape on, and Journey belted out one of my favorite tunes as we sped across Bell Island.

Buzz didn't answer his door, and we checked the barn, expecting to find him there. But he was gone.

"He was here last night. I didn't knock this morning." Kim had been living in his loft for a few weeks.

We searched the barn, finding the alien gear absent, along with his trap and cache of weapons. "He left us." The UFO had been dragged to the second barn a month prior, and we'd spent countless hours trying to decipher how it all worked. Buzz had been convinced he was close to a breakthrough.

I was about to go check on it when I spotted the note taped to the back of the barn door. I ripped it off and read the message.

Friends,

Sorry I didn't tell you about my departure. I found some unsettling information on the UFO and had to hit the road. Thanks for everything. You reminded me I didn't need to be a loner. I was reminded I could count on people, and for that, I'm eternally grateful. Never forget you are capable of great things. Each of you.

Bones, I know I said I'd keep an eye on Nana, but Parker has accepted the task for me. She's in good hands.

Kimberly, you are a breath of fresh air in a polluted world. Enjoy your freedom.

Elliot…

The writing changed, as if he'd stopped to think about what to say.

You're brave beyond expectation, and selfless in a way I thought didn't exist any longer. I've left something for you. It's the most meaningful token I have, and I wanted you to have it. To remember me by.

If we ever need to save the world again, you can be damned sure I'll come find you.

Ethan 'Buzz' Scott

Hanging from the door handle was a ribbon with a star-shaped medal at the end.

"That's a Medal of Honor. They only gave out like two hundred of those," Bones said in awe.

I held it close, wishing Buzz hadn't vanished this way. But he must have had his reasons. "Let's go."

The ferry ride was uneventful, and the three of us stood on the top deck, discussing the coming months. We would reunite for Thanksgiving, but that wasn't soon enough. I knew things would change, but maybe that was for the better. Bones had his own life to experience, and it would do him well to leave Bell Island for some new experiences.

We dropped him off at the bus terminal, and after numerous goodbyes, handshakes, and hugs, we watched as his bus took him south, last stop: Sin City.

"Shall we?" I opened the Camaro's door, and Kim grinned, hopping into the passenger seat.

"What do you feel like? Thai? Mexican? Indian?" I asked, now that we had so many options.

"I heard there's a good diner near my new place. Want to check it out?" Kim asked as I threw it in drive. When the coast was clear, I pushed the gas, ripping down the road.

"I could eat," I said, laughing.

I noticed an orb of light, and looked to the west, only to see the sun blazing in the sky.

While we'd removed the Spheres from Bell Island, I suspected Earth was rife with them. And where there were Spheres, there'd be Travelers.

But in that moment, there was only us.

The End

ABOUT THE AUTHOR

Nathan Hystad is an author from Sherwood Park, Alberta, Canada.

Keep up to date with his new releases by signing up for his newsletter at www.nathanhystad.com

Sign up at www.shelfspacescifi.com as well for amazing deals and new releases from today's best indie science fiction authors.